THE
ROAD
TO
NOWHERE

CHARLES LEMAR BROWN

Broken L Press

To my mom and dad—
for more reasons than words can express.

Chapter 1

Will Tucker was a cantankerous old bastard. Fifty years of ranching in the heart of Oklahoma had left him iron hard and leather tough. He had earned every wrinkle on his clean-shaven weathered face. Years of riding fence aboard an old hammerhead roan had left him slightly bow-legged, and the hours spent perched on his old John Deere tractor had given him a permanent squint. Deep-set hazel eyes, a saturnine nose, and silver hair gave him an almost aristocratic appearance—at least until he opened his mouth. He rarely spoke, but when he did, the deep gravelly Okie twang in his voice got the attention of everyone around. At five ten and a hundred and eighty-five pounds, he was seldom the biggest or tallest man in the room, but he had a way of making everyone he met feel like they were looking up at him.

Today Will rode his favorite mount, a big red roan quarter horse. Together, they plodded methodically north toward a tree line a half mile away. At fifteen and a half hands, the quarter horse was an animal that turned heads. On a normal day, the gelding would be pulling hard, wanting to run, but he could sense the frustration in his rider and so held back.

The problem, as Will had labeled his current dilemma, was not one that could be taken care of with a simple ride around the family's vast cattle ranch. It was not the kind a little duct tape and bailing wire could fix, and that was what had Will's mind in turmoil. He liked life simple.

"Red, I'm pissed." Will finally spoke to his horse.

Red pulled against the reins and then relaxed. Will smiled at the simplicity of the horse's action. With one simple gesture, the horse had said you are still the boss, but I am ready whenever you are. All you have to do is give the signal. He and the horse had been together a long time, and sometimes Will thought the dang animal knew him better than any human, maybe better than he even knew himself.

"Okay, then old boy, let'er fly." he said with a clicking sound and leaned forward to get Red moving.

Red sprang forward into full gallop. The horse and rider moved as one. A quarter of a mile, a half mile, the land blurred past. Another quarter of a mile and the tree line loomed large. Will eased him back to a canter as they passed through the trees and into a clearing lined with scrub oaks and mountain cedars. They crossed the clearing at a trot and Will reined him back to a walk as he found the head of a cattle trail leading off to the northwest.

A half mile further and Will pulled up at the edge of a pond. Several red-eared turtles perched on a snag at the water's edge surveyed the newcomers warily. When Will dismounted, the largest of them slid quickly into the safety of the water. He removed his old worn sweat-stained straw Stetson hat and slapped it against the thigh of his faded, creased Wranglers to remove dust. The remaining turtles disappeared.

Red stood front feet in the water and drank. Will stared silently out across the land. He loved this ranch. He could smell dirt from a freshly plowed field, see a small bunch of his Hereford cattle off to the west, and hear the call of a western meadowlark searching for company. How anyone could not love this land was beyond his comprehension. The few years he had been away during the war, all he could think about was getting back. Once back, he had refused to leave, and for over fifty years, there had been no reason to do so. Now the time had come, and he did not like it—not one little bit.

Will took a canteen down from the horn of his saddle, unscrewed the cap, and drank. Recapping the canteen, he wiped his mouth on the sleeve of his blue denim, pearl-snapped

Wrangler work shirt. A calf bawled, and Red's head snapped up—ears back, eyes searching. Will rubbed the horse's neck, replaced the canteen, gathered the reins, and mounted.

The north fence was still a mile away, and he wanted to check it before supper. As he rode, his eyes studied the land. Not in an obvious way, but in the more natural way of an animal accustomed to its place in the world. He had ridden over every inch of this land, both with his father and with his grandfather, so many times that he knew it as well as he knew his own face. Each had taught him much.

He had tried to do his part. He had added acres to the land he had inherited. He had done his best to pass on the love of the land to his sons and his grandson. Perhaps if Wyatt had lived, it would have been different. Wyatt had truly loved the ranch. Will had never doubted the future of the Rolling T when Wyatt was alive. The small family cemetery near the ranch's northwest corner came into view. Frustrated, Will shook his head.

At the entry to the cemetery, Will pulled Red to a stop and looked over the split-wood rail fence that surrounded the graves. His grandparents, his parents, his only brother, his daughter-in-law, and Wyatt all rested within. He remembered too well the day they had gotten the call. Wyatt had been in an accident. An eyewitness said he had swerved to avoid a head-on collision with a red vehicle. Wyatt had lost control and slammed head on into a tree. The red car had never even slowed down, the driver was never found. Their little family had not been the same since. Bo, Wyatt's older brother, had slowly drifted away from ranching and towards other interests. Will knew it was because the ranch held to many memories of his brother. It was not that Bo did not do his share of the work or help keep the ranch going, it was simply that Will could tell his heart was not really in it.

Will's eyes drifted to his brother Fred's grave. On two different occasions during the war, his brother had saved him from death. He had personally seen Fred do the same for at least three other soldiers. Will himself had been awarded a silver star for a charge he made that enabled a group of injured soldiers to be rescued. What the official record of the heroic deed failed to mention was that Will had thought Fred was among those pinned down by enemy fire. It was not until after everyone was safe that Will would find out his brother's orders had been changed and he was elsewhere, leaving Will to wonder if he had known Fred was not there, would his actions have been different.

The two of them had always been close. They had grown up riding this very land, but the war and the atrocities they had seen there had given them a bond not many would understand. It had also given them the one thing they could never agree on—who really deserved the silver star.

With a click of his tongue Will started Red forward once again. At the northwest corner post, he turned and started east. As he rode, he watched for slack in the barbed wire, wooden posts that would need to be replaced soon, and tracks of any animals that might have passed this way. This was all part of his normal Saturday afternoon routine and usually one of his favorite times of the week. The problems and frustrations of the past several days typically faded away as he rode, but the events of the previous week continued to wear on him. He shifted in the saddle, made a mental note that the corner post at the east end of the fence line was looking a little weathered, and then he turned the horse to the south. He and Bo had replaced the old wooden fence posts here with new T-post last summer. Using the metal post was the smart thing to do, he knew, but he sure missed the look of the old weathered wooden ones.

The sun was easing towards the western horizon by the time he had gotten back to the barn. He curried Red and turned him out. The red, step-side Chevy pickup parked in the gravel beside the western-style, cedar-sided ranch house told him Bo was over for a late supper. Fried chicken, mashed potatoes and gravy, and homemade rolls usually sounded good after an afternoon of riding, but Will just couldn't seem to find his appetite.

*****

Margaret Tucker watched out the kitchen window as her husband curried Red and turn him out. Something was eating at Will, but she was no fool. If she asked him about it, he would just grunt and wave a hand in denial, so she would wait. She was good at waiting. When you live in the middle of nowhere, you had better be. She was a kind, patient, and very caring woman. At five foot eight, she was almost as tall as her husband. At one hundred and twenty pounds she moved with the grace of a model. Dying her hair would have made her look half her age, but she chose not to dye it. It was sprinkled with just enough gray to give her a regal appearance, and she usually wore it in a bun on top of her head.

She removed her white kitchen apron and hung it in its place on the back of the pantry door. Smoothing the front of her blue calico dress with her hands, she stepped back and surveyed the solid oak table that sat eight. It was topped with a red and white checkered tablecloth. Three places were set, each with a solid white Corelle plate, knife and spoon to the right, and a fork atop a white cloth napkin to the left. Above and to the right of each place setting was a quart mason jar half filled with ice. A platter of fried chicken was placed near one end of the table and around it were bowls of mashed potatoes, gravy, corn on the cob, and homemade rolls.

"Smells good, Maggie," Will called half-heartedly from the mud room.

"Thanks," Maggie replied, "It's ready when you are."

"Be right there." Will knocked the dust from his clothes and boots and washed his hands in the wall hung sink next to the back door.

Maggie placed a pitcher of sweet tea on the table as Will stepped through the door. Fifty years of marriage at the end of the month and she still got butterflies when he walked into a room and smiled at her. She straightened her dress once again, stepped around the table, and kissed him on the cheek.

"How was your ride?" she asked.

"Fine," Will answered, then added, "Fences looked good."

Bo came in from the living room. A younger version of Will, he was an inch taller and ten-pounds lighter. A shiny, slick-shaven head kept the grey from showing, but it did nothing for the streaks that shot through his mustache and goatee. Once he had worn a smile that was contagious, now he seldom smiled at all.

"Looks delicious, mom," he stated flatly as he pulled out a chair and slid into it.

Will took his place at the head of the table, and Maggie sat down beside him, across from Bo, who stretched his arm across the table and took his mother's hand as Will took the hands of his wife and son. Together, they bowed their heads.

Will prayed, "Heavenly Father, thank You for this day. Thank You for this family. Thank You for this food. Please bless it to the nourishment of our bodies. We ask it all in Jesus' name. Amen."

Maggie gave each of the men's hands a little squeeze before she released them. Will reached for the fried chicken, and Bo grabbed the bowl of mashed potatoes. Bowls and platters where shuffled until all three had full plates. Will worked on a corn cob briefly then set it at the back of his plate.

"Did last night's supper bother anyone else?" he asked as he picked up his fork then set it back down again.

Last night had bothered Maggie, but how to put her feelings into words just wouldn't come, so she kept her peace. She was glad, on one hand, that Will had opened the conversation and that she knew now what had been eating at him all day, but on the other hand, she was at a loss as how to further the conversation. Bo swallowed a mouth full of chicken and wiped his mouth.

"Yep, Pa," he answered, then added, "The whole situation plum pisses me off, 'scuse the French Momma, but it does."

"Have you talked to that boy?" Will asked staring hard at Bo.

That boy was William Mark Tucker. Trey to his family because he was the third William in line and Bo's only child, Will and Maggie's only grandchild. Four years ago, he had been valedictorian of his senior class and a pretty good high school baseball pitcher. Murray State College in Tishomingo, Oklahoma, had recruited him to pitch for the Aggies, but he had turned that down and accepted a full ride academic scholarship to East Central University in Ada, Oklahoma, so he could be with his high school sweetheart. On the previous day, Trey and Lisa, now his fiancé, had graduated from the university and had been treated by Will to supper at Santa Fe Steakhouse in Ada.

"Yep." Bo stared hard back, "I've talked 'til I'm blue in the face, but he ain't listenin'. He's smitten."

"When's he comin' home?" Will asked.

"Supposed to be in late tonight," Bo answered around another bite of chicken, swallowed then continued, "He's gonna drop Lisa off with her friends up at Will Rogers airport before he comes in. Why?"

"You're not eatin', darlin'," Maggie said glancing over at Will.

"Give me a minute," Will responded and stared aimlessly at his plate.

"Pa, you got something on your mind?" Bo wiped his mouth, laid his napkin down, and sat waiting.

After a long minute, Will spoke, "My grand pappy use to say, 'Son, when you have a problem, you mull it over good, figure a way to fix it, then get to fixin'." He twisted his mouth sideways, thought a minute more, then added, "I been thinkin' 'bout this problem all day long, and I think it's time to get to fixin'."

"And just how do you plan to do that?" Maggie asked.

Will smiled and raised an eyebrow.

Bo grinned, "I've seen that look before. What have you got up your sleeve?"

"Okay, but first, did either of you notice Trey's reaction when that cute little waitress asked him if they'd been in Calculus

II together?" Will asked.

"Yeah," Bo nodded his head, "He looked like he wanted to swallow his spoon and crawl under the table."

"And his fiancé looked like she could have driven her steak knife into the waitress and not even thought twice about it." Will added.

"I felt bad for her." Maggie said.

"For who? The waitress or Trey's fiancé?" Will asked.

"The waitress," Maggie answered, then, "She seemed like such a sweet child. She sure didn't deserve the way Lisa treated her or Trey for that matter."

"Yes, and if I had to guess, Trey caught hell all night long and maybe all day long too." Bo reddened.

"Yep." Will nodded and picked up his fork.

Maggie and Bo watched as he loaded it with mashed potatoes and gravy and took a bite. He chewed, swallowed, cut a piece from his chicken breast, and placed it in his mouth. Bo, not knowing what else to do, picked up his fork and began to eat. Maggie waited patiently until each had taken several bites.

"Do you have a plan or not." She shook her head as she asked the question.

"Course I do," Will answered around another fork of mashed potatoes.

"Care to share?" Bo queried as he pulled a hot roll apart.

Will swallowed, placed his fork so that it rested on the right side of his plate, wiped his mouth, took a long swig of sweet tea, then slowly nodded.

Bo stopped eating, took a drink of tea, and wiped his mouth. Maggie pursed her lips and drew her eyebrows down hard.

"Okay, okay," Will held up a hand, "Don't get you're…"

"Don't finish that sentence." Maggie cautioned, lowering her head and raising her eyebrows.

Will held up the other hand and leaned back laughing, then asked, "Maggie is your great-niece still getting married out in California?"

"I'll play along," Maggie answered, "Yes she is, why?"

"Didn't you say we got an invite in the mail?" Will returned.

"Oh, so you were listening?" Maggie replied.

"I'm always listening," Will stated.

Bo chuckled.

"What's so damn funny?" Will snapped.

"You two act like an old married couple." Bo laughed again.

"How dare you call your momma old." Will feigned shock.

"Enough," Maggie nearly shouted.

Will enjoyed the banter, but he knew when he'd pushed far enough. Now that he had the attention of both of them and knew they had similar thoughts about the situation, it was time to lay out his plan.

"I think what Trey needs is some time away," he said, "time away from that fiancé, time away from Caddo County, time away from Oklahoma. I think it's time for a little trip."

"Okay, I'll agree," Bo chimed in.

"Me, too," Marge agreed.

"Bo can't leave because he's got summer baseball," Will reminded them.

"I don't think he'll go by himself," Maggie said, "He really doesn't know those folks out there that well. As a matter of fact, except for my sister Amelia, none of us do."

"Don't worry," Will said with a nod, "He'll be driving us."

"Us?" Maggie looked puzzled, "Us, like you and I?"

"Yep." Will smiled.

"Pa, when was the last time you left Oklahoma?" Bo's voice registered shock.

"Two years before you were born," Maggie answered, then to Will, "You sure about this?"

"Bad as I hate travelin', I hate what that girl is doin' to our grandson even more," Will nodded his head in affirmation, "She's changed since they went off to college and what's more Trey has allowed her to change him. It's time to get to fixin' the problem, and it looks to me like we're gonna have to do it since he seems to have his head too far up… well, y'all get the picture. Bo, do you think you can get Bud Wilkerson to help you with the ranch while we're gone?"

"I think so, but how are you gonna convince Trey to go?" Bo asked.

"Ain't gonna be no convincing. He got a full scholarship, but not a meal ticket. The deal was I paid his meal ticket, and he worked it off during the summer. He still owes me a summer of work," Will answered.

"Yes, but that was ranch work, Pa," Bo said.

"Never stipulated what kind of work," Will grinned mischievously. "Looks like this summer he's a chauffeur."

Maggie shook her head. "That's not funny, Will."

"Sure, it is," Will shot back.

"When do you want to leave?" Maggie asked.

"After church tomorrow good with you?" Will asked in return.

"Lordy, Will, you got to give a lady time to pack," Maggie fussed. "How 'bout first thing Monday morning."

"Alright, then," Will nodded towards Bo's plate. "Your dinner's gettin' cold, better eat up."

Bo laughed, picked up his fork, filled it with mashed potatoes, and began the process of cleaning his plate. Maggie shook her head in disbelief, and the three continued with their supper, feeling better now that there was a plan for fixin' the problem.

Lord, help Trey, Maggie thought to herself and wondered if her son and husband were thinking the same thing.

Chapter 2

Trey eased his red Nissan Altima into a space on the south end of the church in Fort Cobb. The building was a single-story, light brown brick structure with dark brown shingles and a wooden sign out front identifying the property as the First Baptist Church. A silver sedan pulled through the circle driveway and dropped off an elderly lady at the front entrance, then pulled around to the additional parking on the north side of the building.

Two spaces down from where Trey had snagged a parking place, he noticed a dark blue F150. A gray-haired man in a western suit got out, circled the vehicle, and opened the door for his wife. The two of them walked hand in hand towards the front entrance. Trey wondered if they had always held hands or if it was something that came with age. He and Lisa seldom held hands. His eyes strayed from the couple back to the truck they had exited. He wasn't a Ford man himself, but it was a nice truck. He sure missed his old Silverado, but Lisa thought the Altima said 'accountant' more than a big Chevy pickup.

He opened the door, slid out of the vehicle, straightened his pressed white western shirt, adjusted his belt buckle, and started for the front door of the church. His dark-brown, pleated, Wrangler Riata dress pants stacked up just right over his tan, square-toed ostrich boots. Inside the church, he weaved a path through the folks congregated in the foyer visiting between Sunday school and the morning service and found his way to the men's room. In the mirror, he did a quick check of his hair and then straightened his western print necktie. Staring at his reflection, he suddenly realized how much he looked like the picture of his dad that sat on the hutch in Granny and Pappy's living room. His hair was longer, and he combed it over to the right instead of straight back the way his dad had in his younger years, but the resemblance was uncanny.

Leaving the restroom, Trey found the foyer empty except for a small boy who was stretched on tiptoes trying to get a drink out of the aluminum water fountain. Trey remembered when he had trouble with the very same fountain, crossed to the child, and hoisted him up long enough to get a drink.

"Thanks mister." The boy ran off laughing into the sanctuary.

Mister? That seemed a little odd. Mister was his dad or his granddad. He wasn't old enough to be a mister yet. *To the boy I'm a mister, to my dad and grandad I'm still a snot-nosed kid. Interesting,* Trey thought, *I guess not everything you learn comes from college and books. I guess, age is definitely relative.*

Folks were milling around visiting, hugging, and shaking hands when Trey entered the sanctuary. A dozen men shook his hand, and several older ladies grabbed him for a hug as he made his way down the center aisle towards his family's pew. Officially, there were no assigned pews, unofficially, you could look forward to dirty looks, hateful attitudes, and a whole lot of unChristian-like spirits if you sat in the wrong pew. It was just better to sit where you were supposed to rather than to tempt the Fates.

Trey slid in beside his grandmother. She leaned over and gave him a hug just as the youth pastor stepped up to the pulpit and asked the congregation to bow their heads so he could lead them in prayer. When he finished, he made a few announcements and then turned the service over to the choir director.

A short, wide man in brown corduroy pants and a red polo shirt rose from a bench and approached the pulpit, and the youth pastor stepped aside. Under his direction the congregation sang "Holy, Holy, Holy" and then "How Great Thou Art". At the end of the second selection, he announced that the twelve-member choir would sing 'All Hail the Power of Jesus Name". As the choir sang, Trey glanced past his grandmother at his grandfather. Will Tucker sat straight in the pew, head and eyes forward, watching the choir sing. On the other side of Will sat his father, Bo, who flipped aimlessly through a Sunday School Booklet.

As the choir sang, the power of their voices vibrated from the rafters and settled in Trey's mind. It seemed that lately, Lisa definitely wielded a lot more power in his life than Jesus—or anyone else for that matter. He wondered if that was somehow sinful.

Before he could arrive at an answer, the choir finished singing and Pastor John Paul stepped to the pulpit, arranged his Bible and notes, cleared his throat, and stared out across the congregation. He was a tall man, four inches over six feet, and on a good day, would tip the scales at one hundred and seventy pounds. With deeply sunken eyes of pale blue and a long hawk-like nose, he looked like a taller version of Jim Carey's character in the movie, *A Series of Unfortunate Events*.

"Good morning and God bless." His voice was a deep raspy baritone when he spoke.

The service lasted the customary forty-five minutes. Will and Maggie listened intently, Bo leafed through his Sunday school lesson for the following week, and Trey fiddled with his cellphone. Twenty minutes into the sermon, he received a text message from Lisa.

Where are you? she wanted to know.

Trey quickly texted back, *At church.*

Why didn't you text me this morning when you got up? came the next question.

I thought you might not be awake yet.

Trey noticed that his grandmother was watching him.

I would have gotten it when I woke up, you should have texted. Trey could almost feel Lisa scowling all the way from the Bahamas. Maggie shook her head and patted him on the leg. Trey blushed when he realized his grandmother had seen the texts.

The rest of the service was a blur. Once at a high school

baseball practice, he had been standing too close to the batter's box, waiting for his turn to bat, and a foul ball had struck him on the side of the head and knocked him out cold. For days afterwards, he had suffered the effects of a concussion. Most of the time, everything seemed foggy, not unlike the feeling he felt now. He wondered if this was what love was supposed to feel like or if something was wrong with him. Every time Lisa was angry or even just unhappy with him, he felt like he had been dropped in a box and the lid had been slammed shut. It was hard to breathe, and it felt like a huge weight was pressed against his chest.

It had not always been this way. The years they dated in high school had been nice. Of course, there was little for them to disagree on back then and Trey had learned early on it was better if he just went along with her wishes than to deal with her anger. It had not been until she had been invited to join a sorority that things had begun to change. At first, he had been excited for her and even talked about trying to get into a fraternity so they could do things together. When it became clear this was not a part of her plans, they had argued. It seemed like life had been one never ending argument afterwards. He hoped that once she returned from her Bahama trip, she would put all of that behind her and their life would return to the way it had been.

*****

Maggie felt her grandson's tension and put an arm around his shoulders. She slowly and methodically patted his shoulder, and by the end of the sermon, the tension was almost gone. The pastor prayed, then dismissed the congregation.

"Let's go get some lunch," Maggie suggested.

"Y'all might as well ride with us," Will said and headed toward the front door.

*****

Trey gave his father a questioning look. Bo just gave him one of his 'you'll figure it out soon' grins and followed along after Maggie and Will. Trey shook his head and fell in behind his father.

At the door, the pastor was shaking hands and wishing everyone a blessed week. Trey stopped long enough to exchange brief pleasantries and had just stepped outside when someone grabbed his arm and squeezed it. He turned and looked straight into the darkest eyes he had ever seen.

"You're Trey Tucker, right?" the young lady asked.

"Yeeees," He stammered feeling the red creep up his neck and the lid on Lisa's box slamming shut. He had an enormous urge to look around to see if Lisa was watching the scene unfold.

"I'm Lupita, Coral's little sister." The girl flashed a bright smile.

"Okay?" Trey could not hide his confusion.

"Coral, Coral Jones, you graduated with her." Lupita raised one dark eyebrow.

"Oh, Coral Jones, yes." Trey finally nodded.

"Sorry to bother you," Lupita apologized, "but I promised Coral I'd tell you Hi the next time I saw you at church. She lives in Phoenix with her husband. He's in the Air Force. Anyway, Hi from Coral."

"Thanks, tell her I said hello back if you would please." Trey said.

"Sure will." She turned and was gone.

Trey turned to look for his father and grandparents and found them grouped in front of a recent model black crew cab Chevy Silverado. He realized all three of them had been watching the exchange between him and Lupita. His grandfather looked pissed, his grandmother looked sad, and his father was grinning like a shit eatin' opossum. Trey felt completely lost as he moved towards the trio wondering where his grandfather's old white Chevy truck had gone, and why they were all going to lunch together. Nothing seemed to make much sense today.

As Trey approached, Will opened the rear door and assisted Maggie into the backseat of the black Silverado. Bo opened the passenger door and climbed in. With a shake of his head, Trey rounded the truck and opened the back-passenger side door as Will pulled the driver's door closed.

"New truck?" Trey queried.

"No, your Pappy just had his old white one painted black," Bo smarted off.

"Bo, you behave yourself," Maggie scolded.

Will chuckled. "Wonder where he gets that shit?"

"You know dang well where he gets it," Maggie said sharply adding, "and it's Sunday, William Henry Tucker, so you watch your language."

"Yes, ma'am." He suppressed another chuckle, but not the grin.

Will backed onto Fourth Street and started south. After two blocks, he turned left past the Fort Cobb United Methodist Church onto Main Street. Two blocks after that, he pulled into a space in front of Pat's Café and Saloon. Named for its owner, Patrick O'Donnell, the building was a massive two-story, red brick building. Trey remembered the first time his grandfather had brought him to eat here. Will had told him that the building had originally been a furniture store. Shortly after it had gone out of business, Pat had shown up with his wife, Sam, short for Samantha, purchased the place, remodeled it, and opened a combination café and saloon.

Trey loved Pat's. He loved the western décor, the mismatched tables and chairs, but most of all the food. Normally, he would have been more than happy with Pappy's choice of diners, but traditionally, the after-church meal was chicken-fried steaks, corn-on-the-cob, mashed potatoes and gravy, and Granny's homemade hot rolls. And usually, it was made and served by Granny at the big house out at the ranch. Confused and wary, he entered the café with his family.

Inside, Will weaved a path through the restaurant to the far back of the room and chose a table for four. He pulled a chair out for Maggie and pushed it forward gently as she seated herself. Then he took the chair beside her with his back to the wall. Bo sat down beside his father and Trey took the remaining chair.

"I've always loved this place," Trey said to no one in particular.

"Ain't gonna find nothin' like this in Tulsa." Will sneered as he unrolled his cloth napkin, removed the utensils, and arranged them on the table in front of himself.

"Now, Will." Maggie placed her hand over his and squeezed.

Trey watched as his grandfather visibly relaxed under her touch. He had seen it many times before, but it always amazed him the way his grandmother could erase anger and frustration with a simple touch.

"What's going on?" Trey asked, "I feel like I've missed something."

"Everything's fine," Maggie told her grandson. "Let's just eat, then we'll talk about a little trip your Pappy and I have planned."

"Will Tucker takin' a trip? Well don't that beat all?" Samantha O'Donnell, Pat's wife and their waitress, interrupted and then asked, "Is everyone having the usual?"

The usual was a grilled chicken breast blanketed with a slice of Monterey Jack cheese and covered with a mixture of sautéed mushrooms, jalapenos, and onions, served with an order of steamed broccoli for Maggie. A nine-ounce Sirloin steak cooked medium rare, a loaded baked potato, and a side salad with ranch for Will. Bo's order matched his fathers and Trey's steak was medium well with a double order of French fries. Everyone wanted the usual.

As Sam headed for the kitchen with their orders, the front doors opened and more of the after-church lunch rush arrived. By the time Trey and his family got their meals, every table in the dining room was taken and several patrons had slipped through the archway that separated the café from the saloon and taken seats at tables there. The smell of food filled both rooms, and the hum of a dozen or more conversations filled the air. Someone laughed across the room. Trey cut a slice from his steak, placed it in his mouth, and felt the flavor of the lightly charred meat dance across his taste buds. It felt so good to be home, even if it was just for the summer.

The buzz of his cell phone indicated he had a text from someone. He pulled it from his pocket and checked to see who had sent it.

Where are you? It was Lisa.

Quickly, he laid his fork aside and texted back, *At Pat's*.

Why? flashed across the screen almost immediately, and even without a voice, the message that Lisa was angry was loud and clear.

Eating with Pappy, Granny, and Dad. He flushed as he hit send.

Why? You usually have lunch at your Granny's came the next message.

"Can't that wait?' Will asked looking at his grandson as he slid a piece of steak into his mouth.

I'll call you later. Trey texted quickly, nodding at his grandfather.

Whatever. Came the reply.

The meal continued without interruption, and soon Sam stopped by to inquire about desserts. Maggie declined, while Will and Bo asked for a slice of pecan pie, and Trey ordered blackberry cobbler with vanilla ice cream on top. Sam gathered as many of the dirty plates as she could carry and returned to the kitchen. Minutes later, she returned with the pie and cobbler.

"Okay, I've waited long enough. What's going on here?" Trey demanded. "And what is this little trip you and Pappy are taking?"

Maggie smiled sweetly. "We're going to California."

"Really?" Trey looked at his grandmother in surprise and took a bite of cobbler and ice cream.

"Yes," She replied, "and *you're* going to drive us."

Trey wasn't sure if he was going to spew the cobbler across the table into his grandfather's lap or choke on it. He tried to swallow. When that didn't work, he tried to chew. California? He could not go to California. What was Granny thinking? What would Lisa say? Oh, she would say plenty. She would use screws to fasten the lid on the box and then bury it six feet deep. This was not part of *her* plan. He tried to swallow again. Still a no go. How could he say no to Granny? She and Pappy had been so good to him. But how could he go to California? This was not good. Not good at all. With difficulty, he managed to swallow.

Laying his spoon down, he finally managed a hoarse whisper, "Seriously?"

"Yes, darling," Maggie confirmed.

Trey looked to his grandfather. Will winked and smiled, "Leavin' in the morning, bright and early."

Bo spoke up before Trey's mind could fashion another question, "You take good care of your Granny and Pappy when y'all are on the road, you hear?"

Without thinking, Trey answered, "Yes, sir."

Chapter 3

Trey pulled his vehicle onto the gravel drive alongside his grandfather's old white farm truck. He had hardly slept the night before. A call to explain the situation to Lisa had ended in a fight. According to her, she didn't want to talk to him for a while. It did not take a rocket scientist to know she was unhappy. She said she needed time to think.

Five minutes later, a text let him know that she did not want to hear his voice, but enough time had elapsed to kindle her anger into a full-blown forest fire. A running volley of texts ensued.

How can you do this to me? The first one read.

You know I work for Pappy during the summer, Trey reminded her.

RANCHING, Came the reply.

I guess this summer they want me to drive them to California he responded.

You don't have to be an asshole about it, Lisa texted back.

How am I being an asshole? Trey wanted to know.

Really, like you don't know.

I think it would be better if we were actually talking instead of texting. Trey tried to reason with her.

I don't want to talk to you. And I'm though texting you.

A long twenty minutes passed before she texted again. The cycle repeated itself throughout the night, finally ending around three-thirty with one last message questioning the future of their engagement.

Trey rolled out at five o'clock, showered, dressed, and

arrived at his Granny and Pappy's at six on the dot. Granny sat on the front porch in her favorite wooden chair with a cup of coffee cupped between her hands and her boots perched on the lower board of the porch railing. Granny's coffee was always strong and black, and she drank it with no cream or sugar.

"Mornin' favorite, grandson," Granny greeted Trey as he climbed the steps and then asked, "Have a bad night?"

"Mornin', Granny. I've had better." He gave a half smile as he passed her and headed into the house.

"Well, you look very nice this mornin'," Granny spoke over her shoulder as he cleared the door and made a beeline for the coffee pot. Trey usually avoided coffee or if he did drink a cup, he added cream and sugar, but after texting with Lisa most of the night, he felt like he could use a cup—strong and black—that morning.

As for looking nice this morning, he might have looked it, but he certainly was not feeling it, and if Lisa could see him in his relaxed-fit Wranglers she would scowl in disgust. *She* preferred him in dress slacks and a button-down shirt, and so he seldom got to wear jeans.

Bo sat at the kitchen table with a steaming cup of coffee in front of him. He was wearing a pair of blue Nike shorts and a white shirt with the Mustang logo across the front. His baseball cap lay on the table beside his cup. He blew across the surface of the dark black liquid, took a sip, placed the cup back on the table, and watched as his son poured a cup.

"You look like shit," Bo said. "Have a bad night?"

"You could say that—a long night at the very least." Trey sighed and took a sip of the coffee he had just poured. The thought crossed his mind that he might ought to find a mirror and see what was causing folks to ask him about his night. Was it really that obvious?

"Time to move," Will shouted from the porch.

Trey looked at the nearly-full cup of coffee in his hands and then at his dad. Bo shrugged, took a drink, stood up, and headed for the sink. Trey poured out what was left of his coffee and started for the front door. At the door, Bo put a hand on his son's shoulder and gave it a squeeze.

"What's that for?" Trey asked.

"Luck. Concern. Hope. Love. You take your pick." Bo looked into Trey's eyes, "Love ya, kid."

"Love ya, too, Dad." Trey slipped through the door.

Will had pulled his new black truck around from the barn, had the tailgate down and was busy arranging suitcases under a vinyl bed cover. A large, brown, metal, antique suitcase with a leather handle and metal clasps sat half under the cover. Will pushed a brand-new, black cloth case further into the bed alongside a matching carryall.

As tired as he was, Trey managed a smile at his Pappy. Dressed in a white Sunday shirt, brand new, freshly-creased Wrangler originals, black Dan Post Ostrich-leg boots, and his best straw cowboy hat, he looked ready for a Saturday night rodeo. Trey stepped down from the porch, walked to his car, popped the trunk, and grabbed his duffel. Maggie finished her last swallow of coffee, handed her cup to Bo, and gave him a big hug.

Trey watched as Bo kissed his mother on the top of her head, released her, set the cup on the porch rail, and followed her down the steps to where he stood. The familiar combination of White Diamonds, coffee, and Downy fabric softener that was Granny warmed him to his core.

Bo stepped to the back of the truck and stuck his hand out to his father. To Trey's surprise, Will took the hand and pulled Bo in for a hug.

Trey rounded the back of the truck and stood staring at the two men. The scent of Stetson cologne made him wonder if the morning breeze was bringing it from his father, his grandfather, or both. He shook his head, tossed his bag into the truck, and stuck his hand out to Bo. Bo grabbed him, gave him a big bear hug, and set him down gasping then turned him loose and took a step back.

Laughing, Will tossed him the keys, pushed the old brown suitcase into place, shut the tailgate, snapped the cover in place, and said, "Let's hit the road."

"I love you, Bo," Granny said as she climbed in the back seat on the driver's side, "Keep an eye on things, son."

"Yes ma'am," Bo answered, "Love you too."

Will was already in the passenger seat looking straight ahead when Trey opened the door and climbed in. He started the truck, adjusted his seat then the steering wheel, put it in drive, and headed down the driveway. In the rearview, he watched his father wave from the front yard. At the end of the driveway, he started to turn left onto East 1280 Road.

"Wrong way," Will stated still staring straight ahead.

"Quickest way to Interstate 40 is to take Highway 146 and then 150 across. It meets up at Sayre," Trey explained his plan and once again started to turn out onto the road.

"I don't want to take Interstate 40. I don't like big highways." Will nodded to the right indicating the directions he wished to travel as he spoke.

Trey pulled out his I-phone, tapped it a couple of times, watched the screen, looked at his grandfather and said, "Pappy, it doesn't make any sense to go that way. It will put at least an extra day on our trip. We really should take I-40."

"Fort Sumner is not on I-40, and we need to stop there first," Will explained.

"Fort Sumner? That is way out of the way if we're going to Napa Valley, California. Did I miss something? Aren't we supposed to be going to Napa Valley?" Trey stared at his grandfather and then into the rearview at his grandmother for help.

"We'll get there by and by," Will said. "First to Fort Sumner. I want to see where Billy the Kid is buried."

"Are you kidding?" Trey's usual deep voice sounded squeaky in his own ears.

"No," Will replied flatly, "and you can put your smart-ass phone away. Your Granny has an Atlas; she'll navigate."

Trey looked to the rearview again. Head down, Granny was studying the Atlas. Bo stood at the foot of the porch steps still waving, only now he appeared to be laughing as well. Trey shook his head and turned right.

Lord, what had he gotten himself into?

*****

Two long hours later, Will instructed Trey to pull into a convenience store in Wellington, Texas. Trey eased the truck into a parking slot two spaces from the front door beside a red Mustang convertible. As he put the vehicle in park, a young blonde woman in a red sundress came from the store dragging a screaming little girl of about three years by one arm. The child pulled, squirmed, and fought to no avail. The blonde mother finally got control, picked the writhing kid up, forced her into the backseat of the convertible, and strapped her into a booster seat. The volume and pitch of the screaming reminded Trey of an ambulance as the little red automobile left the parking lot. The whole scene reminded him of Lisa. He wondered if she had acted that way as a child, suspected that she had, and figured it got worse as she grew older.

He exited the truck and opened the back door for his grandmother. Will came around the front of the truck, took Maggie's hand and helped her up onto the curb. Together, hand-in-hand, they walked to the door. Will opened it for her and Trey and then followed them into the store.

As Trey stepped through the door, the scene of the spoilt child still running through his head, he wondered if he wasn't acting just a little like the youngster himself. Maybe he had not physically screamed and thrown himself around, but he had been throwing a mental tantrum ever since being told he was going to have to drive his grandparents to California. Lisa had always been very vocal and dramatic when it came to what she wanted. He was more withdrawn, but he knew that in his own way, he also was being obstinate.

Inside, a limited selection of candy, chips, and overpriced condiments lined a few shelves. Two small booths with chipped white linoleum on the tables crowded the far wall near a chest-high turn rack of dusty greeting cards. In the back corner at the end of a short row of cooler doors half-stocked with carbonated products, beer, and bottled water was the only restroom.

"Looks like a one-holer, Momma," Will commented with a nod. "You wanna go first?"

"Sure." Maggie smiled and headed towards the back corner.

As Trey eased past him, Will picked up a pack of beef jerky, flipped it over, and stared at the back of the package. Behind the counter a bored-looking young woman with shoulder-length, red hair broke into a smile when Trey wandered over to the show case and stared in at the burritos and pizza pockets drying under the heat lamp.

"Can I get you something, darlin'?" she asked Trey in a soft Texas drawl and stepped to the end of the counter.

"No, ma'am, just lookin'." Trey reddened trying hard not to notice the Long Horn symbol stretched tightly across her ample chest. Concentrating hard on the line of burritos, he kept his head and eyes down. Even knowing that Lisa was in the Bahamas did not keep him from feeling like she was standing right behind him with a scowl on her face and a nasty accusation on her lips.

"Let me know if you change your mind." With a flirty grin and a little extra swing in her hips, she waltzed back to the cash register and perched herself on an old metal stool.

"Will do," Trey answered without looking up from the food. The fragrance of her perfume sailed through the smell of grease, and he wondered briefly what brand it was. He heard his Pappy snort, turned in time to see him replace the beef jerky with a look of disgust, and start for the bathroom. He wondered what his grandfather had found so repulsive about it.

His grandfather started for the back of the store passing his grandmother on the way. Will grunted as he passed her and shook his head. She frowned at him, caught Trey's eye, then looked past him at the cashier. Without turning, Will knew from his Maggie's expression that the girl was still watching Trey. Trey moved toward her sheepishly.

"I don't think Pappy likes the beef jerky here," he muttered.

"You may be right." She nodded and then asked, "You need anything while we're stopped?"

"Maybe a bottle of water," he said and kept walking.

*****

Inside the bathroom, Will fought back the nauseous feeling in his gut, urinated, washed his hands and splashed cold water on his face. He dried off with a paper towel, then stared in the mirror for a long minute. It was time to get to fixin'. He hoped it wasn't too late. Hoped he hadn't waited too long. Hoped he could fix this before time ran out. He closed his eyes, bowed his head, and stood very still. Slowly, the ache in his stomach receded. He opened his eyes, turned around, opened the door, and almost ran into Trey who was waiting patiently just outside for his turn in the restroom.

"You okay, Pappy?" Trey asked, adding, "You look pale."

"I'm fine, just fine." Will held the door open and motioned Trey inside. "It's all yours."

Trey stepped in and pulled the door closed.

Will wandered over to the cooler where Maggie was pulling bottles of water from a shelf. She was the most beautiful woman he had ever known and had been from the time he had first laid eyes on her. She turned and handed him two bottles of water.

"You want a Dr. Pepper or a cup of coffee?" She smiled.

"Neither. I just want to look at you." He raised one eyebrow.

"Will, you old devil." She faked a look of shock and giggled.

Will opened the cooler door beside her and pulled out a Sprite, "My stomach's actin' up a bit," he said. "Nerves I guess."

*****

When Trey came out of the bathroom, his grandparents had paid out and were waiting at the front of the store. Maggie was visiting with the little red-haired woman, and Will was holding a plastic sack and only half listening to the two women. Trey wondered how he was going to get out the front door without another embarrassing situation with the girl. He felt the usual dull ache in the pit of his stomach start. His heart beat faster. The palm of his hand felt sticky. He started forward, faked an interest in the candy aisle, and then stepped up behind Maggie.

"Ready to go?" he asked, using his grandmother as a barrier between himself and the cashier.

"Yep," Will answered.

"Hope ya'll have a nice trip," the girl said as they moved towards the door.

"Thanks," Maggie returned, "and I hope you have a good day."

The door closed behind them, and Trey felt himself begin to breathe again. Will opened the door for Maggie, and she climbed in the backseat and opened up her Atlas. Trey was behind the wheel and pulling on his seat belt by the time Will found his seat and pulled his door shut. He looked at his grandson and thought, *Time to get to fixin'.*

Chapter 4

"I ever tell you about my first horse?" Will asked as they pulled back onto Highway 83.

"No," Trey and Maggie answered in unison.

"I was fifteen the first time I saw him," Will began, paused and stared off down the road for a moment before he continued, "He was a big black gelding with a white blaze on his nose. He was the most beautiful thing I'd ever seen."

"He hadn't met me yet," Maggie interjected from the back seat.

Will smiled, "Yep. My Pa told me to steer clear of that horse. Said he was no good. Had a mean streak in him. He said you could tell it by the eyes. 'Course I didn't listen."

"Why haven't I heard this story before?" Maggie wondered.

"Cause I haven't told it to you before," Will said. "Anyway, I worked all summer, raised enough money, and bought that horse. When I got it home, Pa just looked at me, shook his head and said, 'Just like washin' white sheets in the Red River, guess you gotta see for your own self.'

"Reckon so," I told him.

Trey turned west. As he passed a First Baptist Church, his cellphone buzzed. He worked it free from the left front pocket of his Wranglers and entered his pass code. Will watched as his grandson read the text. The color slowly drained from Trey's face leaving him pale and ashen, then in a flash, a deep crimson rushed from beneath his collar, up his neck, and across his face. His knuckles turned white as he tightened his grip on the steering wheel and the iPhone.

Mean horses were one thing, but mean girls, now there was something no man in his right mind would want to tackle and here his grandson was about to be tied to the meanest one he had ever met. *If I can't get this fixed*, Will thought, *it might be best just to shoot him now and save him years of misery.*

*****

Maggie could not see Trey or the cell phone, but she could feel the tension from the back seat. She caught Will's eye. Seldom in their marriage had she seen Will angry. He was slow to anger and that was one of the qualities she loved about him. He was angry now.

"So, what happened with the horse? You didn't finish your story?" she asked hoping to redirect both her husband's and her grandson's attention.

"I worked with that horse for nearly two years," Will continued when Trey set his phone in the cup holder in the center console. "I was sure, that eventually, I would tame that animal. I figured I'd be a real dandy sitting up on the most beautiful stallion in Oklahoma. Then one day, I was working in the corral, and without thinking, I turned my back on that horse." Will shot a sideways glance toward Trey who was staring out the window as if in another world. The red had left his face and his knuckles weren't quite as white, but the boy's teeth were clenched, and his jaw muscles strained.

"Do you know what that horse did?" Will asked.

"No. What did he do?" Maggie asked from the back seat.

"Trey?" Will spoke his grandson's name.

"What?" Trey glanced Will's way and then turned back his attention back to the road. "I'm listening, Pappy, just got a lot on my mind. Sorry. What did the horse do?"

"He reared up and tried to cave in the back of my head with his front hooves," Will answered.

"What did you do?" Maggie raised her voice.

Trey threw a worried look at his grandfather. Will was staring straight ahead not seeing the road but imagining a beautiful black horse standing up on its hind legs thrashing at a young cowboy. "I heard him snort and looked back over my shoulder just in time to see his hooves start for me. I closed my eyes and tried to run but couldn't. It all happened too fast. I dropped to the ground and heard two extremely loud explosions, I opened my eyes, sure that I'd been kicked twice in the head and was dead. And there was my Pa standing over me with the big Smith and Weston .44 Revolver he always carried."

"What?" Trey shook his head, "He shot your horse?"

Will nodded his head, a little sadness etched across his brow. "Yes," he said, "but he saved my life."

"That's rough," Trey sighed softly. "Kinda see why you don't tell that story often."

"Learned a valuable lesson that day, son." Will turned to his grandson.

"What was that?" Trey asked.

"Beautiful on the outside can hide a whole lot of ugly on the inside if you let it." Will nodded at his grandson.

"I'll keep that in mind the next time I'm in the market for a horse." Trey said.

Will shook his head, exhaled sharply, and looked over his shoulder at Maggie. He could read her thoughts.

Nice try, but I think it's gonna take a little more fixin'.

*****

Twenty minutes of awkward silence later, Trey slowed the truck down at the Memphis, Texas, welcome sign. Following the signs for State Highway 156, he turned left, then after three blocks, he made a right onto Noel Street. A block later, the street became red brick.

"This reminds me of the streets in Pauls Valley." Maggie finally broke the silence.

"What?" Will asked.

"The red brick street we're on," Maggie explained. "It reminds me of the street in Pauls Valley, Oklahoma."

"Yeah, now that I think on it." Will nodded, "It does me too."

"Never been there," Trey said.

"Lots of places you've never been, I reckon." Will saw an opening and ran with it, "Probably lots of places you'll never see when you are all tied down to an accountant's desk in Tulsa."

The street took them through the heart of downtown Memphis. After several blocks, the red bricks disappeared, as did the store fronts. The street was lined with residential homes and an occasional small business. At the other edge of town, they passed a Dollar General and a Thriftway Foods grocery store. Ten minutes later, Memphis was just a fading memory as they slowed once again for the town of Lakeview.

According to the sign at the edge of town the population was a whooping one hundred and seven people. Eight blocks long and not a lake in sight. *Blink twice and you wouldn't even know you'd been here*, Trey thought to himself. He wandered how many of these little Podunk towns they were going to have to slow down for before they reached California.

His phone vibrated in the cup holder, and he picked it up. He hated to mess with it while he was driving, and usually, he just read it and pulled over to text back, but he was not sure how Pappy would feel about stopping. He read the message, *I guess you're just too busy with your own little adventure to call me or send me a text. You can be such an asshole.* His jaw clinched, and he put it back into the cup holder. He would have to get to it later. Nothing he could do about it now.

Will watched from the corner of his eye as Trey dropped the phone back into the cup holder, "You need to answer that?" he asked.

"I'll get it later," Trey replied. "It could take a while."

The phone vibrated again. To Trey, it seemed her anger caused the intensity with which it pulsed to escalate, and he had no doubt that she was seething because he had not answered her first text, but his hands were tied.

It stopped and then almost immediately started again. He could picture her, left hand on her hip, phone held in her right hand, looking like her head was about to explode. Knowing there was not a thing he could do at the moment, he ignored it, stared down the road in front of him, and prayed she would stop texting. Anger at being in this situation, frustration at not knowing what to do about it, and embarrassed that it was happening in front of his grandparents caused a blush to creep up his neck.

"Maybe you should pull over and just call the girl," Will suggested when it started to vibrate once again in the cup holder.

"I'd rather not right now," Trey said with a shrug.

"How 'bout shuttin' it off then," Will shrugged back. "The damn thing sounds worse than a kid whining at a Walmart store. You can turn the thing off, can't you?"

"Yes," Trey answered, wishing he could turn it all off, Lisa, his grandfather, the phone, everything. Maybe then he could think for two seconds and figure some way out of this hell he found himself in.

Trey stared out the window at a buzzard floating high above. Slowly, another came into view and then a third. The sky was a perfect blue, and the fresh green grass mingled with the brown and yellows of what was left of last years was just beautiful. He wished he could enjoy the ride and forget about the phone. He wished they all could.

Again, the phone started. Trey picked it up, glanced at the screen, winced, and returned it to the cup holder without shutting it off. Ahead, he could just make out a green sign on the passenger side of the road. As they grew closer, he realized it was a bridge over a waterway. As they passed a sign that read 'Prairie Dog Town Fork Red River' the phone vibrated again.

With his right-hand, Will pressed down on the button that lowered the window, and with his left, he took the phone from the cup holder. Before Trey could object, he tossed the phone out the half open window. It bounced once on the flat surface of the concrete guard rail and careened over the edge.

Without thinking or looking to see if any cars were near, Trey whipped the steering wheel to the right and came to a screeching halt just past the bridge abutment, sending gravel every which way. Wide-eyed, he stared at his grandfather and then slung open the door, slid out of the truck, raced back along the road, and looked over the side of the bridge. At least thirty feet down on the creek's rocky dry bed, he could see what was left of his shattered phone.

A rusty old blue Ford truck passed going the opposite direction. It stopped at the end of the bridge, turned, and started back. When it pulled to a stop right beside him, an elderly man in a tattered, grey Stetson hat leaned across the seat and asked, "You okay, son?"

Trey turned around and stared at him. The man that stared back had what looked to be a two-week growth of shaggy whiskers that almost passed as a beard. His teeth where crooked and yellowed by tobacco. He wore a faded red western shirt with the sleeves cut away for ventilation. The smell of body odor, Red Man, and beer reached Trey just as another vehicle passed in the other lane.

"Hey, you, okay? Can I help you with something?" the man asked again.

"My cellphone," Trey muttered.

"Sorry, young fella," the old man laughed. "If it's got anything to do with this newfangled tech-no-logical stuff, I'm of not help at all," and he pulled away.

Trey shook his head in dismay and looked back over the bridge rail at the riverbed once more. A last look at the pieces of his phone strewn among the rocks and he started towards the truck.

When he climbed back in the vehicle, he was so angry his hands were trembling. He didn't trust himself to speak, and when he did, his voice didn't even sound like his own.

"Why did you do that?" Trey asked staring straight ahead.

"Sometimes you have to shoot the horse to save the cowboy," Will stated flatly.

After several minutes of tense silence, Trey managed to pull himself together, put the truck in gear, and pull back onto the road. His thoughts were a jumbled mess. Separating them so he could deal with each problem individually was the only way he knew how to take care of them, but where did he start without his phone. Like most people his age, everything was on the phone; numbers, addresses, not to mention all of his photos. He tried to remember the last time he had backed the phone up to his computer or to the Cloud. He wasn't sure. At least he had Lisa's number memorized.

So, start with Lisa. She was already hopping mad—or maybe even ready to have a hissy fit as Granny would say--and when he did not text her back, things would go from bad to worse. Maybe at the next stop, he could find a temporary phone until he could get to an AT&T store. Maybe he should call his dad and have him order another phone. Or perhaps, he could call AT&T from the motel tonight. Surely, they would stay in a motel. Surely, Pappy…?

Next problem, Pappy. For the first time in his life, he felt like screaming at his grandfather. He felt like it but wouldn't. He wasn't much of a screamer. He knew himself well enough to know that he was a brooder. Trey had always been a planner, a fixer, the calm behind every situation, and down deep inside, he knew that particular bit of his DNA came from the man sitting in the seat next to him. Trey had never in his life heard his grandfather raise his voice. Will handled every situation as it came with the same calm demeanor be it bad or good.

Identify the problem. Decide on a solution. And get to fixin'. As the words ran through his mind, Trey gripped down hard on the steering wheel. He wanted to look at his grandfather. Wondered how Will was able to put thoughts in his head from across the seat.

Staring down the road, he chided himself for thinking crazy thoughts, realizing Pappy had placed those words into his skull many years ago. As the miles slipped by, he remembered the first time Will had ever talked to him like a grown up instead of like a little kid.

It had been the last month of his freshman year in high school. They had buried Trey's mother that January, and the whole family was having a hard time of it. The house was like a tomb without her. Pappy tried to keep Bo busy around the ranch as much as possible, and frequently he took Trey with him on one chore or another. On that day they had gone to the old barn to check on an old John Deere Pappy kept around in case the new one broke down or they needed two tractors at the same time. When they got to the barn, the tractor was gone.

"Load up," Will had told him.

The two had crawled back into Pappy's old beat-up farm truck and headed back to the house. To Trey, it had all seemed very exciting. Someone had stolen the tractor, that was obvious. He remembered thinking that a trip to Anadarko to the sheriff's office would make for an interesting day, and maybe afterwards, Pappy would take him out to eat. The excitement ended when Will pulled into the driveway of the ranch house, pulled the truck right up to the front porch, put it in park, and climbed out.

"Sit tight," He ordered Trey.

From his seat Trey watched as his grandfather climbed the steps and entered the house. Through the old screen door, he watched as his grandfather pulled down the old gun belt and pistol that hung on a special wooden peg beside the fireplace. Will checked the loads, threw the belt around his waist, buckled it in place, and tied the holster in place low on his right leg. When he stepped back out onto the porch, Trey felt like he was staring straight into an old John Wayne western. Granny came around the house with a worried look on her face. Will laid his hands on her shoulders, kissed her on the forehead and nodded.

Trey remembered watching her standing there beside the

porch as he and Will turned around and headed back down the drive. Fifteen minutes later, they pulled into a set of ruts that lead to a dilapidated old sheet metal pole barn at the back of a pasture. Trey could still remember the smell of pig manure. Inside the barn was the tractor and two young men.

"Sit tight," Will ordered again. "Be right back."

Trey remembered how his heart had nearly thumped out of his chest as his grandfather walked up to the barn. The two men had stepped around in front of the tractor. They wore dirty, grease stained bibbed-overalls and no shirts. One of them had his overalls tucked down into an old pair of combat boots. The other was barefooted.

"Clem," Will spoke to the fellow in the combat boots, "what are you doing with my tractor?"

"Needed some parts," Clem answered, "Didn't figure you'd mind. You hardly every use it."

"I do mind." Will said.

"Well, that's a problem," Clem scuffed his boot in the dirt, "We already pulled the parts."

"Your problem, Clem." Will's voice was flat and cold, "I expect...

"Don't really care what you expect," the barefooted man interrupted. "This here is private property, so you best hightail it out of here."

"Ted, I'm talking to your brother, not you." Will never took his eyes off Clem.

Ted's hand moved towards the nearest pole and Will drew. Trey stared in disbelief. He never saw the movement. One instant Will was talking, the next there was a gun in his hand, and it was pointed at Clem's face.

"If he touches that .12 gauge, I will shoot you in the face." Will spoke in a voice as calm as if he was asking those guys for the time.

"Dammit, Ted!" Clem's voice cracked, "don't do it, you'll get us both killed."

"Ted, you step over here by Clem, and you both have a seat," Will instructed.

With Ted and Clem seated, Will walked just inside the barn door. The pistol still trained on the two men, he inspected the tractor, and then picked up the shotgun as he stepped back outside.

"Clem, this is Saturday," Will looked down at the older of the two. "If my tractor is not in perfect running condition and back in my barn by the time I get home from church tomorrow, I'll be back. And if I have to come back, I won't come talkin'. Are we clear?"

"Yes, sir, Mr. Tucker." Clem had looked downright green around the gills.

"That's my shotgun," Ted snapped as Will walked away.

"You're on probation. Ain't allowed to have firearms." Will said over his shoulder as he opened the truck door and passed the shotgun to Trey, "I'll drop it at the Sheriff's office. You can pick it up there when your probation is over."

"How'd you know they had the tractor?" Trey asked his grandfather as he backed the truck away from the barn.

"I didn't know for sure," Will answered, "About a week ago, I saw Ted at the bait shop, and he asked me how much I wanted for that old tractor I didn't use anymore. When I told him it wasn't for sale, he smirked like I'd said something funny. When I saw the tractor was missin', I figured it was mostly likely him and his brother."

"What if it had't been there?" Trey asked.

"Then this would have been a wasted trip," Will chuckled, "And you'd have gotten that meal over in Anadarko you were so anxious to get."

They rode the rest of the way home in silence. The next day after church, Trey had ridden with Will to their old barn. The tractor was inside, and when Will turned the key, it purred like a kitten. News travels fast in a small town, and to Trey's knowledge no one had stolen anything off his Pappy's property since.

On the way home from the barn that day, Will had said, "Trey, you're becoming a young man. You aren't a kid anymore. What kind of man you will become is up to you. It is your decision. Do not ever let it be someone else's or you will never be your own man. Do you understand?"

"I think so Pappy," Trey answered honestly.

"Good," Pappy smiled.

Identify the problem. Decide on a solution. And get to fixin'. Full circle, Trey's thoughts brought him back to the present.

The gas gauge was under a quarter of a tank as he slowed to enter Silverton. He passed a Tex-Mex Barbeque café, the post office, the courthouse, and a flower shop, before he found a gas station. Trey pulled to a stop beside the pumps and shut off the engine.

"We need gas," he said flatly, "And you owe me a new phone."

Chapter 5

The Llano Estacado is one of the largest mesas in North America. Located in northwest Texas and eastern New Mexico, it took nearly two and a half hours to cross it. The summer sun reached its zenith and began its race to the Pacific Ocean. A red-tail hawk perched atop an electric pole scanned the field as the Black Silverado rolled west. Just west of Tulia, Texas road construction slowed traffic briefly. Flat prairie and dry farms lined the rural roads. Circle irrigation gave the landscape a strange, eerie, modern art feel that Will found irritating.

At Dimmit, Texas, the high school baseball field drew Trey's attention. The summer program was in full swing. Trey caught a momentary glimpse of a single pitch and swing as they passed by. The memory of Lisa sitting in the stands cheering for him as he stepped up to the plate surfaced. What had changed? She had always found a way to get him to do what she wanted him to, this he had realized even early on in their relationship. But lately, it was as if she didn't know what she wanted and just seemed to be happy making him run in circles while she tried to figure it out.

A sudden desire to turn the truck around and go see who would win caught him off guard. He hadn't been to a baseball game since his last one in high school. Somehow, he never thought he'd ever miss it. Maybe now he did just a little. He wondered if he could still throw a fast ball ninety miles an hour, and if giving up that scholarship to play at Murray State had been a mistake.

"Anyone else gettin' hungry?" Granny asked from the backseat.

"Maybe a little," Trey answered.

"How 'bout you, Will?" she asked.

"Whenever ya'll are ready," Came the flat reply.

"Sign back there said Bovina was thirty-two miles. Maybe we can find a nice little place there for lunch," she said.

Half an hour of silence passed between Dimmit and Bovina. Twice Trey noticed two large dairy farms, but mostly it was mile after mile of farmland irrigated using the same circular method that seemed so prevalent in this area. According to the city limit sign at the edge of Bovina, the population was one thousand eight hundred and sixty-eight. Trey was expecting to see businesses as he entered the town and slowed to the posted speed, but instead, the streets were lined with residences.

"I believe we need to turn left and make our way up to Highway 60," Granny spoke from the backseat. "That seems to be the most likely place to find a restaurant."

Trey followed her directions and headed north. Several blocks later they rolled past the town's post office. Granny pointed out the city hall to the left and suggested they ask someone about possible eateries.

"If I had my cellphone, I could just do a quick search and find us a place." Trey spoke aloud.

"Yes, but if you still had your cellphone, its constant binging would have driven us all crazy, and so we wouldn't need a place to eat," Will shot back.

With no logical return and no desire to argue the point, Trey shook his head and pulled into a parking space in front of the bricked, false-fronted building. He stepped out of the truck and headed for the door, still mourning the loss of his cellphone. If it had not been broken, he could have used it to find a restaurant. Instead, he would have to do it the old fashion way.

Inside, he found a counter and behind the counter a very sweet, very plump middle-aged lady. At the sound of the door opening, she looked up from the magazine she was reading and flashed a smile.

"Can I help you, young man?" she asked.

"Yes, ma'am," Trey answered. "I was wondering if you could suggest a good place to eat here in Bovina."

"Well, now, we don't have a lot to choose from right here in town." She pursed her lips and seemed to be thinking for a few minutes, and then added, "If you want a really good burger, you could try across the tracks at the burger shop."

"That sounds just fine, ma'am." Trey said, "Could you give me some directions?"

*****

The digital clock on the truck's dash indicated the time was five minutes after eleven as Trey eased into the small parking lot at the burger shop. A series of red wooden placards advertised burgers, drinks, and fries. Except for their truck, the place was empty. A sign on the front door indicated the hours of operation were from eleven a.m. to seven p.m., Monday through Saturday.

Trey parked and got out of the truck to the smell of burgers grilling. He closed his door, stepped back, and helped his grandmother out of the back seat. She thanked him as Will came around the front of the pickup and took her hand. As frustrated as he was, Trey could not help but smile as he followed the two of them to the shop's door. Will held the door for Maggie and then followed her inside. Trey found himself wishing he and Lisa were more like his grandparents. He stepped in behind them and waited a moment to let his eyes adjust to the change in light.

"Y'all have a seat wherever ya want." from somewhere in the rear of the place came the sweetest voice Trey had ever heard.

Maggie pointed at a table in the far back corner and Will nodded approval. When they reached the table, Will pulled Maggie's chair out and seated her and then took the chair beside her. Trey chose the chair beside his grandmother and across from Will.

As he lowered himself into the seat, a waitress came through a set of metal doors with menus in one hand and a tub of ketchup bottles cradled under her other arm. Short and small of frame, but with a toughness about her that showed in the way she walked, she had her long blonde hair pulled back into a ponytail. The gravelly tone in her voice matched her looks perfectly.

"Howdy, folks, my name is Teresa," she said as she handed each of them a menu, "Welcome to Bovina. What would y'all like to drink?"

"Coke, please," Maggie spoke first and then looked to Will.

"I think I just want a Sprite," he said, then when Maggie gave him a questioning look, he admitted, "Still feeling a little queasy."

"I'll take a Dr Pepper if you have it," Trey ordered.

Teresa set the tub of ketchup on the table to his left and stepped back through the metal doors. Before the doors had quit swinging, she reappeared with three tall, amber-colored plastic cups filled with the drinks they had ordered.

"Y'all know what ya want?" she asked as she passed the beverages out.

"I think maybe I'll have the junior cheeseburger, hold the onions, please?" Maggie smiled and handed her menu over as she spoke.

"Want to make that a meal?" Teresa asked returning the smile.

"What do I get with the meal?" Maggie asked.

"Fries, a dill pickle, and if we still have some, I'll throw in some of Dan's famous stuffed jalapenos." Teresa said.

"Sounds wonderful, I'll take the meal," Maggie said.

"And you, sir?" she turned to Will.

"Sir?" he put his hand over his heart and feigned serious hurt. "You make me feel old."

"So, sorry," Teresa played along.

"Okay, then," Will removed his hands from his chest and pointed a finger at his menu, "I'd like the grilled cheese and an order of French fries, but if that's a meal, hold the pickle and jalapenos, please."

"Very well," Teresa said as she turned to Trey, "and what for you, young man?"

Trey's mouth opened to order, but his brain sidetracked him. He figured he couldn't be more than a couple years younger than she was. He realized that they were all staring at him, and he felt the blood creeping up the back of his neck and looked quickly down at his menu to compose himself.

"Sorry," he said when he looked back up. "I'll have a double bacon cheeseburger meal, please."

"You got it," Teresa said with a wink, took his menu, stepped to the doors, and shouted the order to someone in the back.

When Trey looked back at his grandparents, both were sporting grins. *Glad y'all find my discomfort so amusing*, he thought, but said, "What?"

"Nothin'," Maggie answered.

"Awful sweet, ain't she?" Will said.

"Pappy, I'm engaged," Trey reminded him.

"Bein' nice ain't a sin, ya know? And admiring a woman doesn't mean you're committin' a sin," Will argued.

"Yeah, I know," Trey said aloud, but added to himself, *kinda depends on who you ask.*

*****

Trey noticed his grandfather had slipped a five-dollar bill under the ketchup bottle as the three of them got up from the table after finishing their meals. Maggie excused herself to the restroom so Trey followed Will to the pay counter. Teresa used a calculator to tally their tab and then hit a couple keys on an old cash register. Will paid in cash and told her to keep the change.

"Y'all come see us again." She nodded at Will and winked at Trey over his shoulder.

Trey blushed again, but managed to say, "Thanks, we sure enjoyed the meal." Maybe, just maybe, that would shut his Pappy up for a little bit.

Will smiled. "Are you ready to hit the road?"

"Think maybe I better run by the men's room first," Trey answered.

"Probably ought to myself," Will admitted just as Maggie stepped up behind the two.

*****

"Which way from here?" Trey asked over his shoulder as he pulled back onto the highway.

"Just stay on Highway 60," Maggie said from the back seat, "It'll take us all the way to Fort Sumner."

"How long 'til we get there?" Trey wondered out loud.

Granny consulted the Atlas and then said, "Oh, 'bout an hour and a half or so. We should be there around two o'clock. That's if my calculations are correct."

Fifteen minutes later, Trey slowed as they entered the city limits of Farwell, Texas. Farwell turned into Texico at the Texas-New Mexico state line. Trey found it a bit strange that a city would be called by two different names simply because it straddled a state line but said nothing aloud.

Trey had barely gotten back up to speed when he hit the first of a series of speed limit signs that slowed him back to forty-five miles an hour going through Clovis. He figured at their current rate, he could have ridden one of Pappy's horses and made better time. Luckily, there were few traffic lights, and he had to stop at only one.

A half hour of silence passed before Trey saw the makings of another town in the distance. A green sign indicated that the Melrose Cemetery was off to the north at the next intersection.

I may need to look into a cemetery plot, Trey thought to himself as he passed the sign and wondered what Lisa was thinking now that she hadn't heard from him all morning long. He could see his tombstone, a simple, flat, marble slab, and on it written: Here lies Trey Tucker, God bless his soul, killed by a woman's fury when she lost control.

A set of rusted old red railway boxcars along the left side of the road caught his attention as he slowed to the posted speed limit. Someone had extended the roof of each and turned them into horse stables complete with corrals. A big paint gelding tossed his head at the truck as it passed by. It reminded Trey of Pappy's story of the horse that had been shot and the comment about the broken cellphone. So, his grandfather thought his fiancé was mean and beyond fixing. Well only time would tell if that was true, but he failed to see how a trip to California was going to change anything. He loved Lisa. Their wedding was only a couple of months away, and when this trip was over and he was back in Oklahoma, he was sure everything would be okay.

"Turn just before that Allsup's." Will pointed up at a sign two blocks away as they entered Clovis. Trey nodded, and as he slowed for the coming turn, noticed the airplane across the street from the convenience store. He was driving slow enough that he could see the white writing on the blue sign--F100A Super Sabre.

"Just pull over there," Will pointed to a spot beside the aircraft, "and give me a minute." He unbuckled his seatbelt, opened the truck door as it came to a stop, and stepped out.

Trey caught his grandmother's eye in the rearview mirror. She shrugged as if to say, 'your guess is as good as mine' then shifted in her seat and watched her husband step over the weathered, white knee-high pipe railing that surrounded the plane and the rest of the city park.

In the passenger's side mirror Trey could see his grandfather walk to the sign in front of the plane, lay his palm on it and bow his head.

"Does Pappy ever talk about the war?" he muttered.

Eyes still on her husband, Granny answered, "To me, only once, and that just a brief few sentences the day we buried his brother."

Will finally moved from the sign to stand in the front of the plane. "Did you know your Pappy was awarded the silver cross?" Granny whispered as she watched her husband reach up and touch the underside of the fuselage.

"I did not. Why doesn't he have it out for folks to see?" Trey answered.

"He put it in the casket with his brother," Granny's voice waivered. "He told me later that your Uncle Fred was the only reason he enlisted in the Army in the first place. Fred got drafted and Will didn't feel like he could let Fred go by himself, so he enlisted. He always said that Fred deserved that star far more than he ever did."

"Why was that?" Trey asked.

"I asked him that very question." Granny turned back around in her seat. "'Because he did' was all he would say, so I left it alone."

Will's minute stretched into several, and just as Trey was thinking about leaving the vehicle himself, his grandfather stepped back over the pipe railing and returned to the truck. Once back in his seat with his seatbelt on, Will nodded, and said, "I'm ready if y'all are."

The way his Pappy's voice cracked brought a lump to Trey's throat. He had never given much thought to all that his grandfather had been through. Will had always just been Pappy, the man who was always there for him. The idea that Will had himself needed someone's help somewhere back down the line had never really dawned on him.

Trey checked his mirror for any traffic, whipped a U-turn back onto the street, turned right at the stop sign, and they were on their way once again. In less than three minutes, the little town faded behind them. In that tiny space of time, Trey went from thinking about his grandfather's life and all he had been through back to worrying about Lisa's anger. It was beginning to feel like no matter where he turned or who he thought about, all there was for him was guilt. Guilt because he couldn't fix the problem with

Lisa. Guilt because he did not really want to be on this trip. Just guilt piled on more guilt.

Two miles outside of Melrose, Trey watched a dirt devil creep northeast across a recently plowed field. The top of its vortex some thirty or forty feet above the earth, it moved slowly, stalled out for a long ten count, and then started once again on its path, sucking up dirt as it went. Trey had never seen anything like it. Not to say there weren't dust storms and an occasion vortex of dirt back in Oklahoma, but nothing that would catch a person's attention like this one. He looked for a message in it but found none.

A Rafter J Ranch sign designated ownership to what must have been a large parcel of land because the buildings of the homestead were far enough away on the horizon to be mere specks. Looking out across the land, Trey wondered what the Rolling T would look like without all the scrub oak and cedars. It occurred to him that he had no real idea how much acreage his family actually owned or how many head of cattle they ran on the land. He hated to admit it, even to himself, but he had been looking forward to the summer's ranch work and was wishing a little that he was back there astraddle a horse instead of picking his way through every Podunk town in the southwest.

Windmills dotted the landscape, and in the twenty minutes it took to reach the ghost town of Tolar, New Mexico, Trey noticed three different trains rolling east along the tracks to his left. Never in his memory could he recall seeing the entire length of a moving train all at once, but then the land was flat, and the road was straight. As the third train flew past, he realized that everything seemed to be heading east--the trains, the dust devil, the few cars passing on the road, everything. It didn't seem right—him heading west away from Lisa when the natural flow of nature moved east. Was this a sign of things to come? He decided he did not really believe in signs and chalked it up to circumstance. He figured once he got back to Lisa and they were both headed in the same direction, all would be fine.

Trey slowed as they entered the limits to the town of Tolar.

Not because there was a speed limit sign but because it had become habit to slow down when he came to the edge of a town, but this was not a town, once it maybe had been, but it was no longer.

"Kind of dead around here," Will stated the obvious.

"Reminds me of some of the ghost towns you see in the old western movies," Trey said.

"It's a lot different than on television," Maggie offered. "I mean seeing it in person has a very unique feel that you don't get from watching a show."

"That one there," Will pointed at a rather small structure weathered, and worn with half of its roof missing, "reminds me of the old house my grandparents first lived in."

"Where was that?" Maggie asked.

"Not far from the family cemetery," Will told her. "The house is gone but the foundation is still there. It's just overgrown with cedar trees."

"What happened to it?" Maggie looked from the ruins to her husband.

"It stood empty for years after the folks passed away," Will answered, "Then one summer a grass fire burned it to the ground. Before all the cedars grew up around it, me and Frank use to play like it was our fort and we were under attack from the Comanches."

Trey studied the shamble of structures as he listened to his grandparents. The largest portion of the dilapidated buildings stood off to the left. Only a couple of buildings stood to the right between the highway and the railroad tracks. As Trey accelerated away from the last of the shanties, he found himself wondering what had happened here. Two miles further along, he found his answer.

"Pull over right there." Will pointed to a wide spot in the road.

It took no small amount of finesse to get the truck off the black top and onto the gravel pull-off without throwing Will and himself into the dash and Maggie into the back of his seat, but he got it done and pulled to a stop beside one of the state of New

Mexico's official scenic historic markers. A weather wooden plank background with a large brown aluminum sign screwed to it told the story. At the top of the sign in large white letters three words—EXPLOSION ROCKS TOLAR—and beneath it the story.

Will unlocked the door and stepped out before Trey even had time to put the truck into park. By the time he and Maggie made it around the truck, Will had finished reading the sign and turned to a large piece of iron to its right. Maggie stepped up to his side and put an arm around his waist. Will slide his arm past her shoulder, down across her back, grabbed her at the waist, and pulled her tight against his side.

Trey always got a warm, fuzzy feeling inside when he saw his Granny and Pappy stand together holding each other. He couldn't remember a time in his life where they weren't close. He wondered if what he and Lisa had would be like that in the years to come, and then realized he had thought about Lisa, but not about how she was going to react when he was finally able to reach her again. With the realization came the customary empty pit in his stomach. Instead of letting it overcome him, he turned his attention to the story of the explosion on the sign in front of him.

A train hauling one hundred and sixty-five bombs for the Pacific Theater during World War II had derailed in Tolar. At noon on November thirtieth in nineteen and twelve, it had caught fire and the bombs had exploded leveling nearly every building in the town, vaporizing five hundred feet of track, and sending pieces of the train flying in all directions. Trey finished reading the sign and turned to read the one above the large piece of iron in front of Will and Maggie. The sign above it explained that it was a section of the undercarriage of train car that had been found some five hundred feet south of the tracks where the train exploded.

Gotta wonder how big the explosion is going to be and what kind of debris is gonna fly when I finally get to talk to Lisa, Trey thought to himself.

Chapter 6

True to Granny's calculations, it was almost two before they reached the first signs announcing Fort Sumner. A billboard advertised a Motel 8 just two miles ahead on the left. Trey was amazed at how quickly the terrain had changed after they left the historical marker. The vegetation was still pretty much the same, but the flat view of endless land all the way to the horizon had given way to the occasional rolling hill. He decided he liked the new landscape better. Not as much as he liked the land back home, but better than what they had driven through earlier in the day. The word *home* resonated in his head, and he realized that for all of his life that word had been synonymous with the ranch. Moving to the city with Lisa would change that, or would it? Would the ranch always be home? Somewhere he had read or heard, home was where the heart was, so if his heart was truly with Lisa, then he guessed his home would have to be in Tulsa.

A quarter of a mile past the Motel 8 billboard Trey tapped the brake and let the truck decelerate to fifty-five miles per hour. A small brown sign on his left caught Will's attention; Fort Sumner Historical Site and then some more words he didn't have time to read as they cruised pass, but at the very bottom of the sign was a line he caught that read: Billy The Kid's Grave and a white arrow pointing left.

"Gotta take the next left." Will pointed.

Trey slowed, made the turn, and then gave his grandfather a questioning look as they passed another billboard that indicated the Billy the Kid Museum was two miles ahead on the road they had just left.

"Sign back there said to turn this way." Will shrugged and pointed as they passed another Billy the Kids Grave sign suggesting they were on the right road.

They passed a mile of residences before they came to an intersection. The words on the little green sign read Billy the Kid Drive.

"This is not the way I pictured it," Will said. "There's way too many houses, too much civilization."

"Not exactly what I was thinkin' when you told me we were goin' to see Billy the Kid's grave, either," Trey admitted having a hard time believing there was a cemetery ahead as he watched one residence after another slip by.

In the back seat Maggie studied her atlas. When she and Will had discussed possible side trips for their travel to California, it had come as a bit of a surprise to her that Will had chosen Billy the Kid's grave, but she had learned long ago not to overthink or ask to many questions. If Will wanted to open up, he would, and if he didn't, all the nagging in the world would not budge that door.

"Why Billy the Kid's Grave?" Trey asked.

At first, Trey thought his grandfather was not going to answer, then Will said, "Way before they made that movie, *Young Guns*, my generation knew who the Kid was and his story. Some folks thought he was just a common criminal; others saw him as a hero. I always figured he was a bit of both, a true outlaw, but one with a code. His story always intrigued me and if it hadn't, well, my life might have been much different. He is a big part of the reason I met your grandmother."

Before he had time to question how Billy the Kid fit into the story of his grandparents meeting, Trey rounded a curve and spotted a large building with a big parking lot. Across its front above the wrap around walkway were the words: Old Fort Sumner Museum. The parking lot was empty except for a pair of

Harley motorcycles parked to the right of the front door. Trey eased the truck to a stop in the spot just to the left of the cycles.

An arrow on a large brown sign at the end of the building pointed along a sidewalk that led the way to the cemetery where Billy the Kid's grave could be found. Trey put the truck in park, set the brake, and shut off the engine. Still not sure what was expected of him at this point, he unfastened his seatbelt, opened his door, stepped out of the truck, and opened the back door for his grandmother.

"Will, you go on ahead," Maggie said as she stepped down out of the truck. "Trey and I will catch up to you in a minute. I want to show him something here on the map."

"Alright." Will shot a wink her way and disappeared around the side of the building.

"What is it, Granny?" Trey asked.

"Nothing really," Maggie patted his arm. "I just thought we'd let your Pappy have a minute to himself since it was his idea to visit this place. We'll give him a little head start and then catch up to him."

Trey wondered why his grandfather needed a head start, decided not to question his grandmother, and simply nodded instead, "Okay, Granny."

"On second thought," Granny picked up the big Atlas book and pointed to a page, "Here's where we are, and right here is Fort Sumner, and honey, it is not a very big town."

"Okay, Granny." Trey repeated.

"I just hate to lie to your Pappy," she chuckled. "I said I wanted to show you something on the map, and now I have."

Trey grinned as the warm fuzzy feeling that only his Granny could cause began somewhere in the middle of his chest and radiated outward. It had always amazed him that she was so thoughtful. His Pappy was a lucky man. He only hoped that someday his wife cared for him as much as Granny did for Pappy. His wife? Should that thought not have been that he hoped that Lisa cared for him that much? Was it a sign? Was this trip getting to him? What if he and Lisa never had a relationship like his grandparents? He shook his head. This trip was definitely getting to him, and he could not, would not, let it.

The thought of Lisa and her temper fits caused his grin to fade. The warm fuzzy feeling disappeared, and that old familiar emptiness laid heavy on his heart. He needed to call her. Needed to 'get to fixin'' as Pappy said. Needed this terrible sinkhole in his stomach to go away. If all else failed, surely he could figure out how to use the motel phone to call her. How had life gotten so screwed up—and all over a stupid phone?

*****

Will followed the sidewalk around to the back of the building and stopped. The small, well-maintained cemetery had a chest high adobe wall surrounding it. A series of sidewalks lead visitors from one grave site to another. The first grave Will noticed was marked with a wooden plank headpiece. Rough block-style letters were carved into the wood—JOE GRANT, SHOT JAN. 10 1880 BY WM. BONNEY. Atop the wooden marker someone had stacked several small stones.

Will made his way along the path stopping to read every one of the headstones as he came to them. Each told a story, and many of them were part of the Billy the Kid saga. Most of the stories, he already knew or had heard somewhere along the way. There was a somber yet peaceful feeling about the place. He couldn't quite put a finger on it, but the feeling seemed deeper and grew deeper still as he approached the grave he'd come to see.

Billy's grave sat towards the back of the cemetery at the end of one of the concrete pathways. A large metal cage that reminded Will of an old-time jail cell was placed over three graves. The whole of the cage floor was covered by a layer of concrete. In the back left corner of the enclosure was a large, weathered white headstone. Three names were carved into it. Tom O'Folliard in the upper left corner, William H. Bonney in the upper right

53

corner, and Charlie Bowdrie centered at the bottom, and above them all was the word PALS.

Will looked through the wrought iron bars at the word PALS and thought of the people in his life he would have used that word to describe. They were all people who would stick by you through hell or high water. Of course, Maggie would have to be at the top of the list. She had stuck with him through thick and thin, had loved him even when he did not love himself. Frank, his brother, would be high on the list as well. If not for Frank, Will knew he would have never made it home from the war. As he thought about it, he decided he should add Bo to the list. Bo had never failed to show up any time he needed a hand. Trey should also be on the list, and if this trip went to his liking, perhaps he would be, but that remained to be seen. It would be so much easier if the boy could just see what a mess he was about to make of his life. But then as they say: Love is blind and wisdom is wasted on youth.

Another smaller stone of gray was set in the concrete and bolted down in a metal cage of its own. This one for Billy only. Carved into it were the day he was born, the day he was killed, the words THE BOY BANDIT KING, and in quotes "He Died As He Lived". A heaviness started deep inside Will's chest and spread outward as he read those words. Here laid a kindred spirit. A cattleman, a fighter, a lover of land, someone with a deep sense of right and wrong. Had he been born a century earlier, Will thought, it could well have been him lying under this concrete encased in a cage.

All his life Will had been a rancher, a cowboy, a man of the land, and he couldn't think of five words that could better explain how he felt about his own life than: He died as he lived. The thought of himself in an old folk's home had always scared him more than he would ever admit—even to himself. He hoped the good Lord would allow him to pass quickly and quietly somewhere on the ranch. He wanted to be like Billy. When it was his time to go, he wanted to die as he had lived on the ranch.

Movement behind him caused a shadow to creep along the edge of the walkway beside him and filter its way into the cage. Maggie stepped up beside him, slipped an arm around his waist, pulled his arm over her shoulder, and asked, "Why the cage?"

"To keep folks from taking the headstones," Will explained.

"Look at all those bullets and coins." She pointed through the bars.

"I saw them. Folks must've been payin' their respects as best they could," Will said as he reached in his pocket and tossed in a couple of quarters.

"And there on the bars," Trey pointed at a line from the movie *Young Guns* that was written in white on the black bars.

Will read it aloud, "I'm darin' you, Billy".

"I love that movie." Trey chuckled at the twang in his grandfather's voice.

"Me, too." Will loved hearing Trey laugh. "I'm ready when y'all are."

"Don't you want to read some of the other headstones?" Maggie asked pointing out several, "I think they have a story to tell, too."

"Not really," Will answered. "I read a little about them before y'all made it around here, and I already know Billy's story pretty well. I just wanted to see his grave. Now that I've done that, I'm ready to go, but if y'all need more time, I'm not in a hurry."

"Do you want to step into the museum and see what they have in there?" Maggie asked.

"Nope," Will answered, "and I don't want to stop at the one in town either."

"Alrighty then," she said with a wink. "I guess I'm ready if you and Trey are?"

"Trey?" Maggie asked.

"I'm fine to stay as long as y'all want, or go on either one," he answered.

As he followed his grandparents back down the sidewalk

and around the building, he thought about how much extra time this little detour had caused. It seemed like a lot compared to the half an hour they had actually spent looking around the cemetery.

*****

Trey followed his grandparents back down the walkway and around the side of the building. At the edge of the building Will stopped, looked off into the distance, and then as a grin began to spread across his face, he said, "Back when I was young, me and my brother use to play at being old time sheriffs and outlaws and such. He always wanted to be Wyatt Earp or Bat Masterson or Pat Garrett. That left me to be the outlaw and most of the time, I was Billy the Kid."

"It's kind of hard to see you as an outlaw." Maggie laughed.

Will chuckled and said, "You're right, darlin', but had I been born a century earlier, I figure my life might have been a lot different."

"How so?" Trey asked.

"It's like this, Trey," Will answered, "We've all got a little bit of outlaw in us. Who we decide to run with will either feed the outlaw or starve it out. The time and place we are born often does the same. I've seen men from good God-fearing families turn out bad because of who they decided to follow, and I've seen some mighty bad men led away from an outlaw life by a good woman they were lucky enough to have cross their path. And don't think for one minute that it is only men who have it in them, women do too." A quick glance at Maggie, and a wink at Trey, and he added, "It's just that they hid it a lot better than us men do."

"Will Tucker, you better watch it, you…" Maggie's face flushed, "You… well, you… you old outlaw."

"See what I mean, Trey?" Will grinned, "We better load up before this old outlaw gets himself into more trouble than he can get himself out of in this lifetime."

*****

Except for road noise, the truck was silent on the five-minute drive back to the highway. Trey turned left and the town appeared before them. A Super 8 was the only modern-day chain motel in town, he started to pull into it when Will stopped him.

"I like the looks of that one," Will said pointing at the Billy the Kid Country Inn across the street.

"Okay," Trey said, and on his grandfather's orders, pulled into a parking place in front of the office door. The motel was single story and built in an L-shape. Each room had a door that opened directly into a designated parking place. Trey wondered if this was the kind of establishment they would be staying in throughout the trip.

Without a word Will opened the door, stepped out of the truck, and disappeared inside leaving Trey to wonder about the sleeping arrangements. They had not discussed one or two rooms, and until this very moment, he hadn't really given it much thought. When Will returned with two old-style metal motel room keys, Trey breathed a sigh of relief.

"I'm not all that hungry tonight," Will said as he got back into the truck. "I thought maybe we'd just grab something and bring it back to our rooms. That okay with y'all?"

"That works for me," Granny said. "You're not getting sick, are you?"

Trey heard the worry in his grandmother's voice and wondered too if something was wrong with his grandfather. It had been a very emotional day, so perhaps it was just nerves, Trey thought to himself. He knew the stress of having to talk to Lisa tonight was definitely getting to him.

"Nah," Will smiled over his shoulder at her, "Just ain't used to riding this much." He turned toward Trey and asked. "Take out okay with you?"

"Sure," Trey answered. "I'm not really that hungry either."

Trey noticed that his grandmother was shaking her head in

the back seat and could almost read her mind. She was thinking that her grandson's appetite was gone because of this trip and the mess it was getting him into with his fiancé. Her husband's appetite was gone because he was worried about their grandson and the young man's future.

Two blocks further into town, they found a Dariland with a drive-through, takeout window. Trey pulled up to it, ordered two chicken sandwich specials and a hot ham and cheese with fries and soft drinks. Their order was handed out through the window surprisingly quickly, and a few minutes later, they were back at the motel, dragging food and luggage into their rooms. Trey dropped his bags on the queen bed, turned the thermostat on the air conditioning unit down as far as it would go, and went to his grandparents' room next door.

Granny was laying out their food on a small, round, white wooden table with a single pedestal-style leg. The chairs matched the table but there were only two, so Trey stepped back outside and brought in one of the faded green plastic chairs he'd passed on his way from his room. After Will had graced the meal, they ate without much conversation, each lost in their own thoughts. The rustle of the paper their sandwiches were wrapped in and the hum of the air-conditioning unit kept the silence from feeling uncomfortable.

"I need to run an errand," Will spoke as he finished his hot ham and cheese, pushed the majority of his fries towards Trey, and stood up. "I'll be back shortly."

"Can you pick up a few snacks. Maybe some crackers and something to drink while you're out?" Maggie asked and then dumped what was left of her fries into the container with Will's.

"Sure can," he answered her, then to Trey, "Be needing the truck keys."

Trey dug the keys from his pocket and handed them to his grandfather. Will kissed Maggie on the cheek, whispered, "I love ya," and headed out the door.

"What errand does he have to run?" Trey wondered aloud

but was thinking to himself, *I'm gonna gain ten pounds on this trip if I'm not careful.*

"I learned a long time ago not to ask," Maggie said and patted him on the shoulder as she stood up. "Best to just let him go and get the answer when he gets back."

*****

Trey was sitting in a green plastic chair when his grandfather brought the truck to a stop in front of the motel doors. He crawled out with two white Family Dollar store bags in his hands, pulled a second chair away from the wall, sat down next to his grandson, and handed him one of the bags.

"What's this?" Trey asked as he reached into the bag.

"The phone I owe you," Will stated in a flat tone.

Trey opened the bag and pulled out a prepaid Tracfone. It was an LG Classic flip phone with a yellow 3M sticky tab stuck to it.

"This is not quite the same as my phone," Trey said and then read the phone number on the sticky note.

"Nope," Will said, "It's better, it works."

"Pappy…" Trey started.

Will cut him off with both palms held up defensively. "Use it 'til we get home, and I'll get you one like your old one. The Dollar Store didn't have much of a selection, and I don't know much about the durn things anyway. The lady working there had to help me find that one."

"Okay," Trey agreed with a nod.

The two of them sat quietly and listened to the sounds of the little desert town for several minutes. An old, square-bodied, red Ford truck passed headed east with a cab full of teenage boys and two more seated in the bed. A memory of cruising the main drag of Fort Cobb with his friends the summer before his sophomore year of high school came to Trey's mind. Try as he might, he could not recall whose truck it was, or even who was old enough to have been driving.

"Trey," Will's deep voice brought him back to the present, "why are you so set on moving to Tulsa?"

"It's where Lisa wants to settle, and I guess I'm good with that," Trey answered.

"But are you really?" Will pressed. "Is that really what you want out of life?"

"What do you mean?" Trey asked.

"I mean," Will paused and sighed. "I mean do you really want to live your whole life being told exactly how, when, and where to do everything? Do you want to be your own man or just somebody's project?"

"It's not like that, Pappy," Trey argued, managing to keep his voice level while the voice in his head screamed that his grandfather was one hundred percent correct.

"Yep, Trey," Pappy said. "It's exactly like that." And without another word, he rose from the chair, bag in hand, walked the short distance to his room, opened the door, went inside and closed it, leaving Trey glaring at the Super 8 Motel across the street.

*****

Lisa picked up on the third ring, "Who is this?" she demanded in what Trey had long ago come to understand was her sweetest voice. The background music and noise told him she was at a party or a club.

"It's me," He told her, holding his breath against the wrath he was sure was coming.

"Me who?" she asked.

Trey envisioned her with a finger in one ear pressing the phone against her other so she could hear better.

"Trey!" he yelled into the phone.

There was the sound of a door opening and then closing, and suddenly, the music vanished, and there was only silence. Dead silence that for an instant left Trey thinking the damn cheap-ass phone was not working.

"I don't know this number," Lisa said. "You've got five seconds then I'm hangin' up."

"It's me, Trey," he said.

"I heard you the first time." Lisa's tone went icy cold.

Trey could picture her face. He'd seen the transformation too many times over their relationship. Happy and sweet around family and friends turning into ice-cold anger as soon as they were alone. "Whose phone number is this? You've got two seconds left."

"It's mine," he answered. "At least, it is for right now. My iPhone was broken, and I had to get a temporary flip phone from a Dollar Store for now." He saw no need in explaining to her the events that had led to the broken phone.

"So, I guess next you're gonna tell me that's why you haven't been answering my texts and calls all day long." Her tone still dripped icicles.

"Yes." Trey wasn't sure if it was a question or a statement but decided to answer anyway.

"Yeah, right," Lisa shot back, "and where are you now?"

Trey ignored the 'yeah, right' and answered, "Fort Sumner, New Mexico. Pappy wanted to see Billy the Kid's grave."

"Billy the Kid's grave…" she snapped, "that's just wonderful, and so much more important than I am." The chill in her voice told him that it was going to take a lot to fix this issue. "I sure hope you're having a good time. You've all but ruined my trip."

"Really? It sounded like you were having a pretty good time when you answered the phone," He snapped back at her, and then said, "Sorry, it's been a long day."

"Yes, it has. And here I thought I might actually get to enjoy this evening, but thanks to you it looks like that's shot, too." Her voice went even colder.

"I said I was sorry." Trey countered trying hard to control the anger and frustration swirling around in his chest.

"I guess *I'm sorry* is supposed to fix everything, huh?" she shot back and then without waiting for a response continued, "I'm not sure how much you really want this to work. It seems to me like you were more than happy to ruin my plans for the summer by running off with your grandparents on some trumped-up vacation or wedding or whatever the hell this thing you are doing is. I think you're just getting cold feet, and I'm not gonna put up with it. You better figure out really quick what you really want or else."

"Or else what?" Trey asked.

"Oh, you don't what to go there." The chill in her voice reached a whole new level.

"Darlin', I really don't want to argue with you." Every beat of Trey's heart felt as if it was going to burst right through his ribs and out of his chest. "Can we just maybe take a breath and try this again? I really want this to work, and I really do love you."

"So, this is what you call love?" she asked.

"Lisa you're being unreasonable," he said, and immediately wished he could put the words back into his mouth.

"Unreasonable? Unreasonable!" her voice rose with each new word. "I'll tell you what's unreasonable! You! You are unreasonable. Me not being able to enjoy my graduation trip with my sorority sisters is unreasonable. And all because of you."

"Really? Well, darlin'," Trey said through clenched teeth, "why don't you just go back to the club with your sorority sisters and have a good time. And you give me a call when you feel like being civil."

"Don't hold your breath!" she screamed, and then the line went dead.

Trey lay back on the bed and stared at the ceiling. He hated it when he let himself get angry and frustrated, but Lisa had always been able to push his buttons. This was not the first time she'd threatened to end the relationship, and somewhere back along the line, he'd lost track of how many times it had happened.

So why do you still let it get to you when she does it? His granny's voice popped into his head.

"It's not like she will go through with a breakup, she just wants attention, and she loves drama," he whispered.

A half hour passed slowly by before he reached for the phone once more. After several rings Bo answered with his usual, "Yep."

"Dad, it's me, Trey."

"Whose phone are you calling from?" Bo asked.

Trey gave his father the details of the day's trip, including how his phone got broken.

Bo chuckled, but Trey failed to see any humor in it. He filled Bo in on the problems and the conversation he'd had with Lisa. He wasn't sure if he just needed someone to talk to, or if he really wanted his father's advice.

"So, you're on a trip with your Granny and Pappy, and Lisa is running around the Bahamas in a skimpy bikini, and she's mad at *you*? Doesn't make much sense to me," Bo said.

"Yeah, doesn't make much sense to me either," Trey agreed. "I'm at my wit's end. What do I do?"

"I don't know that I have an answer for that question," Bo answered, "What does your gut tell you?"

"Nothing, it just feels empty and kind of lost," Trey's voice waivered, "I just keep thinkin' if we can make it through her trip to the Bahamas and my trip to California with Granny and Pappy, things will change. Maybe go back to the good times."

"And when were the good times?" Bo asked.

"Three maybe four years ago," Trey answered, "At least in my mind that's when everything started to come apart. Before that she was a bit controlling, but somehow it seemed to get much worse after she joined the sorority."

"Maybe tomorrow will be better," Bo suggested, and then added. "Son, you need to figure out what you really want in life, in a relationship, and in a wife, and you've got this trip to figure it all out. I can't fix this one for you. Only you can do that."

"Well, tomorrow can't be any worse," Trey said.

"Be careful there, son," Bo warned. "It can always get worse."

An hour later, as Trey crawled under the covers, his father's words were still stuck in his head, he thought, *Surely dad's wrong. How could it possibly get worse?*

Chapter 7

At five-thirty, Trey was awakened by the alarm on his new flip-phone. He had been too angry the night before to get a good night's sleep, and he'd been too angry to call his grandfather to ask about travel plans for the next day. He had simply set his alarm and gone to bed figuring his grandfather would want to start at his usual time of six o'clock.

When Trey stepped out with his bags in tow, Will was stowing the last of his and Maggie's luggage under the tarp in the truck bed, and she was making one last check of the rooms. The desert night had given way to the rising of a huge, round, red sun in the east, but the temperature was still on the chilly side. Trey wondered if perhaps he should have packed a heavier jacket.

"Good mornin', grandson," Maggie greeted him as she pulled the door to their room shut.

"Good mornin', Granny," he returned the greeting and with a nod to Will, "Pappy."

"Mornin'," Will nodded back and held his hand out for Trey's bags, "You ready to hit the road?"

"As ready as I'll ever be," Trey answered honestly, maybe a little too honestly.

Will appeared not to notice. Maggie on the other hand, was well aware of the tension. She made a quick decision not to mention breakfast in the hopes that a few miles might lighten the mood.

The truck packed and everyone in their seats, Maggie told Trey to keep west on Highway 60. "When we hit the town of

Vaughn, we'll catch Highway 285 towards Encino, but that's not for nearly sixty miles."

The miles slid slowly past, and Trey wondered if or when he should expect a call from Lisa. He figured it was anyone's guess.

Will stared at the road ahead not seeming to really see much. Not that there was much to see in Trey's opinion. The terrain was the same mile after mile. Sparse vegetation covered sandy desert as far as the eye could see, broken only occasionally by a few rolling hills.

*****

Maggie checked the atlas from time to time, not for any other reason except it gave her something to do. A half hour out of Fort Sumner she began to notice an abundance of hip-high cactus with arms branched out in what appeared to be no particular pattern. Towards the end of the topmost arms were large purple flowers. She found them interesting and wondered about their name. She decided she should probably pick herself up some reading material the next time they made a stop and made a mental note to look for a book on cactus.

*****

A few miles outside of Vaughn, they caught up to a train headed in their direction. As they passed boxcar after boxcar, Trey was reminded of a scene from a movie where someone in a truck was trying to outrun a train to the next crossing. In the movie the driver had barely made it across the tracks, breaking through the crossbars just before the train went speeding past. Seemed kind of like his relationship with Lisa. Always a crossing just ahead. Always a need to beat a train to it. Always the chance of a major train wreck if he didn't make it in time.

And then they reached the outskirts of Vaughn and were

brought to a stop behind three other vehicles caught by the train. *So much for outrunning trains*, Trey thought to himself, *I hope this isn't an indication of how things are going to go with Lisa.*

*****

When they finally got into Vaughn and passed a Conoco station, Trey gave the fuel gauge a quick look. The needle indicated the tank was half full—or perhaps it was half empty. He wondered if he was that guy. *Mr. Glass-Half-Empty, always looking at life from the negative side.* After a moment's thought, he decided he was too optimistic to be that guy.

"We're at half a tank," he announced as an Allsup's sign came into view. "Should we stop?"

Will looked back over his shoulder at Maggie who picked up the Atlas once again and traced a finger along one of its many highways.

"If y'all can hold out for another hour, I thought we'd stop at this place called Cline's Corner. It is right on Interstate 40, and surely we can find some gas and some breakfast there," she suggested.

From the front seat, both men gave a grunt to let her know they had heard, but neither actually spoke. It looked like it was going to be long day of silence after all.

"Maybe while we're stopped, I'll see if I can find some reading material," Maggie said aloud.

When neither Will nor Trey bothered to respond, she leaned forward and said, "Can one of you please find a country station? I think I'd like to listen to some music."

Trey looked at his grandfather, but Will seemed to have not heard her, so in between quick glances at the road ahead, he turned on the radio and found a country station. Bebe Rexha and Florida Georgia Line singing *Meant to Be* came through loud and clear. 'If it's meant to be, it'll be' kept repeating over and over again. By the time the song ended, Trey was beginning to wonder

66

if it wasn't some kind of message and if he and Lisa were really meant to be.

Encino sported a post office but not much else. Just west of the town, Highway 285 veered north and Highway 60 took a more westerly direction. Alongside the road in a gravel pull-off, a man was set up beside an old rusty white van selling beefy jerky and pinion nuts. Trey wasn't sure what pinion nuts were, but the beef jerky sure sounded good. He realized he was starting to get a little hungry and hoped they weren't far from where Granny and her Atlas planned for them to stop for breakfast. He got his answer when he noticed a sign that said Cline's Corner was twenty-seven miles ahead.

*****

As the miles rolled by Will pondered over last night's conversation with Trey. That his grandson wasn't talking to him very much that morning didn't bother him. He had said what needed saying, and he had every confidence that in time Trey would realize he meant it for good. Movement up ahead broke his train of thought, and as they grew closer, Will realized it was a herd of cattle milling along the edge of the highway. A huge Hereford bull caught his attention. The rest of the cattle were all cows, and none were Herefords. His thoughts turned to cattle and the ranch, and he wondered why the rancher had decided to put a Hereford bull on a mixed lot of cows. He had never ranched in New Mexico, so all of his rational was mere speculation.

"You see that Hereford bull?" he asked pointing it out to Trey.

"Yes," Trey answered.

"Why do you think the rancher but that bull in with that mixed herd of cows?" Will asked.

"I don't know." Trey shrugged, "Maybe since most of those cows look to be at least part Angus, he's hoping for some Black Baldy calves."

"Kind of what I was thinkin'," Will agreed. "Might make a cattleman out of you yet."

Trey grinned and shook his head, "I'll admit I do miss the ranch work, but Pappy, I am going to be an accountant."

"We'll see." Will grinned back feeling a little homesick and wishing he was back on the ranch riding Red.

Soon the terrain and vegetation made a noticeable change that caused Will to forget the cattle and concentrate on the landscape. Constant rolling hills dotted with cedar trees and covered with green grass took the place of the barren cactus view they had been seeing nearly the whole time they had been in the state.

"Man, I never thought I'd be so happy to see a cedar tree in all my life," Maggie said from the backseat.

"It is definitely a welcome change of scenery," Will agreed.

There was hardly time to get used to the new view before Interstate 40 appeared on the horizon and they got their first look at Clines Corner. At first, Trey thought there must be some mistake. He had been expecting a large, thriving city or at least a decent sized town. As they arrived at a combination gas station, gift shop, restaurant, RV park, he realized this was more of a stop off than an actual town.

"Not exactly a thriving metropolis," Maggie said as Trey pulled into an open gas pump.

"Big enough for gas and a meal," Will said seemingly unmoved by the place's lack of size. He handed Trey his credit card and stepped from the truck.

"I think me and your Granny will go on in and scout the place out," Will said as Trey opened the truck door. "You go ahead and park and come find us when you're finished filling up."

Trey nodded as his grandfather pushed the door shut. Staying angry was getting tougher with each mile. He knew the conversation the night before had been meant to help him, that it had been said out of love, and that it had not been easy for his grandfather either.

As he slid the credit card into its slot and removed the gas cap, he again watched his grandparents walk hand-in-hand across the parking lot towards the front door of the establishment. Waiting for the gas to pump, he decided that perhaps his grandfather was right. Maybe Lisa was running his life a little too much. But how to fix the problem this late in the game was beyond him. Too much time had been spent on the relationship for him to just give up on it. There had to be something he could do. If he just put his mind to it, he would figure something out—he always did.

The hard click of the pump brought his mind back to what he was doing and away from his Lisa troubles. He returned the pump handle to its place, screwed the gas cap back in place, stepped into the truck, and found an open parking spot as near to the front door as he could.

He decided, or rather his growling stomach did, that worrying about Lisa would have to wait as he hurried across the blacktop and into the store. Inside, he found a long, narrow gift shop to his left, an area much like a convenience store to his right, and a narrow hallway leading to restrooms straight ahead. He spotted his grandfather standing beside a glass box with what appeared to be the head of a Native American Indian in it.

As he got closer, he realized it was a fortune telling machine and that there was another one just a little further down the hallway. The one his grandfather stood next to did indeed have the head of a Native American in it. He had on a full, eagle feather head dress, and for one dollar, the machine would spit out a card with lucky numbers, your fortune, or a phrase of wisdom. On the front glass where the words Medicine Man at the top and Speaks at the bottom. The second machine was much like the first except it had what Trey figured was a Gypsy man with a turban and Zoltar Speaks on the front glass.

"Your Granny's still in the restroom," Will said. "I'm gonna take a look around." He handed Trey a dollar bill and a card and walked away.

Trey looked down at the card in his hand. On the front of the card was a picture of the Native American Indian from the machine and the words Medicine Man Speaks and on the back was a message, You Control Your Own Destiny. Below that in his grandfather's handwriting was another phrase that read: Honesty is better than sugar-coated bullshit.

Trey stared at the words his grandfather had written and then pulled out his billfold, wedged the card behind the paper money, and slid it back into his hip pocket. Then he stepped to the Zoltar machine and fed the dollar bill his grandfather had given him into it. Zoltar's hand began to move, and a computerized voice spoke, "Cheer up my friend and listen to the proverb from Zoltar. A smile is worth a hundred frowns in any market. Oh, yes, and lucky for you, the Great Zoltar sees much happiness ahead for you."

At the end of the speech a card like the one from the other machine shot out of the slot except with Zoltars' picture on the front, and the message on the back read, Life is here and now, not yesterday and tomorrow. There was also a series of numbers that were supposed to be lucky. Shaking his head, Trey placed this card in his wallet with the first one and headed for the bathroom. *Put a smile on your face, be happy, live in the day,* all good advice he guessed, but none of it gave him a clue as how to deal with the mess that was Lisa. *Surely things have got to get better soon*, he thought.

*****

The sound of someone sobbing softly caught Maggie's attention as soon as she entered the restroom. Several women, some with little daughters in tow, had entered and left the bathroom while she was in it, but none had bothered to address the sounds from the stall. Finally, as Maggie dried her hands on a handful of paper towel, she could take it no more. She tossed the wet paper towels into the trash and went to the stall door at the end of the room.

"Ma'am are you, okay?" she asked.

The sobbing stopped, followed by a series of sniffles, and then the sound of toilet paper spinning off its roll, "Yes… no… maybe . . I don't know." A woman said between sobs.

Maggie thought for a moment and then said, "Are you physically hurt? Do you need a doctor?"

"No, ma'am, I'm not hurt," the lady said. "I've done something really stupid, and I don't know what to do about it."

"That's good then," Maggie said, but something wouldn't let her turn and walk away. "I mean it's good you're not physically hurt. Why don't you come on out here, and let's see if we can figure out what to do about this stupid thing you've done?"

"I couldn't burden you with my problem," the lady whispered.

"Come on," Maggie urged. "You can't spend the rest of your life in there, now, can you? Surely there's someone who will be wanting to know where you're at."

"Okay, then," the woman said.

Maggie heard the lock sliding back and then the door eased open.

The young lady in front of her was nearly as tall as Maggie herself, and she had dark brown eyes and jet-black hair that hung straight down over her shoulders. She was slim built with an olive complexion and a natural beauty that shined through tear swollen eyes and wet cheeks. A red bandana print sundress that fell to an inch above her knees matched the straps on her sandals. A small diamond on a gold necklace sparkled when the overhead lights hit it.

"Hi, there," Maggie said with a smile. "I'm Maggie, what's your name?"

"Tess." the girl answered as her lip began to quiver. In her right hand she held a medium-sized pink suitcase. A shoulder bag that reminded Maggie of the ones the hippies hauled around with them back in the sixties lay on the floor.

Without a thought Maggie reached out and pulled her

forward. Tess laid her head on Maggie's shoulders, and the flood gates opened once again. Maggie rubbed her back gently and all the time whispering, "There, there, now, it's gonna be okay. We'll figure this thing out and fix it, darlin' girl."

*****

Will and Trey had browsed the gift shop and the convenience store, and Trey was beginning to worry about Maggie when she came down the hallway from the restrooms with a young woman in tow. Trey wasn't quite sure how to react when Maggie introduced her and announced that she would be riding with them as far as Placerville, California.

"What?" Trey could not believe his ears.

"I believe what your granny is saying is that this young lady needs a ride out to California, and we're gonna take her along with us," Will explained and flashed a brilliant smile.

"I thought we were just stopping for gas and breakfast," Trey stammered.

"That's right, breakfast. I forgot that we were going to eat here." Will turned to the young woman, removed his hat, extended his hand, and said, "I'm Will. Are you hungry?"

"I'm Tess," the young woman shook with him, and then answered, "No, sir, I'm not really hungry."

Will turned to Trey, "This young man is my grandson, Trey Tucker. We were just about to have a bite to eat, and we'd be happy if you'd join us."

Before Trey could think or react, Tess released Will's hand and reached out and took his. The feel of her hand in his sent a jolt of electricity through his entire body. Part of him wanted to jerk the hand away quickly, but a bigger part wanted to hold on to it forever. She dropped his hand, and he removed his hat and stammered, "Nice to meet you."

What in the world is wrong with you? he scolded himself. *You don't even know this girl. And what is Lisa going to say when she finds out about her. So much for Zoltar and the Medicine Man and their advice. So much for hopes that things would soon be better. This trip just keeps going from bad to worse.*

"Trey, why don't you take this young lady's suitcase and put it with ours, then come and find us in the restaurant," Will said, then turned to Tess. "Would that be okay with you. No sense in toting it around the store."

Tess answered with a nod and handed the luggage to Trey. Without another word the three of them turned and started for a table leaving Trey staring after them—bewildered.

Chapter 8

After a very quiet, very awkward meal, Maggie insisted that she and Tess would need some reading materials.

"You and Trey find some snacks and drinks," Maggie told Will, "while me and Tess take a quick look around the gift shop?"

"We can do that," Will said. "Meet you back at the front in a few minutes."

Trey followed along while Will gathered up a box of crackers, several small bags of various types of chips, and three different kinds of candy bars.

"What do you think we should get to drink?" Will asked.

"I'm fine with water," Trey answered, "but I have no idea about Granny and that girl."

"That girl has a name. It's Tess." Will gave him a sharp look, "What's your problem? Why don't you like her?"

"I don't like her or dislike her, Pappy," Trey answered, "How could I? I don't even know her. And for that matter, neither do you or Granny. She could be some kind of con artist for all you know."

"Is that a fact?" Will chuckled.

"Yeah, it's a fact," Trey snapped, "and what's so funny?"

"You are." Will's chuckle turned into laughter. "Never thought I'd see the day a little snip of a girl could scare you so bad. Is it Tess or is it the idea of Lisa finding out about her that scares you more?"

Trey's jaw tightened as he clenched his teeth. He picked a twelve-pack of bottled water off the shelf and started for the checkout counter, not caring whether Will followed or not. His grandfather's chuckles followed him all the way to the front of the store.

*****

Maggie gathered up an assortment of magazines, a small book on cacti native to the New Mexico area, and a brightly colored Navajo blanket. Maggie watched as Tess followed along wide-eyed staring at the items on each shelf but not seeming to really see any of them. Maggie figured after the morning Tess had been through, she must be bone-weary and spent.

"What do you think?" Maggie picked a pink neck pillow off a shelf and offered it to Tess.

Tess took the pillow from Maggie, frowned and said, "I'm sorry, ma'am, I'm afraid I'm a little out of it. You and your husband seem like really nice folks, but if I'm being honest, I'm a little wary. I normally don't accept rides from strangers, but I kind of feel like I'm on the ropes."

"That's okay, child," Maggie smiled. "Maybe you just need a little rest and a reset.".

"Are you sure that it's okay if I go with you?" Tess asked, feeling unsure. "Your grandson doesn't seem to like the idea very much."

"Oh honey," Maggie added a wink to her smile and then put an arm over Tess's shoulder, "don't you fret yourself about Trey. He's havin' troubles that have nothing to do with you. You let me worry about him."

"Yes, ma'am." Tess almost smiled, and even that much was beautiful, but it still didn't quite reach her eyes.

Maybe in time, Maggie thought and remembered something her grandmother used to say. What will be, will be. What won't be, might be anyway. And God has the final say in it all.

Will and Trey were waiting at the checkout counter of the gift shop when she and Tess arrived at the front of the store. Trey had a case of water under one arm and held a bag full of the snacks they had selected in his other hand. Will pulled out his wallet and nodded toward Maggie. She placed all their items on the counter beside the register. A tall elderly gentleman in a black t-shirt with a portrait of Val Kilmer as Doc Holiday from the movie *Tombstone* on its front and the words *I'm Your Huckleberry* below it, keyed in the price of each item. When he had bagged the last of the merchandise, he smiled, showing a perfect set of pearly white teeth beneath his handlebar mustache.

"That'll be sixty-three dollars and thirteen cents, folks," he said as he passed the bag over the countertop to Will, who handed him a hundred-dollar bill.

The cashier checked to see that the bill was not a forgery, placed it in the register below the tray, then he pulled the correct change from the draw and counted it back, coins first and then bill by bill until he reached one hundred.

"Don't see that very often anymore," Will commented.

"What's that?" the man asked.

"Someone actually counting money back," Will answered. "Mostly these days, folks just toss the change at you in a big handful, and you have to hope they got it right."

"Been at this a long time," The man smiled. "I guess it has just become habit."

"Well, I appreciate it," Will said.

"Thanks." He nodded, and then turned to Tess. "I'm glad to see you're doing a bit better young lady."

"Thank you," Tess smiled weakly and nodded.

*****

"I think maybe I better visit the men's room one more time," Will announced. "I'll meet y'all at the truck."

After a quick trip to the restroom, which was not really necessary, Will stopped by the counter once more and waited while Handlebar Mustache Man finished checking out a middle-aged lady in a long flowing dress that he thought might be what Maggie called a moo-moo. It was covered in a red rose flower pattern and fit the lady rather snuggly. As she gathered her bag from the counter, she caught Will looking her way and with a smile that showed off her crooked tobacco-stained teeth, she said, "I like your hat, cowboy."

Unprepared and shocked, Will tipped his hat and stammered, "Thank you, ma'am."

"Mmm," she winked and said over her shoulder as she walked away with an extra swing of her hips, "And a gentleman to boot."

Will nearly forgot why he'd sent the others on to the pickup. The cashier chuckled and said, "Don't you mind, Sally. She's a local. Got her a place over in the RV park. Moved out here a few years ago hoping the climate would help her health. And it might just do it to if she'd stop smoking two packs of Marlboros every day. She's a big flirt, but she's harmless."

Will just shook his head, "You don't miss much that goes on around here do ya?" he asked.

"Nah, I guess not," Mr. Mustache answered with a grin.

Will stuck his hand out, "I'm Will, Will Tucker."

They shook hands over the counter, and the man said, "I'm Ben, Ben Adleman. Nice to meet ya."

"Likewise," Will said. "What can you tell me about the young lady that checked out with us earlier?"

"Well now," Ben twirled the left side of his mustache and then did the same with the right side before speaking, "She came in here, maybe about an hour before you all showed up. Came in with a man I would have pegged for an older relative if it hadn't been for the way they were hanging onto each other. Mind you, I'm not judging, just saying. Nowadays, it's hard to tell age, but I figured him to be a least ten years her senior, if you know what I mean."

Will nodded and before he could ask about the man, Ben continued, "They headed back to the restrooms, and after a few minutes I noticed in that mirror up there," he pointed up at a big round mirror affixed to the wall high up near the ceiling that gave a view down the hallway, "that the young lady had come out and was kind of hanging out by the Zoltar machine. She must have been there a least ten minutes because I got busy checking out customers and forgot about her. Then when there was a break in the line, I looked up and she was coming down the hall acting like she was looking for someone. Almost like she was lost."

Ben took a breath and Will asked, "What happened to the man?"

"I was just getting to that," he continued once again. "She started looking around the gift shop, and I asked her if she needed help, but before she could answer, the man steps around the corner, and she tells me no but thank you. He takes her by the arm, and they head back down the aisle towards the restaurant, and I lost track of them when another customer stepped up."

Ben paused once more. Will was beginning to think he should have asked for the short version but held his tongue.

"Next time I saw them, she was coming around that endcap there with the baseball caps on it, and she was crying her eyes out. Before I could say a word, she shot past me and out the front door with the man right on her heels. I had another customer, so it was a minute before I could step out to check on the situation, but when I did, she was coming back across the parking lot toting that oversized bag-purse thing she had with her a while ago and that pink suitcase on wheels with a pullout handle. She was still weeping to beat the band, and that man was just standing there with his hands on his hips, glaring at her. When he saw me sizing him up, he jumped into a car, slammed the door, and sped out of the parking lot. It was silver, the car was, one of those foreign job. I don't know the brands, but it's the one with the four circles linked together. You know which one I'm talking about?"

"Yeah," Will nodded, "That's the Audi, I think."

"Anyway," Ben shrugged, "I followed her in, and asked her if she needed help. She said no, she'd figure it out somehow and disappeared into the restroom again. I was thinking I should get one of the ladies who works here to go check on her when your wife walked out with her. Is she some kin of yours?"

"No," Will answered, "Just a family friend." He didn't see any reason to admit that she had only been a friend of the family for about a little over an hour.

"Well, I'm glad she got ahold of you all," Ben stated, fiddling with the right side of his mustache once again, "I don't think Mr. Audi was any good for her."

"I agree with you. Any man that would leave a woman stranded out here ain't much of a man," Will said and turned to leave. "Hope your day goes well,".

"Safe travels," Ben said in return.

*****

Trey saw his grandfather coming and pulled around to the front of the parking lot. Will opened the door and stepped up into the cab with a smile that Trey found irritating for some reason. As Will clicked on his seatbelt, he turned to Maggie, raised his eyebrow, opened his eyes wide, and asked, "Plans still the same?"

"Don't see why not." Maggie smiled back.

Turning to Trey, Will said, "I think we're ready to roll."

Trey found his way out of the parking lot and at the stop sign, flipped on the blinker to turn right towards I-40. A big rig with a picture of fries blowing out of a McDonald's container on the side of its trailer and the words *Going, Going, Gone* was stopped, waiting for an old, dirty, white, dented flatbed farm truck to pass so it could turn in. Trey waited patiently for both of them to clear out. The going, going, gone reminded him of an auctioneer, and he worried that it might be a sign of the direction his relationship with Lisa was headed.

As the truck approached, Will pointed north, and said, "You'll need to turn left."

The truck passed, the semi began its turn, Trey turned, a look of utter confusion on his face, and asked, "Why?"

A smile once again played at the corner of Will's mouth. "Because that's the way to Arches National Park, and that's our next stop."

"What? Why?" Trey's eyes narrowed, causing the skin at the top of his nose to scrunch up.

"Arches National Park is what," Will said, "and the why is because your Granny wants to see the arches." He gave Trey a look of exasperation.

The driver in the car behind them tapped the horn causing Trey to check his rearview mirror. In the time it had taken the semi to clear, a line of six cars had backed up behind him. The man in the first vehicle had both hands raised illustrating his impatience and frustration. Trey gave him a wave over his right shoulder, turned left, then immediately pulled off onto the shoulder and put the truck in park.

He glanced in the rear view at his grandmother. "I thought we were going to a wedding in Napa Valley."

"We are sweetie," she said, "but there's a few stops we have planned on the way. Just a couple of places me and your Pappy would like to see while we're away from the ranch. I can't remember the last time we took a trip for fun, and one never knows. This could be our last one."

"Really?" Trey shook his head, realizing that bad to worse was fixing to get *even* worse but feeling the need to ask anyway. "Well, I kind of figured on a three-day trip out to a wedding, a couple of days there, and three days back, but I guess I was mistaken, so when exactly is this wedding supposed to take place?"

"Not 'til next Thursday," Maggie answered. "Maybe we should have let you know our itinerary before we left out. Oh, and you," she turned to Tess, seated across from her, "I didn't think to tell you we'd be taking the long way around to get to California. I hope you don't mind. We'll be glad to help you with food and motel rooms."

"No…" Tears welled in the girl's eyes threatening to

overflow, but she quickly wiped them away, "I'm sorry," she sniffled. "I mean no, I don't mind it taking longer. I'm in no hurry to get back. But I have money and can pay my own way. I don't want to be a burden. I really appreciate the ride."

At least a dozen questions came to Trey's mind, but the sight of the beautiful young woman in tears and embarrassed beyond belief behind him told him they could wait. Without another word, he pulled back onto Highway 285 and started north. Fifteen minutes later, he glanced back to see Tess sound asleep with the Navajo blanket wrapped around her and her head resting on the neck pillow against the passenger door. Trey's phone began to vibrate in his left pocket, and as he dug it out, he thought, *Lord, how am I gonna explain this mess to Lisa*? Luckily, it was a spam call wanting to talk to him about extending the warranty on his vehicle. *First time in my life I've ever been glad of a spam call*, he thought as he dropped the phone into a cup holder in the truck's console.

*****

Highway 285 turned into I-25 south of Sante Fe and then into Highway 84 just north of the city. Seventeen miles further north, it became 285 once again. The route reminded Trey of how screwed up his life had become. Three days ago, he knew exactly what road his life was supposed to take, and he was at peace with his future. Now, it seemed like every time he saw a road sign, it indicated a different road, and the destination at the end was not a given.

Ten minutes north of Pojoaque, New Mexico, Tess sat up and looked around the truck. Granny stuck the receipt she was using as a bookmark into the Cactus book, turned, and smiled at her.

"Have a good nap?" she asked.

Wiping at the edge of her mouth, Tess blushed. "Yes ma'am. I didn't think I could sleep, but I guess I drifted off."

"You must have needed the rest," Maggie offered. "Your

body will let you know when it needs rest and when it needs to eat. You didn't eat much at the restaurant. Would you like a snack?"

"No thank you, I'm okay. And thanks again for giving me a ride back home," Tess answered. "Where are you all from?"

"Oklahoma," Maggie told her. "Right in the middle of the state, pretty close to Nowhere."

"So, out in the country then. Are you farmers?" she asked.

"Ranchers," Maggie told her, "Cattle ranchers."

"So, Tess," Will spoke from the front seat, "what do you do in Placerville, California?"

"Cook," she answered, "and waitress. I work… well, I guess I should say, I *worked* at the Taproom, a restaurant and bar combination place."

"So, you cook the food and then do the waitressing, too?" Will asked.

"Not exactly," Tess answered. "I started out as a waitress and worked my way up to a cook. I really like to cook, but sometimes when they need me to waitress, I take a shift."

"Do you ever tend the bar?" Maggie asked.

"Not yet," Tess said, "You have to be twenty-one to tend bar in California, so I can't legally work behind the bar for another ten months, but I do serve drinks once the bartender gets them ready."

Will caught Maggie's eye and gave her the slightest wink. Maggie recognized the 'well done' look that passed between them and appreciated Will's confidence in her. Even if all that happened was that Tess rode along with them to Placerville and they dropped her off, at least Trey would figure out that being in the same vehicle with a girl wouldn't kill him.

*****

Trey mulled over how to break this new set of complications to Lisa. First, that this trip was going to be more than a weeklong, and he would not be able to pick her up from the airport. Part of him was actually relieved that he wouldn't be there when she got off the plane. Perhaps a little time out between them would ease her temper.

And then there was the news about his grandmother giving Tess a ride. He considered just not telling Lisa about it. But there was no doubt in his mind that if the trip got brought up in future conversations, one of his grandparents was likely to mention her. It became a question of whether to tell her both bits of news at the same time and deal with one humongous explosion or spread it out so the fallout would be less painful. He had just about decided on the second course of action when Tess woke up and the questions began.

As much as he tried to just ignore the conversation and concentrate on Lisa, Trey felt himself being drawn in and had to resist asking questions of his own. Within minutes thoughts of Lisa faded away, and he found himself wondering if the slight gravely texture of Tess's voice was always there or just a byproduct of the crying she had done earlier in the day. He found himself hoping it was her normal voice. And then he thought, *where in the hell did that come from?*

Maggie told him that another highway change was coming up, and Trey noticed that they were once again on Highway 84. By the time another hour had passed, Trey knew that Tess had graduated high school with no desire to attend college. Her dream was to one day own her own restaurant. She said she had thought she was going to Kentucky to do just that, but then that got messed up. She didn't elaborate, and neither Maggie nor Will pushed the issue. Trey acted indifferent and stared straight ahead as the miles and the conversation rolled on, but in truth, he was hanging on every word, and the questions he had continued to accumulate.

During a lull in the conversation, Maggie picked up the atlas, ran her finger up along the line labeled Highway 84, and said, "We've been at it a while. I need a restroom and a stretch-my-legs break. There's a little town ahead called Chama. Let's stop there, okay?"

When Trey began to slow at the edge of town, Will pointed up ahead at small animals scurrying along the edge of the shoulder and then darting off into the desert sand.

"Look at those prairie dogs?" Will said.

Maggie and Tess leaned forward over the seat's back and looked through the front windshield.

"Yes, I see them," Trey answered. "Never been anywhere where they were this close to the road or this close to a town." Just as he finished his statement, an overly-brave, overly-fat little prairie dog decided the sand on the other side of the highway looked browner and made a run for it.

Maggie grabbed Trey's shoulder and squealed, "Oh, no!"

Tess covered her eyes with her hands and shouted, "Don't hit it!"

Before Trey had time to brake the little critter disappeared from his view, leaving him to wince in expectation of that uncomfortable and heart wrenching thud that too often proceeds rodent stupidity. The thud did not come, and he looked quickly to his rearview only to see both his grandmother and Tess turned around in their seats, looking out the back glass.

Mr. Prairie Dog was dashing headlong across the opposite lane as fast as his stubby little legs would go and nearing the fog line on the other side of the road. As he crossed the white line, both women threw up their hands and squealed in unison, "Yes, he made it!"

Trey turned from watching the women in the back seat, patting each other on the shoulders, to look at Will. Evidently, his grandfather thought something was funny because he was smiling like a possum eating grapes through a chicken wire fence, and his old eyes were sparkling. His grandfather's smile turned into a chuckle, and then a full-fledged guffaw.

Trey watched as his grandfather's joy spread first to his grandmother and then to Tess. He could not recall a time when he had heard either of his grandparents laugh so hard. The way they looked at each other touched a chord deep in his heart. The love in that moment between Will and Maggie was visible, tangible, the kind he wanted, the kind he hoped to have someday.

His eyes met Tess's, and he wondered about her story. What had caused her to leave California? Why had someone abandoned her in the middle of nowhere? Even as he watched her laugh, he could see the sadness in her eyes.

A Phillips 66 Speedway looked like it might have clean restrooms, so Trey pulled off the highway and into its parking lot. Will pulled out a handkerchief and dabbed at his eyes.

"Why don't we go ahead and fill the gas tank while we're stopped," he suggested, and Trey found an empty pump and pulled to a stop.

Will handed his credit card across and said, "We'll meet you inside," and was still chuckling when he opened the door and climbed out of the truck.

Trey exited the truck, helped his grandmother out, and as the gas filled the tank, he watched Will open the door for Maggie and Tess to enter the store. The swish of Tess's dress and the way her hips moved reminded him of a model from a television commercial. He tried to recall which commercial and couldn't. Then realization hit, and he felt the hair on the back of his neck stand up. What in the world was he thinking? He was in a committed relationship. He looked around quickly to see if anyone had noticed or read his thoughts. His simple, little well-planned life was sure getting complicated all of a sudden.

Chapter 9

As Trey pulled away from the gas station, Maggie pointed over his shoulder and said, "We need to go straight across there and onto Highway 64."

Before they were ten minutes outside of town, Tess was curled up against the door again, and by the time they crossed over into Colorado, she was sleeping soundly. At the state line, the highway number changed--again. When they reached the outskirts of Pagosa Springs, Tess was still fast asleep.

"Let's find a place to stay here tonight," Maggie leaned forward and suggested in a half whisper.

"That sounds good to me," Will said out the side of his mouth. "I think I'm about ready to call it a day."

"Just tell me which hotel you want me to stop at and I'll pull in," Trey whispered just loud enough for them to hear, then involuntarily looked back over his shoulder to make sure he had not awakened Tess. She was till sleeping peacefully, and a strand of her dark hair had fallen across her cheek and along the corner of her mouth. "Seven Spanish Angels", an old Willie Nelson and Ray Charles, song popped into his head. Turning his eyes back towards the road in front of him, he caught a quick glimpse of his grandfather staring at him. Will sported a knowing grin, and Trey felt his neck burning once again. *If I make it through this trip in one piece, it'll be a miracle*, he thought

Trey turned west at the edge of town and began to look for a motel. That Pagosa Springs was a tourist town became apparent immediately, what with the San Juan River paralleling the street to the left and an assortment of every kind of souvenir shop one could imagine to the right. "Look at all those stores." Maggie pointed, keeping her voice low.

The sidewalks were full of families and couples strolling along with colorful bags of the treasures they had purchased. Trey had to stop for people in the crosswalks at nearly every intersection.

"Maybe after dinner, we can do a little shopping," Will whispered over his shoulder at Maggie.

The signs for several motels went by as Trey navigated through the stop lights and pedestrians. He had begun to wonder if Will was paying attention when his grandfather pointed suddenly to the right and said, "There. I like the looks of that place. The Pagosa Lodge. Let's see if they have enough rooms to put us up."

Trey drove through the parking lot and pulled the truck to a stop in the drive near the front door of the lodge's lobby. The building was a beautiful structure with weathered wood and natural stone construction. It had that old west look and feel. Trey liked it and thought perhaps one day he might build a house with similar materials on a piece of land of his own. The idea of such a home had no sooner formed in his mind before a voice in his head reminded him; he was going to spend the rest of his life somewhere in downtown Tulsa in a house of Lisa's choosing.

"Give me a minute," Will said as he crawled out of the truck, "and I'll be right back. I'll just step in here and see what they've got available."

"I need a restroom," Trey said keeping his voice low. "You gonna be alright by yourself, Granny?"

"Just fine," Maggie answered with a wave and looked over at the sleeping Tess.

*****

Will and Trey made their way out of the vehicle and Tess stirred restlessly but did not open her eyes. Maggie watched as the young girl wiggled into a more comfortable position under the blanket and then fell still once more.

The sliding glass doors of the motel had nearly shut behind her husband and grandson when Trey's phone began to vibrate. When no one answered, it rang and kept ringing until Maggie leaned up over the seat, grabbed it, flipped it open, and said, "Hello, this is Trey's phone."

"Who is this?" Lisa snapped.

"This is Trey's grandmother," Maggie recognized Lisa's voice but didn't like her attitude, "and just who is this?"

"I'm sorry Granny Maggie," Lisa's tone instantly changed to sweet and innocent. "I didn't recognize your voice. I need to talk to Trey?"

"He's with his grandfather right now," Maggie answered, "and they're in the hotel, getting our rooms for the night."

Whether it was the tone of Maggie's voice or simply the moment when Tess's mind realized the truck was no longer in motion, she awoke and raised her head, looked warily around then turned to Maggie, and asked in a sleepy voice, "Where are we?"

"Pagosa Springs," Maggie answered her and then spoke once again into the phone, "Do you want me to have Trey give you a call in a little bit?"

Instead of an answer, Lisa asked in a tone that could well have frozen fire, "Who was that talking to you? I heard a woman's voice."

With no hesitation and in her kindest voice, Maggie answered, "That's Tess. She's a friend of the family." Then she asked again, "Do you want me to have Trey give you a call in a little bit?"

"Oh, you bet I do… oh, yes… yes, I do," She answered, then with a quick cold, "Thank you. Goodbye," the line went dead.

Will came out of the hotel with three small card sleeves each holding two magnetic keycards in his hand. Trey walked along behind his grandfather pushing a luggage cart. Maggie saw them coming, opened the truck door, and stepped out to meet them.

She smiled as Will handed her the stack of keys. "Looks like we're in luck."

"Yes, ma'am," he said with a nod. "Three rooms. Now, all we have to do is get the luggage up to them. Second floor with a view of the mountains, the clerk says."

As Tess rounded the back of the truck, Maggie offered her a set of room keys. She stared down at the little folded envelope looked up until her eyes met Maggie's. "Miz Maggie," her voice was sweet, "I cannot accept handouts. I will not be a burden or a freeloader. I intend to pay for my own rooms."

Will nodded, pursed his lips, and then said, "Alright Tess, I can appreciate that, so how about this, you reimburse me the cost of your room?"

"Okay," Tess said digging in her shoulder bag and then asked, "How much do I owe you?"

"One hundred dollars and some change," Will answered.

When she looked up and gave him a suspicious look, he stared straight into her eyes, maintained a perfect poker face, and said, "but let's just round it to an even one hundred. That okay with you?"

"Yes… Yes, sir." she said and dug a hundred-dollar bill out of the little brown and white cowhide, western-style lady's wallet she had taken from her bag and handed it over to him.

"Good," Will said exchanging the keys for the money. "Now, let's get our bags upstairs, get cleaned up, and go find us some dinner. And *that*, young lady, I intend to pay for."

With Will's help, Trey got the luggage from the truck onto the cart while Tess stood beside Maggie waiting. Once everything was organized, Trey pushed the cart, following along behind Tess and his grandparents. Watching the three of them, he wondered, *Has Pappy finally met his match. Was this young woman just as stubborn as this bowlegged old cowboy he loved so much.* Somehow, he doubted it, but it was going to be interesting to find out.

"Oh, by the way," Maggie said as they made their way into the lobby of the lodge, "Lisa called while you were inside. She'd like for you to give her a call when you have a minute."

*****

The thoughts running through Trey's head as the packed elevator rose towards the second floor could best have been described as the mental equivalent of a class five Oklahoma twister. The need to call Lisa weighed heavy, but the closeness of Tess in the cramped space clouded his mind. He found her scent, something like rose petals and dew in the morning mixed with just a tint of desert sun, intoxicating, and part of him hated for the ride to end. Then the guilt hit, and he could hardly breathe for thoughts of Lisa and how wrong it was to be enjoying the moment. A harsh bump as the elevator finally stopped caused Tess to stumble forward. She managed to grab the little brass rail beside her but not before Trey felt the full impact of her chest against his back, and a jolt of something like electricity shot through him once again.

Before he could catch his breath, the elevator doors slid open.

He stopped beside the door of Will and Maggie's room as his grandmother used her key on the automatic lock. Once the door was opened, he and Will began to sort through the bags. When the correct luggage was in their room, Will checked the number on the sleeve his grandmother had given him and started on down the hall.

Tess started to follow him, but Maggie reached out and stopped her. "Do you need to call anyone?" she asked and held out her little flip phone.

With a look of confusion, Tess stared briefly at the phone, and then as realization dawned, she said, "Oh, no ma'am. I don't need to call anyone, and I have my own phone, but thanks for the offer." She turned and moved away down the hallway after Trey who had stopped in front of his room and was holding her pink suitcase in his left hand. The look on his face made it evident he didn't have a clue what he was supposed to do with it.

"I'll take that," Tess said as she reached his side. Then with a quick look at the number on her card sleeve she added, "Looks like I'm next door to you."

She disappeared into her room as Trey opened the door to his and pushed the cart inside. It wasn't until he had placed his luggage on the raised shelf provided and put his Dopp kit on the counter in the bathroom that he noticed the door adjoining his room to Tess's.

The beige telephone across the room on a small desk rang and gave him a start. He crossed, picked up the receiver, and a little uncertain said, "Hello."

"Hey, Trey," his grandmother said, "Can you be ready in twenty minutes? We're hungry and ready to go find a bite to eat."

"I think so," Trey answered.

"Okay, then," Maggie said, and hung up.

He placed the receiver back in its cradle and heard the phone ring in Tess's room and the muffled sound of her voice. He reached into his pants pocket thinking he would go ahead and give Lisa a call but quickly realized he had left his phone downstairs in the truck. The call would have to wait.

*****

A short drive further along Pagosa Springs main street and Will spotted Boss Hogg's Saloon and Restaurant. It was a false-front building sporting a green awning. A lighted sign with the establishment's name framing a pig wearing dark shades and a ten-gallon cowboy hat advertised steaks and BBQ. On Will's command, Trey pulled in.

Inside, the four were shown to a table in view of the bar by a young woman in a black Boss Hogg's T-shirt and Wrangler jeans. The table seated four. Will pulled Maggie's chair out for her, and once she was seated, took his own. Caught between thoughts of what Lisa would say if he helped Tess with her chair and what his grandfather would say if he did not, Trey reached to do the same for Tess. She was already in the act of pulling the chair out herself when their hands collided above the chair's

91

back. Both instinctively jerked their hands away and both of them started talking at once.

"I'm sorry," Trey blushed. "Allow me to get that for you."

Tess stepped back and let him pull the chair out. "Thank you," she said as she settled into the chair and picked up a menu. Trey fussed at himself for the charge that surged through his body every time they accidentally touched, but at the same time, wondered: if Lisa was *the one*, then why did he feel like this about a woman he'd just met?

Because they had arrived before the dinner rush and were the only ones in the restaurant, their meals arrived soon after they ordered. Will had a half rack of ribs, Trey ordered a steak, and both Maggie and Tess had chopped brisket baskets. In short order, the table was cluttered with half empty drink glasses and plates littered with the food that would have to be left because their stomachs could hold no more. When the waitress asked if it was all on one check, Will handed her his credit card with a yes, and shot a quick glance at Tess.

"Thank you for the meal, the company, and for everything you are doing for me," Tess said.

"You are very welcome," Will said with a smile.

The sun was quickly sinking towards the western horizon, casting long shadows across the parking lot, when they stepped out of the restaurant. After a short drive back past the lodge and into the heart of main street, Trey found a parking place.

Will and Maggie led the way, moving from one shop to another with Trey and Tess following along behind them. After the first couple of shops, Trey found himself carrying bags, all of which contained stuff his grandmother had purchased. He noticed that Tess did quite a bit of looking but didn't seem all that interested in buying anything. He found himself wondering about her financial situation.

They were several blocks from the truck when Will suggested, "Maybe we should start back. I'm starting to wear down a bit."

Maggie reached out, took his hand in hers, and they started back down the sidewalk. Trey couldn't remember a time when his grandfather had ever admitted to being tired. He hoped this trip wasn't too much for Will then scolded himself for even thinking such thoughts. His grandparents were two of the toughest people he had ever been around. He chalked it up to the fact that neither of them had done much traveling.

Tess walked along beside Trey but kept enough distance between them, so that her hand didn't brush against his. Maggie and Will chatted back and forth, and from time-to-time, Trey could see their smiles when one or the other turned their heads. The way they looked at each other, the way they visibly and completely enjoyed each other's company was something he would never get tired of witnessing.

He wondered if he and Lisa would ever have this kind of relationship. *What is wrong with me*, he wondered. *My wedding day is just a couple of months away, so why am I questioning my relationship with Lisa? Why is there doubt and where is it coming from?* He definitely needed to call Lisa.

*****

The phone rang several times before someone picked up, and a girl's voice said, "Hello, Lisa's phone, I think." Her speech was slurred, and then laughter from what had to be at least a dozen females erupted.

"Hello, this is Trey. Who is this?" he said loudly, hoping to be heard above the giggling. "Can I talk to Lisa, please?"

"This is Samantha… you know Sam?… Lisa's friend, we met once at a party," she answered. "Just a sec, and I'll try to find her for you. I know she's around here somewhere."

Trey's patience grew thin as he listened to the sound of not one but several male voices in the background while Sam went to search for Lisa. Finally, after what seemed like a short eternity but in reality was only a couple of minutes, he heard Sam say, "There she is. Just a minute and I'll give this phone to her."

Seconds later, Sam shouted above the crowd, "Hey Lisa, Trey's on the phone for you."

A deep baritone voice responded, "Who's Trey?"

"You sure took your time getting back to me." She was slurring her words almost as badly as Sam was, but there was no mistaking the venom in her voice.

"We had dinner, and Granny wanted to do some shopping," Trey shot back, feeling the anger already rising, "and this is the first chance I've gotten to call. And who was that guy that asked *Who's Trey?*" he asked through clenched teeth.

"*Oh no, you don't!*" Lisa screamed above the noise.

Trey heard a door slam, and the noise of the party disappeared.

"Don't you even question who I'm spending time with when you're traipsing all over the country with some tramp friend of the family's. Yeah, that's right. Your Granny told me. Who is that girl, and how long has this been goin' on, huh? For weeks? Months? You've probably been planning this little sex-capade for months, just laughing at me behind my back, haven't you?"

Teeth still clenched and heart pumping ninety to nothing, it took all the effort Trey could muster to keep his voice level, "The girl is someone who got dumped at a truck stop and needed to get back to California. I don't know why Granny thought it was a good idea to offer her a ride. I even tried to talk her out of it. I have not been planning anything lately except for our wedding, and that was definitely not behind your back. So, how much have you had to drink, and who is the guy?"

"I don't believe you," Lisa continued to shout. "I don't believe you at all. As for how much I've had to drink, the answer is not enough. And if you must know, some of the guys from our brother fraternity showed up down here. So, how long have you known this Bess bitch?"

The thought that he should just hang up crossed his mind, but he gritted his teeth and tried to explain—again. "Her name is Tess. I just met her today. And I can't believe you lied to me about your trip to the Bahamas being an all-girls trip. That really makes me angry. Now, what's the guy's name, Lisa?"

"Oh, that's a good one," she was no longer shouting, but the chill in her voice had reached a whole new range of cold, "You're such an asshole. You've ruined my whole trip. I worked so hard for four years to get through college, and I deserve this trip, and you're ruining it. And if you must know his name is Slade Marland, and he's just a friend."

Trey felt like someone had pushed the thermostat in the room well above the one-hundred-degree mark but somehow managed still to keep his voice level. "You may think Slade Marland is just a friend, but I guarantee that's not what he's thinkin'. I know who he is, and I know his reputation, and it isn't good. You need to stay away from him."

"Oh, right," her words came out like the hiss of a snake. "Now you think you can tell me who to be friends with, huh? Well, you get rid of your little family friend tramp, and I'll think about stayin' away from Slade."

"That's Granny and Pappy's call, not mine." He felt trapped and a bit nauseous, "What do…"

She cut him off midsentence, "Are you screwing her?"

Shocked and in disbelief, Trey answered, "No, I am *not* screwing her." Then quickly asked, "Are you screwing him?"

"No," she said her voice low and calculating once again, "But if you know what's good for you, you had better get rid of that so-called family friend real quick."

One second Trey felt like he had been lit on fire and the next a cold emptiness filled his very core, "Is that some kind of threat?" he asked, and the tone of his voice surprised him.

"You can take it however you want to… asshole," she told him and the line went dead.

Trey lay back on the bed, and no matter what scenario he came up with, hope eluded him. Saddened, angry, and alone, the wetness on his cheeks was the first sign that of all of his pent-up emotions were trying to find a way out. Turning on his side, he pulled a pillow close, buried his face in it, and screamed over and over again. Sometime later, he undressed and crawled under the covers. When sleep finally came, it was filled with dark dreams.

Chapter 10

Sunrise found Trey dressed and sitting in the desk chair in his room. The curtains on the window were thrown wide open, giving him a view of the mountains. A dream awakened him early, but he could not remember the details. He recalled the sensation of falling, and then he was awake, fighting to get free of the bed covers. Unwilling to return to sleep, he had taken a shower, shaved, and gotten ready for the day.

His bags were already packed and setting beside the door. He had hoped that somehow the distant mountain view and a little time to think would bring about some peace, but it had not. Last night's phone call with Lisa played over and over in his head until he wanted to puke. He wondered if this was just a rough patch, maybe something all couples went through in the months before a wedding, or if it really was the beginning of the end.

Should he have insisted on going to the Bahamas with her? He was sure if he had asked, Pappy would have allowed him to start at the ranch when he got back. But then reality told him Lisa would have never allowed it. That it had been a sorority-fraternity thing from the start was now clear, and since Lisa had never wanted him to be a member of any fraternity, he would not have been welcome.

The phone on the desk next to him rang, and he picked up the receiver. Granny wanted to know if he thought Tess was up and around yet.

"I'm not sure," He looked over at the digital alarm clock on the bedside nightstand. The red numbers showed it to be five

minutes after six o'clock. "Do you want me to knock on her door?"

"Not just yet," she said. "Your Pappy didn't sleep well last night, and we're a little slow getting around this morning. Let's give it another hour, then if we haven't heard from her, I'll give her a call."

Trey agreed and returned the receiver to its place. Twenty-five minutes later, he heard what sounded like a phone alarm buzzing in the direction of Tess's room. A couple of thumping sounds later, he decided it was definitely her. A soft tap on the door adjoining her room startled him. A second tap brought him out of his seat. He crossed to the door, flipped the lock, and eased it open a crack.

Tess peeked sleepy-eyed around her door. Her hair was in disarray, and there were sheet creases along the right side of her face. Trey stared into her dark eyes and found a peace that no mountains anywhere could have offered.

"Oh, you're already dressed and ready," she said, her voice husky from sleep. "I'm sorry. I didn't know what time I was supposed to be ready."

"No worries," Trey said. "We usually meet at the truck at six, but Granny called and said they're running late this morning, so there's no hurry."

Movement behind her caught his attention, and as he looked past her, he realized he could see her in the full-length mirror hung on the wall opposite the door. The thin nightshirt she wore was pink with a white heart pattern and lace along the bottom edge. The way it hung did little to hide the curve of her bottom. She had one leg straight, the other was bent slightly and pressed against the door, and she was barefoot. In the split second it took him to realize what he was seeing, he felt his face turning red, and he shifted his gaze to her eyes.

"Thank you. I'll get around as quickly as possible," she said.

Trey pushed his door shut and heard her set the lock back in place. A moment later he heard a loud gasp. *So, she knew he had seen her backside in the mirror.* The thought made him blush again but then a smile spread across his face as he found himself hoping she was doing the same. Why was it that this girl he barely knew could put a smile on his face and joy in his heart, and the woman he was supposed to marry, whom he had been with for over six years, only brought out anger and frustration? Would the world ever make sense?

*****

Will stared at his reflection in the motel mirror in the bathroom. He already missed his own bed, already felt homesick for the ranch. He felt a deep desire to be back home, saddling Red for a ride instead of traveling down the road for hours every day. That his tossing and turning had kept Maggie from getting a good night's sleep did not set well with him, either. He wasn't a drinking man, not that he had anything against having a drink, and he had on occasion sipped a glass of good bourbon, maybe, he thought, a shot might help him sleep. He stowed the idea away in the back of his mind and began to shave.

*****

Maggie sat on the edge of the bed staring out at the same beautiful mountains her grandson had been looking at a bit earlier and wishing that she was back home on the ranch and in her normal routine. In all her years on the earth, this was the furthest she had ever been away from home. Raised in Hico, Texas, she had had no desire to ever leave until she met Will. Most folks would never have believed it possible that a cowboy from Oklahoma could win her heart—including Maggie herself. Will had definitely changed that, had changed her life. Before Will, she had never been out of Texas. He had swept into town like a strong summer wind and after a very unlikely romance, she found herself married and on her way to Oklahoma. In her mind, it was the single best thing that had ever happened to her.

But this morning, something was bothering her. If she was honest with herself, it had been sometime since she had felt completely at peace. At first, she thought it was the situation with Trey and Lisa. She had known long before Will, or even Bo for that matter, that their relationship was too one-sided to stand the test of time. As a mother and a grandmother, she had known that something would have to be done about it before Trey was allowed to make the mistake of marrying that girl, so she had agreed to come on this trip. Had that been the reason she felt a deep unexplainable restlessness, she knew it would have begun to wane. It had not, so she began to search for the reason. So far, she was coming up empty.

"Good morning, Beautiful," Will interrupted her thoughts. "You look like an angel setting there in that light."

He had finished shaving and had been leaning against the wall watching her for several minutes before he spoke. She turned with a smile and said, "Will, you old charmer, you startled me."

"Yeah," he teased. "I noticed you were deep in thought, figured I better say something before the steam started pourin' out of your ears."

"Oh, you are a rascal, aren't you," she shook her finger at him. "Call me beautiful and an angel and then say something like that."

"Well, you are all that and more," he assured her.

"I don't know, Will," Maggie frowned. "I'm not sure I qualify as beautiful anymore, and I'm quite certain the title of angel was never mine to bear."

"Nonsense!" Will crossed the room, pulled her up from the bed into his arms and kissed her—long and passionately. Then he looked deep into her eyes and whispered, "You are the most beautiful woman in this world. You are more beautiful today than the day we met, and I'll whip anyone who dares say different. As for being an angel, your most definitely have to be. How else could you have possibly put up with me all these years?"

"Now, that last part, I can't argue with." Maggie's smile returned along with a sparkle in her eyes, "I sure love you, Will Tucker."

"And I sure love you, Maggie Tucker," he said and sealed it with another kiss.

*****

A few minutes before eight, the last of the luggage was loaded into the bed of the truck. Maggie had spotted a little café next to Boss Hogg's the night before and wanted to try it out for breakfast. Will wasn't crazy about the idea of dining at a place called Two Chicks and a Hippie but decided not to press the matter, especially since he wasn't all that hungry anyway.

To Will's surprise it was as good a breakfast as he had ever had anywhere. He ordered 'The Basic', choose his two eggs over easy, the pork sausage, and the sourdough toast. The country taters that came with the meal were a given, not a choice. Maggie ordered a Tall Stack which turned out to be three buttermilk pancakes. Trey ordered a cheese omelet and asked for mushrooms, spinach, tomatoes, and bacon to be added. The waitress asked if he would like it smothered with red, green, or veggie chili. He declined all three with a snarl that put a smile on both Tess's and Will's faces. She ordered the Hippie, which included two pancakes, two eggs—she wanted hers scrambled-- bacon and country taters.

When their meals arrived, Will blessed the food. Trey picked up his fork to eat, and before he had a chance to cut into his omelet, Tess slipped the bacon that had come with her meal onto the edge of his plate. He cocked his head to the side and shot her a look out of the corner of his eye.

"What?" she asked and raised one shoulder in a shrug. "You like bacon, and I'm not going to eat it."

"Thank you," he muttered, turned back to his meal, and began to eat.

Across the table Will dipped sourdough toast into the yokes of his eggs. All the while, he was thinking about the way that Tess reacted to his grandson. Maybe Maggie was right when she said that if they left things in God's hands, everything would turn out okay. The exchange between this little spitfire and his grandson had him smiling all the way to his soul.

Trey had eaten half of his omelet and had a fork full on the way to his mouth when a large slice of mushroom fell out of its center onto the middle of his plate. Tess stabbed it quickly with her fork and stuck it in her mouth.

"Hey!" Trey protested.

"What?" Tess looked at him, then pointed at the piece of bacon he had not eaten yet and said, "You got bacon, I got mushroom." Then with a slow wave of her hand, palm down, across both plates she added, "Good trade."

Will nearly choked on a piece of sausage he was about to swallow, and Maggie began to laugh so hard she had to wipe away tears with a paper napkin. Trey just stared at them as if they had lost their minds. What was so funny about exchanging mushrooms for bacon? Head down, a smile on her face, Tess continued to work on her pancakes.

When Will finally got his wind back, he looked across the table at Tess. Her eyes met his, and he flashed a grin.

With the same slow gesture she had used, he moved his hand across Trey's plate and repeated, "Good trade." Then broke into laughter again.

Trey still didn't know what was so funny, but his grandpa's laughter was contagious and before he knew it, he was laughing, too.

*****

Half an hour west of Pagosa Springs, Trey saw the terrain change again. Now they were traveling in mountain country. Pines and evergreens began to stand tall and thick as far as the eye could see. The flat land had disappeared, and everything seemed to be on a slope. Off to the south, the top of Chimney Rock became visible on the horizon.

"I wish I had a camera so I could take some pictures." Maggie pointed out the window at the rock formation.

"I can take some with my phone and send them to you." Tess dug into her bag.

"Why don't we stop at the next town with a Walmart and buy you a camera?" Will offered.

"I think I'd like that," Maggie said and then turned to Tess, "and I'd sure appreciate you taking some pictures for me until then. Should I roll down the window?"

Tess shook her head and said, "Probably be a good idea. The picture won't be good through the tinted window."

Maggie rolled the window down, and Tess snapped several pictures. The smell of mountain air and pines filled the truck before she was finished, and the window was once again back up. Trey navigated one curve after another and listened to the women talking behind him. A couple of hours later, they reached Cortez and with the help of Tess's cellphone found a Walmart store.

"Maybe we ought to grab a snack while were here," Maggie suggested. "Looks like we're still a couple hours from Moab, and we might get hungry before we get there."

Inside the store, Will and Maggie headed for the electronics department leaving Trey and Tess to go their own way. Trey grabbed a pack of Jack Link's original beef jerky, a box of Ritz brand peanut butter crackers, and a twenty-ounce bottle of Dr. Pepper, paid through the self-check lane, and returned to the truck. Dropping the tailgate, he climbed up onto it, set the bag of snacks down, dug the cellphone from his pocket, and called Lisa.

After several rings, voicemail kicked in and advised him to leave a message. He hung up and dialed again. The third time voicemail picked up, he waited for the beep, then said, "Lisa, I've got a few minutes where I can talk in private before Granny and Pappy are finished shopping, so if you get this message, give me a call, please." He flipped the phone closed, set it on the other side of the plastic Walmart sack and rummaged around in the bag until he found the jerky and the drink and settled back to wait.

Twenty minutes later, Trey was still sitting on the tailgate, waiting and watching the front door of the store when Tess walked out. He picked up the phone and sent a text message telling Lisa that he was no longer alone, and he would try to call her again later.

He watched Tess as she started across the parking lot towards him. Halfway to the truck he saw her look his direction. Their eyes met, and he knew from her expression that she realized he had been watching her. She was dressed in a solid blue sundress in the same style of the one she had worn the day before and a pair of tan leather sandals. The faded denim jacket she had worn over her dress earlier in the day, she had removed and now wore tied around her waist. When she got close to the truck, she did a little spin and curtsied when she came out of it.

"Why'd you do that?" Trey asked.

Tess hopped onto the other end of the tailgate and set her bag next to his. "I don't know," she swung her legs back and forth, "Because you were staring, I guess."

"Was not?" he argued.

"Yep, you were, and it made me feel… well, special, I guess," she shot back.

Staring at the faded oil-stained pavement below his boots, he tried to figure out why this slip of a girl was getting under his skin. It seemed to him that when he and Lisa argued, even if she was in a playful mood, he always felt like she was belittling him. But here with Tess, arguing felt more like flirting.

Trey had been trying to figure out a way to start a conversation with Tess but having no luck. Tess had produced an apple from her bag, taken a bite from it, wiped the juice from her chin, and said, "Well, I guess we can sit here in awkward silence… or you could say something in return.

"Ain't much good at talkin'," Trey said. "Don't take it personal. I just never seem to know what to say or if it's the right thing to say."

"You'll never know if you don't speak up," Tess said with a sideways look then took another bite from her apple.

"How's your apple?" Trey asked.

Tess chewed, swallowed, and turned to look at him, "That's the best you have? How's your apple? Really? And next I'm guessing you're going to ask me how I like the weather?"

"Hey, I'm trying here," Trey shot back. "You said speak, I spoke. This ain't something I'm used to doing."

"So, what? You're the strong silent type?" Tess squared her shoulders mimicking him and asked, "All your girlfriends just want someone who looks good but doesn't talk much?"

Trey sat quiet for a few seconds and then muttered, "Yea, I guess that would sum it up pretty good."

"I like a man who knows how to talk," Tess said, "and one that isn't afraid to speak his mind."

"Alrighty then," Trey nodded and took a drink of his Dr Pepper.

When it became apparent that he was not going to say anything further, Tess looked up at the sky and asked, "So, what do you think of the weather we're having today?"

In the middle of a swallow, Trey chuckled and nearly choked on the soft drink. Tess giggled. When he could breathe once again, he said, "It's a little hot, but I guess it ain't too bad. How do you feel about it?"

When Will and Maggie arrived at the truck a short while later, Tess and Trey had made it past the weather and were discussing activities they had participated in while they were in high school.

"See y'all beat us out," Maggie said. "Have you been waitin' long?"

"No, ma'am," They answered in unison, looked at each other, and then smiled and hopped down off the tailgate at the same time.

"That's good." Maggie smiled.

"Well, we've got a camera and looks like everyone has snacks now, so let's get movin'," Will said.

"I hope I can figure this camera out before we get to the park," Maggie said.

"I can probably help with that," Tess told her. "I know my way around a camera pretty well."

"Well, aren't you just full of wonderful surprises?" Maggie said as Trey put the tailgate back up and started around the end of the truck.

Yes, she is, Trey thought as he opened the door and slid into the driver's seat. *Yes, she is.*

Chapter 11

Not far out of Cortez, the evergreens and the grass started to thin, and the mountain ridges gave away to rolling hills of broken desert and an occasional patch of irrigated farmland. There were fewer cattle to be seen. Trey caught glimpses of sheep foraging on the sparse vegetation.

Maggie and Tess tinkered around with the new camera in the back seat. It was a little Canon PowerShot, perfect for a beginner and so easy to explain that, within the first hour, Maggie, with Tess's help, had the basics figured out. Will stared out the side window. Trey drove and tried to work through the tangles of his own mind, making little progress.

"So, Miz Maggie," Tess said, "how did you and Mr. Will met?"

"Oh, goodness," Maggie giggled. "That's a long story."

Tess raised an eyebrow. "Well, I think we might just have some time on our hands."

All thoughts of Lisa or Tess or any of life's problems disappeared from Trey's mind, and he found himself waiting to hear the story. He wondered why he had never heard it before, and suddenly realized that he did not know much of the family history at all. He felt a bit ashamed. This young woman was showing more interest in his family's story after knowing them for barely a day than he had shown in all of his adult life.

Trey noticed that his grandfather turned away from the window and gave his wife a wink over the back of his seat. Maggie smiled and then began, "I was just five months out of high school, the first of my family to finish, and I was waitressing at the café that had just opened."

"The Koffee Kup." Will interjected, "And it was spelled with K's instead of C's. I always thought that was neat."

"Me, too," Maggie agreed with a nod, then continued. "I was working when in walks this handsome young cowboy, spurs jinglin', prancin' along like he's the cock of the walk."

Trey shot his grandfather a sideways look. The idea that his grandfather had ever been young had never really crossed his mind, and he found it a bit hard to imagine.

Will just grinned and shrugged.

"He sauntered over to one of the empty booths like he was king of the world." Maggie looked across at Tess and rolled her eyes.

Tess giggled.

Trey had no trouble envisioning Will walking into a place and drawing everyone's attention. He had seen it happen too many times in his life. Will just had a way of being noticed without even trying.

"I *was* the king," Will said, "maybe not of the world, but definitely of the state that day. I was just passin' through, coming up from a little town down in south Texas where I had won myself a brand-new, silver belt buckle at the rodeo."

"For what?" Tess wanted to know.

"Bareback bronc riding," Will answered holding up his left index finger to signify first place and with a bit of a flourish ran his finger and thumb around the brim of his hat as if to say, that's how it's done.

Trey had never seen this side of his grandfather. The man he had grown up with was quiet, humble, and very reserved.

Maggie went on, "When I reached the booth, he had scooted back against the wall and had one spurred boot hanging over the edge of the seat and his straw cowboy hat resting on his knee. He looked up at me and said, 'Well, Hello, Sweetheart'."

Will interrupted, repeating, the "Well Hello, Sweetheart,"

but he strung the second syllable of the word hello out for at least a four count, and his southern drawl was much exaggerated.

In the rearview mirror, Trey watched as his grandmother rolled her eyes once again, nodding in agreement.

Tess let out a hearty chuckle that warmed Trey to the core.

"Yes," Maggie said. "That's exactly how he said it."

"And what did you say?" Will chided.

"I said," Maggie answered pursing her lips and moving her head from side to side with each word, "I ain't your sweetheart, mister, and if you wanna eat in here you better get both feet square on the floor."

"Oh, my gosh!" Tess laughed out loud.

"That's exactly what she said," Will agreed with a nod, "and exactly how she said it, except she was standing up with a hand on her hip and the forefinger of her other hand was pointed at my face like she was gonna shoot me dead if I didn't listen."

"So, what did you do?" Trey looked across at his grandfather as he asked.

"What I've been doin' for the last fifty years," Will answered. "I listened to her and dropped my leg off the seat onto the floor quicker than you could say boo and sat up ramrod straight."

"And then?" Maggie asked from the backseat.

"And then," Will grinned, "I looked her right in the eye, and said 'Well, you ought to be'."

"I ought to be what?" Maggie asked.

That's when Trey realized they were reliving the scene right there in the pickup, and it was making them both a little feisty.

Will grinned, "I said, 'You ought to be my sweetheart'."

"And I said, 'I don't date cow… boys'." Maggie separated the cow from the boy and dragged out the last word.

"How 'bout ranchers?" Will shot back.

"Yeah, right," Maggie laughed, "Keep dreamin', cow… boy. Now, what do you want to drink."

"Sweet tea," Will said.

"And that's where I figured the story was over," Maggie admitted.

"But I knew it was just the beginning," Will said

A windmill farm on the horizon announced the likelihood of civilization, and a discussion about the huge white turbines in front of them put Maggie's story on hold.

"Kinda ruin the view if you ask me," Will said, nodding ahead at the horizon.

"Just another form of energy, I guess," Trey suggested. Like his grandfather, he hated the way the giants messed up the natural view.

"I hope the day never comes when you can see one of them from the ranch," Will stated as a sign on the edge of the highway appeared announcing their approach to the town of Monticello, and below the name the logo—The Land Above the Canyons. As they navigated through the little town, the word quaint popped into Trey's mind. He thought that a bit odd since it was not a term he commonly found in his vocabulary, but in this case, it fit perfectly.

From Cortez, they had traveled on highway four-ninety-one, crossing from Colorado into Utah while Maggie and Will were telling their story. Trey had noticed the *Welcome to Utah* sign but had not wanted to interrupt the story. Now as he approached an intersection, he found that he did not know which way to turn.

"Granny, I'm going to need a little help here," He said as he neared a stop sign.

Maggie opened the Atlas, and after a quick check said, "My goodness, time sure got away from me. We're already in Utah, and I never even realized we crossed the state line. You need to turn right onto Highway 191."

Trey made the turn, and the residential area quickly gave way to open areas and scattered farmhouses. An old wooden barn with weathered and chipped red paint, caught Trey's attention and reminded him of home.

Prairie dog mounds began to dot the landscape, starting near the edge of the highway, and the young pups scurried towards the nearest hole when they passed. Trey was sure glad they did not have the little fellows digging holes and tunnels on their ranch. Their ranch, it had been a while since he had thought of himself as part of the ranch. It felt good to think that way again.

Six miles north of town, the road made a sharp s-curve on a steep grade, and at the bottom, the canyons opened up, and it was breathtaking.

"It looks like someone took every possible color of sand and layered them one on top of another then walked off to see what nature would do with it." Will said as he looked out across the landscape.

"Not in a hundred years could one person ever hope to photograph all of this beauty" Maggie said as she reached for her new camera.

A large dome-shape form ahead on the left side of the road caught Trey's attention and at first, he thought perhaps it was some manmade structure used for advertisement. As they got closer, he realized it was a gigantic, naturally-occurring sandstone formation left after thousands of years of erosion. A gravel turn out had been made for people to stop and view it. Without asking, he turned his signal on, slowed, and pulled onto it.

By the time Maggie grabbed up her camera, Trey and Will were outside the truck, and Tess was not far behind them.

"Goodness, Pappy." Trey removed his hat and wiped the sweat from his brow. "It's hotter'n blue blazes out here."

"Probably wouldn't feel so bad if we hadn't been ridin' 'round with the A.C. running," Will told him. "Just think about how we do things back home. We get up and around early in the mornin' when it's cool, so as it warms up, we don't notice it as much."

"Hadn't really thought about it like that," Trey said, "but it makes sense."

"Of course, it makes sense," Will stated flatly.

Maggie snapped shot after shot of the dome and then began to insist on everyone taking portraits with the formation in the background. First, it was Will and Trey, then after much persuasion, Tess and Will and Trey. Tess took over the camera from there, and Maggie took her place. Then Will wanted a shot with Tess, Maggie, and Trey but couldn't figure out the camera. After a lot of patient coaching from Tess, he succeeded on his third attempt at getting the picture. On Tess's suggestion, the last photo taken was of Will and Maggie facing each other with the dome formation in the far-left background.

Tess handed the camera back to Maggie, pulled her phone out, snapped a selfie with the dome behind her, then she looked at Trey and asked, "Would you like me to take one of you?"

"No, but thank you for offering," he said not sure how to get the picture from Tess's phone to his, especially without Lisa asking questions about it in the future.

Tess shrugged, and the four of them made their way back to the truck. Trey was surprised at how quickly the inside of the vehicle had heated up while they were playing and made a mental note to at least crack the windows if they got out again.

Once back on the road, Tess asked, "So what happened next?"

"Next?" Will asked in return.

"You know, next in the story," Tess fastened her seat belt, "Tell us more about how you two met."

Will looked back over his shoulder at Maggie, and then said, "I had a chicken fried steak dinner followed by a big slice of lemon meringue pie, then I left Maggie a dollar tip and walked out."

"A dollar was a lot of money in those days," Maggie said, "and I figured he was just showing off because I'd hurt his pride."

"Well, you had," Will laid a hand on his heart. "I had only planned on stopping in Hico because I wanted to see the Billy the Kid Museum. Brushy Bill Robert had died there back in nineteen fifty, and I'd always wanted to visit. Anyway, after meeting Maggie, I decided to stay awhile. I checked around town until I found a rancher who needed some horses broke. He offered me fifty dollars a month, room and board, and my only job would be breaking horses. I took it. I didn't tell him, but I would have done it for just the room and board."

"So, you stayed in Texas just for Miz Maggie?" Tess asked.

"Yes, I did," Will said. "I called my folks and told them I'd met the woman that I was gonna marry. My mother had a million questions, and I couldn't answer nary a one. My dad only had two questions, how long was I gonna be gone, and did I have a job. He said he wasn't sending me money to trapse around all over Texas chasing some woman, and he and my brother were gonna need help working cows before winter set in."

"So, you had a ranch to go back to?" Tess asked.

"Yes, I did," Will answered, "at least, my family did. It was actually still in my father's name at that time."

"He didn't bother to tell me about his daddy's ranch until much later in the story," Maggie said. "I thought he was just a drifter."

Will chuckled. "The next day after working horses for hours, I took a chance, drove into town, and went back to the restaurant. And when I walked in the door, there she was, waiting on a table at the other end of the room. Well, I real quick like slid into the nearest booth, dropped my hat on the bench beside me, and waited. Directly, she saw me and pranced right over…"

"I did not prance!" Maggie declared.

"Who's telling this story?" Will countered and shot a wink over the seat toward her. "In my version, you pranced. Let's see… so she saw me and pranced over," he repeated, "and just as she got to the table, I looked up and said, 'Well good evening beautiful I hope you had a good day'."

Will paused and once again looked back at Maggie. She gave him a go-on look like she was not impressed, but Trey could tell she was enjoying every minute of Will's shenanigans.

"I'm not sure what she was fixin' to say before I spoke, but I would have wagered my first month's pay that it was something sassy," Will said, "and I don't know if it was me calling her beautiful or telling her I hoped she had a good day, but all of a sudden, she just stood there like the cat had got her tongue. So, I said, 'aren't you gonna to ask me how my day was?'"

"The cat didn't have my tongue," Maggie declared. "I was just trying to figure out how to get you to go away."

"So, it wasn't love at first sight for you?" Tess asked.

"Goodness, no," Maggie shook her head. "Not at first sight, not at second sight, not for many, many sights beyond that. As far as I was concerned, cowboys were just heartache and misery stuffed into Wrangler jeans and pearl-snapped shirts."

"So, had your heart been broken by a cowboy before Pappy showed up?" Trey asked.

"Nope, but my momma's had, my aunt's had, and my sisters' had," she said, "and I was aimin' to learn from their mistakes. Wasn't gonna give my heart to no cowboy."

"So, what did you say to him?" Tess asked.

"I believe what I said was, 'Because I don't care how your day was, and what makes you think you can call me beautiful?'," she laughed at the memory, "and he said, 'Well, what would you like for me to call you then?'"

Will laughed out loud. "She's got a memory like a steel trap. But to get on with the way I remember things, I really caught her off guard. You should have seen the way she stammered. Finally, she said, 'my name's Maggie. You can call me Maggie!'"

"And what did you say?" Maggie asked.

"I said," Will turned in his seat and looked her square in the eyes, "'It's very nice to meet you Miz Maggie. I'm Will Tucker, and I'm going to marry you.'"

"Oh, my gosh!" Tess gasped, "you did not?"

"Oh, yes he did," Maggie said. "You could have knocked me down with a feather, but I wasn't goin' to let him know that, so I just stood there until he finally said, 'I'll have sweet tea, the chicken fried steak dinner, and another piece of that wonderful lemon meringue pie. Oh, and when you're ready, I'd love to take you out on a date.'"

"And what did you say?" Trey was hanging on every word.

"She didn't say a thing," Will said, "just turned around and walked away. I ate in that restaurant every day for a month, just so I could see her. After the third day, I didn't even have to order, she would just bring my drink and food, set it on the table and walk away."

"But every day when I took his food to him," Maggie took over, "he'd look up at me and say, 'Good evening beautiful, I hope you had a good day'."

"And every day she'd just turn and walk away without so much as a smile," Will said.

"I was hopin' that, eventually, he would get the hint," Maggie said.

"So, when did things change?" Trey asked.

"If I'm being honest," Maggie smiled, "it changed the day he told me he was goin' to marry me, but I wasn't about to make it that easy for him."

"No, she wasn't," Will chuckled softly. "It was two weeks to the day before she actually spoke to me again."

Rounding a curve, they found themselves on the outskirts of the town of Moab. Maggie picked up the Atlas and said aloud, "Guess we'd better start lookin' for a place to stay."

"I could use my phone and search for motels in the area," Tess offered.

"You can do that?" Will asked over his shoulder.

"Sure, it's easy," Tess answered, her fingers already tapping on the screen.

Trey just shook his head and wondered where this kind of thinking had been when he wanted to use his iPhone to navigate at the beginning of the trip. He thought of the flip phone in his pocket and its limited abilities. It was good for phone calls and not much else. Yes, if he had to, he could text on it, but having to hit buttons multiple times to get the right letter seemed archaic by today's standards and not something he really enjoyed. But then he could not really say he had enjoyed his recent phone calls to Lisa either. He suddenly realized that this was the first time he'd thought about her since the rock dome formation and wasn't sure if he should be ashamed or not. He decided he wasn't but still felt the need to call her.

Chapter 12

The first two hotels Maggie called didn't have any available rooms. She was just hanging up with the with the second one when Will pointed to a Holiday Inn and told Trey to pull in. While everyone else waited, Will went in to see if they had any vacancies.

A thin young man who towered several inches above Will was on the phone behind the counter. Dressed in a light blue oxford button-down shirt and a navy-blue vest, his name tag read John. He put a hand over the receiver, raised his index finger, and said, "Give me just a minute, sir."

When John finished his conversation, he hit a few keys on the keyboard on the desk, looked up at Will and said, "So sorry to keep you waiting. What can I do for you?"

"No need to apologize," Will told him. "You had business to attend to, plus I'm not in that big of a hurry anyway. But if you have three rooms that would be wonderful news."

"Sir, once again I must apologize," John said, "there is some sort of convention in town this week, and all the motels in the area are completely booked up. However, the call I just hung up with was a cancellation. I only have two rooms, so if you need three, I'm afraid you're out of luck."

"We can make two work," Will said as he pulled out his wallet, "and we're glad to get them."

"They are still being cleaned, so it will be another hour before you can actually have the rooms, but I can go ahead and get you set up if you want me to," John said.

"Sounds wonderful, John," Will handed him his driver's license and credit card. "Set it up."

The paperwork done and keys in hand, Will started back out the front door, then stopped and said, "John, I was just wondering how many beds are in these rooms?"

"Both rooms have two queens in them. I hope that's okay."

"Yes, sir." Will nodded, "That's perfect." And then he stepped through the sliding glass doors.

As soon as he opened the truck door, Maggie said, "I hope you had better luck than we've had. Seems like there's no rooms anywhere in this town."

"Not anymore," Will said with a grin, "because I just got the last of them."

"Oh, thank goodness." Maggie let out a sigh of relief.

"How much do I owe you for my room?" Tess asked.

"Let's worry about that when we get back from the park," Will told her and then nodded at Trey as if to say, "Let's go."

*****

It took less than ten minutes to drive to the front gate of Arches National Park. As the line of vehicles waiting to enter slowly moved forward, Tess watched a line of cars and pickups climbing a road that ran along the cliff above them. Just watching them climb higher and higher along the edge of the weathered sandstone made her a bit nauseous.

When Trey pulled to a stop beside the payment window, she suddenly realized that the sharp turn just ahead was going to take them up that same road, and it was all she could do not to open the door and bail out of the truck. They could pick her up on their way back the hotel. She hated heights so badly that her palms began to sweat, and her heart thumped in her chest like it was going to fall out right onto the floor of the truck.

She closed her eyes when Trey made the turn and began to climb the steep incline that was supposed to take them up and over the rim of the entrance and into the heart of the park. Halfway up, Tess made the mistake of peeking out the window for a quick glance. She let out a moan, scooted to the center of the seat, and slapped both hands over her eyes.

"Is everything alright back there?" Trey glanced into the rearview mirror.

"I'm guessing she's scared of heights." Maggie put an arm around Tess's shoulder and pulled her close. "It's alright, darlin'," she assured Tess. "Just another minute and we'll be at the top."

Tess did not feel reassured or comforted. She snuggled into Maggie's embrace and prayed it would be flat when they reached *the top*. She felt like her prayers had been answered when the road leveled out and began a very slight decline into smooth flat land with a multitude of unique rock formation.

"It's safe now we're on pretty level land again." Trey said.

Tess slowly raised her head and looked around. "I'm sorry," she said and blushed. "I don't do well with high places."

"No need to apologize and no need to be embarrassed," Maggie patted her shoulder. "We're all scared of something."

"I hate it," Tess admitted, "I hate being scared of anything."

*****

Ahead, Trey could see where people were pulling off to the right. At Granny's request, he followed a green Camry that turned into a small parking area.

He noticed that Tess was still visibly shaken as they unloaded from the pickup and joined a group of other tourists who were crowded around a plaque. Information about the Balanced Rock was printed on it, along with how tall the rock formation was and how it had been formed. Trey felt like he should say something to comfort Tess, but he wasn't sure how to go about it. He watched her read the sign, her left hand braced on the wood rail fence in front of it, her right resting on her hip. Left foot flat on the ground, right leg bent, toes on the ground and heel

117

up, she swung her knee slowly from side to side, causing the hem of her sundress to shift slightly with each motion. Mesmerized by the way the fabric danced across her backside, he did not notice his grandfather watching him and smiling. Nor did he notice that Tess had finished reading the sign and was watching him staring at her butt. When she dropped the hand from her hip, he looked up, her eyes met his, and he blushed clear down to his pinky toes.

"Are you feeling better?" he asked, but his voice sounded a little high in his own ears.

"A little bit," she smiled. "Thanks for asking."

Unsure of what to do next, he turned his attention to the Balanced Rock itself. It reminded him of a gigantic teardrop perched on a pedestal two sizes too small. Hovering precariously on an erosion-marred podium, it looked like a strong wind would cause it to topple right off and crash to the ground below. *Kind of like my life right now*, Trey thought, *just teetering there, waiting for the wrong stone to move and it will all come rolling down.*

*****

The sun was falling over the edge of the horizon before they started back towards the park's entrance. The brochure they had been given upon entering the park said there where over two thousand natural arches in the park. Trey was sure that they hadn't seen that many, but then they hadn't actually gotten very far away from the roads and walkways. Even at that, he had quickly lost count of how many they had actually viewed. Maggie snapped photographs until the battery in her new camera died, and by the time they stopped at their third parking lot, Tess had regained her composure and was snapping selfies with the rock formations and arches in the background.

"I'm beginning to feel like an old pro at this selfie stuff," Maggie said as she and Tess stood side-by-side so Tess could snap one of the two of them with the Delicate Arch in the background.

"Yes, you are," Tess agreed. Trey figured she must have taken at least fifty selfies already, and they were just getting started.

"Come take one with us, Mr. Will," Tess said, motioning him over, and much to Trey's surprise, his grandfather complied.

When the three of them were finished, Tess raised an eyebrow at him and said, "How about it?"

"I'm good," Trey declined.

"William Mark Tucker, you're as stubborn as an old mule," his grandmother chided. "I want some pictures with you in them. How else will anyone know you were even on this trip with us?"

"Alright!… alright!" Trey threw his hands up and stepped over beside his grandfather, "I'll be in the picture."

Hours later, he had posed for more pictures than he could count and was beginning to think the sun would never set. As beautiful as the park was, he was not sure he could take much more when Will finally said, "We better head back to town. It's already late and I figure it'll be dark by the time we make the hotel."

To get out of the park, Trey had to take the same road they had taken coming in. The thought of Tess being scared again made his hands clammy. He wiped first one and then the other off on the front of his jeans then alternated holding them palm out in front of the air conditioner vents, letting the cool air and dry them before putting them back on the steering wheel. He was beginning to feel like there was absolutely nothing in his control.

"Enough to piss anyone off," he muttered.

"Did you say something?" Will asked.

"Just muttering to myself," Trey answered.

The ladies in the backseat had taken the park map out and were going back over the day's journey, tracing each road to see if they had missed anything. Trey noticed that his grandfather kept nodding off for short little naps. The truck's automatic lights came on at dusk and by the time they rounded the last curve and started down the section of road that had caused so much trouble earlier, Tess and Maggie were using the light from Tess's phone to illuminate the map.

Halfway down, Trey realized the darkness was hiding the view and keeping him from seeing how far it actually was to the bottom. Instead of a sharp drop to his left, there was only darkness. If Tess had bothered to look out her side window, all she would have seen was the shadowed shape of the mountains as they passed by, but she was concentrated on the map and never even looked up.

Which is a good thing, Trey thought as he drove past the pay booths. Getting down off the mountain had been no trouble at all, which meant he had worried over nothing. It could be that there was a lesson here. Perhaps he was fretting too much about everything, including his relationship with Lisa. Maybe everything would work out just fine in the end after all. Possibly, a positive attitude was all it really took. When he got back to the hotel, he would give Lisa a call. He had checked his phone periodically throughout the day to see if she had called or texted, but there had been nothing. With his new positive and improved mental state, he chalked it up to bad service and figured surely all would turn out well.

Will jerked awake as Trey made the turn into the hotel parking lot, yawned and said, "I almost forgot. They only had two rooms available, so I guess it guys and girls tonight."

"What?" Trey felt his positive mental state slipping away.

"I'm bunking with you tonight," Will answered his grandson first, and then over his shoulder to Tess, "and you and Maggie can share the other room, so there's no need for you to pay for a room tonight."

"That wasn't the deal." Tess reached over the seat and placed three twenty-dollar bills on his shoulder. "I'll pay for my half."

Too tired to fight with her, Will slipped the money into his shirt pocket.

*****

"Trey, how about you make a food run?" Will asked as his grandson pulled to a stop in front of the motel entrance, "and I'll help the ladies get their luggage upstairs?"

Too tired to care or argue and knowing it would give him a few minutes of privacy to try to get ahold of Lisa, he nodded, "I can do that."

"Anyone have a restaurant request?" Will asked.

After a short discussion, Wendy's was agreed on. Trey took their orders, helped get everyone's bags onto the cart, and started for the restaurant.

Instead of going through the drive by window, he went inside the small café. That way he could check the order to be sure it was right. He didn't want to get back to the hotel to find out someone's meal wasn't right or was missing. Lisa always ordered her burgers with no onions, and he remembered how upset she got the few times there had been a mix-up. Somehow, it always ended up being his fault.

A young couple were coming out as he opened the door to go in. He held the door for them and tipped his hat to the lady.

Inside, he placed his order, then found an empty booth away from the few costumers scattered throughout the place and checked his phone. Nothing. A check of the signal told him his service was good. Lisa still hadn't called or left a text, which probably meant she was still angry. He scanned down his contact list to her name and pressed the button. On the sixth ring her, voicemail picked up. He hung up and tried again. Same result. He thought about sending a text and then decided against it, all the while trying to convince himself that the reason she wasn't answering was because of the time difference.

It didn't work.

A sweet little voice with a slight nasal twang called Trey's order number. When Trey went to the counter to get the food, he found that the voice belonged to a short, curvy blonde girl who had dyed the tips of her hair a bright blue. Trey guessed she was a high school student trying to make enough for a car payment and gas money. Yet, another point of contention between him and Lisa. He had always worked on the ranch. If he did not work, he did not get paid. He had never thought of it as an allowance. It was his job. Lisa's parents had given her a credit card before she was even old enough to drive. Trey never knew for sure if there was a monthly limit, but if there was, it had to be a ridiculous amount because what Lisa wanted, Lisa got. She had always thought that him having to work off the money his grandfather paid for his meal card was ludicrous. More than once, they had argued about it until Trey had learned to simply avoid bringing it up.

The name on the plastic rectangle pinned to cashier's blouse read "Stacie". She smiled and handed him a large brown paper bag filled with hamburgers and fries and a carrying tray with four drinks. "There you go."

He verified the order then rolled the top of the bag down in hopes that would keep the fries warm until he could get them back to the hotel, gathered up the drinks and nodded.

"I like your hat," The girl said.

"Thank you, Stacie," he nodded.

At the mention of her name, a look of confusion crossed her face until Trey pointed at her name tag, then she grinned and blushed. He left her standing there still smiling and walked out.

*****

The four of them ate in Tess and Maggie's room. Dog tired and weary, Will gave Maggie a kiss on the cheek as soon as he'd finished his meal, excused himself to get ready for bed, and headed for his room. He hated sleeping away from his wife, and it hadn't happened very often over the years. Once in a while, he had to be away from her overnight on some cattle business with the ranch, but when possible, he was home in bed with her when night came.

Trey allowed time for Will to get ready for bed and said, "I think I'll turn in myself."

He kissed his grandmother on the cheek, nodded at Tess, and made his way out into the hall. He thought about trying to phone Lisa one more time before calling it a night, but he was tired, and he knew it would only frustrate him if she didn't pick up.

Chapter 13

"Hello," A man's deep husky fresh-from-sleep voice answered Trey's call on the fourth ring.

Shocked, Trey nearly dropped his phone but managed one word, "Lisa?"

The muscles in his cheeks flexed hard and his eyes narrowed.

"I think she's in the shower." The man's voice sounded vaguely familiar.

The rustle of sheets and the creak of a bedframe filled Trey's ears. He imagined a man crawling out of a bed, then he heard, "Want me to get her for you?"

"Just tell her Trey called," he said through clenched teeth and hung up.

When Will stepped out of the bathroom, Trey was sitting on the edge of the motel bed, face red, fist balled up and staring at a blank television screen. Will crossed the room, put his shaving kit into his suitcase, turned to Trey, and asked, "You, okay?"

"Yea, I'm fine," Trey lied.

"You don't look fine," Will said. "You look like one of those old Halloween toys made of rubber that you press onto a surface and then step back and wait until the tension releases and the toy springs up into the air"

"What?" Trey asked, finally turning to look at his grand-father.

"You don't look fine." Will said.

"Okay, you're right, I've been better," Trey admitted, his

mouth moving just enough to allow the words out, as he turned his gaze back to the television.

"Wanna talk about it?" Will asked. "I heard you on the phone while I was shaving. Lisa problems?"

"Yep, but I don't want to talk about it," Trey answered, "I'm ready to get out of here if you are. I'll go get a cart if you'll see if Granny and Tess are ready."

"Sounds like a plan," Will said as he zipped his suitcase. "You know, Trey, if you need to talk, I'm always here for you. I know I can be irritating sometimes, but I do have your best interest at heart."

"I know and thanks Pappy." Trey picked up his suitcase and headed for the door.

*****

At the edge of the Holiday Inn parking lot, Trey stopped, looked left, then right, then at his grandfather.

"What?" Will asked.

Maggie and Tess, who had been arranging the snacks and drinks in the backseat, paused.

"Did we forget something?" Maggie asked.

"What is it, son?" Will asked.

"Well, Pappy," Trey cocked his head slightly to the left and gave a shrug, "I have no idea where we're goin' next."

Maggie giggled from the backseat, and Tess cocked her head to one side.

Will grinned.

Trey didn't even crack a smile, just sat there and waited.

"What do you mean, you don't know?" Tess asked.

"Oh, he knows we're going to end up in California," Maggie explained, "but we haven't told him all the places we plan to stop on the way."

"Why not?" Tess asked.

"It's like this," Maggie told her. "When we decided to attend my great-niece's wedding it was kind of a big deal. Me and Will don't travel much… well, that's not actually true… we don't travel at all. So, we thought that while we were headed west, we'd make some stops and see some sights."

"Only they didn't bother to tell me any of this." Trey raised his eyebrows, his eyes never leaving his grandfather's. Neither of them smiled. Trey cocked his head to one side and raised a shoulder.

"Oh," Tess said.

"I picked two places I wanted to see, and Will picked two he'd always want to see," Maggie said.

"What were they?" Tess asked.

"Yes, what were they?" Trey glanced up into the rearview mirror.

"Billy the Kids grave and Horseshoe Bend for me," Will spoke up first.

"And Arches National Park and Lake Tahoe for me," Maggie answered with a flourish as if to say, 'Surprise! Now you know'.

"So, which is it Horseshoe Bend or Lake Tahoe?" Trey asked.

"Horseshoe Bend," Maggie picked up her trusty Atlas. "You need to turn right and head back towards Monticello."

Trey waited for a break in traffic, pulled onto the highway, and headed south.

As Moab faded into the desert behind them, Tess looked over at Maggie and asked, "Can we hear more of the story? You left off when you served him dinner for two weeks, but didn't speak to him."

Maggie put the Atlas down on the seat between them and said, "Yes, I did."

"And when you finally spoke?" Tess's question brought a chuckle from Will.

"I said," Maggie cleared her throat, "I said… 'Will Tucker I reckon if the only way to get you to go away and leave me alone is to go on a date with you, then I'm ready, but if you think I'm gonna marry you, you better think again'."

Trey looked over at his grandfather who was smirking and wondered if he was reliving that moment when he'd finally wore Maggie down. A look in the rearview mirror, and he saw that his grandmother was grinning at Tess in much the same way that his grandfather was smiling. He followed Maggie's gaze across the backseat and found that Tess was staring at him. Before she could look away, their eyes met for only the briefest second, and they shared a smile. Then Tess looked down and Trey turned back to his grandmother who was looking at him in the mirror with a smile of her own. Caught, he thought of Lisa, and wondered if he should feel guilty for sharing a smile with another female.

"Will said to me," Maggie picked up her story again, "'I'll pick you up at six o'clock on Saturday'."

Will chuckled again from the front seat and said, "and she said, 'I'm working Saturday night'."

"Yes," Maggie shot him a look, "And that's when my boss who was standing behind me said not this Saturday night you aren't. I whipped around and asked why not? And he said cause you've got a date with Will Tucker'. Turned out Will had been visiting with him behind my back."

"Technically, it wasn't behind your back because, as you so clearly indicated, we were not at that time in any kind of relationship," Will clarified.

"I was so mad I could have twisted both their heads off, fried'em up, and tossed'em to the hogs, but I wasn't gonna let them know they'd gotten to me," Maggie went right on, "so, I turned back to Will and said, 'I guess it'll be the usual for you then'."

"And I said," Will broke in, "'Oh, heck no, I'm so sick of chicken fried steak. It'll be years before I want another one. Bring me a burger and some fries'." And then he broke into a laugh that ended in a coughing fit.

Maggie passed him up a bottle of water, and after a few minutes, he managed to get it under control. He wiped his eyes on his shirt sleeve, thanked Maggie for the water, and gave her a wink. Trey was beginning to feel like he was just meeting his grandparents for the first time in his life. Once again, he caught himself looking at Tess in the rearview mirror, only this time, no one seemed to notice.

"So, after that it was happy ever after?" Tess asked. "Like in the romance books?"

"Oh, not by a long shot," Maggie said, and Will nodded in agreement.

*****

An hour's drive back through the canyons found Trey once again passing through Monticello. It had been less than twenty-four hours since he had travelled along this stretch of road. When Trey hit the center of town, he found himself at the junction that led either back to the east and Colorado or on south to Arizona, he continued south. As he drove, he started to wonder what his life would be like if he could travel backwards in time. At which juncture would he want to take a different road?

Would it have been when he decided to go to East Central to be near Lisa instead of Murray State where he could have played baseball? Would it have been even further back when as juniors, they had become sexually active? Or even further back when she had let him know she was interested in him?

Trey mulled over and over the events of the end of his sophomore year. Logan Daniels had been Lisa's boyfriend since seventh grade. Everyone just assumed they would graduate, get married, take over his father's construction business, and start having babies. Then after spring break of that year, Logan had left town with his mother and younger brother.

When all the rumors got sorted and pieced together, Logan's dad, church deacon and Sunday school teacher, had been caught in a very compromising position with his secretary in his office at work. To make matters worse, it was Logan, his brother, and his mother who had walked in on them. A surprise birthday for the father had suddenly gone very wrong.

According to the information running through the town grapevine, Mrs. Daniels had returned to her hometown of Tignall, Georgia, where she had grown up as the daughter of a Baptist preacher. Not long after Logan was out of the picture, Lisa had walked into Mr. Cromwell's biology class and sat down behind Trey.

"Whatcha doin' Friday night?" she asked.

Not sure if she was talking to him, Trey had turned in his seat and was surprised to find her looking at him and waiting for an answer.

"Playin' baseball," he said. "We gotta double header at Binger."

"Whatcha gonna do after the games?" she asked.

"Probably be late, so I'll probably go home and go to bed," he answered.

"Or" she said with a smile, "you could take me to the late movie over in Anadarko."

What would his life be like today if he had just laughed at her then, instead of turning six shades of red and stammering out, 'Okay'? He would never know because a person couldn't turn back time.

He told himself he was just mad because he was pretty sure that it had been Slade who had answered her phone.

When I get a chance to talk to Lisa, she'll have an explanation, he thought, but as he drove through little towns with names like Blanding, White Mesa and Bluff, he began to doubt that he could fix the relationship this time—or if he should even try. Just west of Bluff the highway took a sharp turn to the south. Maggie advised him to keep straight onto Highway 163.

At the town of Mexican Hat, they stopped at a Shell station long enough to use the restroom and grab fresh drinks. Trey checked his phone for calls, and when there weren't any, attempted a call himself, but there was no answer.

The bridge out of town crossed the San Juan River. It was a

beautiful high arched structure with a spectacular view of the mountains and canyons to the north. Trey noticed his grandfather staring at something in the water off his side of the bridge and slowed to see what was below. A man, tanned dark by the sun, was holding the reins of a horse that was chest deep in the muddy red water while another man used a bucket to pour water along the horse's back. At the end of the bridge, they disappeared from sight, leaving Trey wondering about the scene. To his way of thinking, it would do no good to wash a horse in muddy water but then what did he know, he had never had to wash a horse in the Utah desert before. Maybe they were trying to break the horse in the water was his next thought.

Trey was still pondering the scene thirty minutes later when he topped a slight rise in the road and Monument Valley opened up ahead of them. The road was straight and seemed to go on for miles. Speed limit and warning signs were posted along the shoulders urging people to decelerate and watch for slow moving vehicles. The many sandy pull-offs were packed with parked cars, trucks, RVs, and people. There where even people in the middle of the highway snapping pictures of each other walking on the yellow lines running down the middle of the road.

"Right there," Maggie pointed over the seat at a space that a large white RV with Colorado plates had vacated, "Right there, pull in right there."

With a quick check of his rearview, Trey eased to a stop to allow the vehicle to clear and then pulled into the spot left. A yellow Volkswagen beetle made a U-turn from the other lane and the driver somehow managed to wedge his vehicle into the space left behind them.

Camera in hand, Maggie was out of the truck before Trey or Will had time to unsnap their seatbelts. By the time Trey made it around the front of the vehicle, the other three were standing at the very edge of the blacktop, staring at the view.

A break in the flow of traffic had left the road empty in both directions. A young couple stepped out to the center line and took a selfie with the valley in the background. As soon as they cleared the road, a young man in khaki shorts, a light blue Ocean Pacific tank top, and leather flip-flops stepped out onto the road, followed by a young lady in a pair of cutoff jean shorts, a yellow bikini top, and a pair of white Keds with the shoestrings removed. The girl looked a little like Tess to Trey, and he found himself wondering what Tess would look like in a bikini.

Trey began to mentally chastise himself for the thought and the lady did a model walk down the road towards the valley while the guy snapped shots on his iPhone. Someone whistled and several of the bystanders gave loud hoots. Encouraged by Mr. iPhone Photographer, the young woman began to overly exaggerate the swish of her hips. Then she put both hands on her hips, took several more steps forward and with a toss of her hair spun around, and started back towards him, hips swaying in the same manner. On the return trip, she added a new facial expression every third or fourth step. First, pursing her lips like she was about to kiss the camera, next, moving her right hand from her hips to cover her mouth while her eyes went wide as if in surprise pointing at the photographer with her right index finger, she shot him a wink, and finally, just before she reached him, she leaned forward, tossed both hands out to her sides, scrunched her nose up, closed her eyes, and gave a little shimmy. The onlookers gave a roar of approval, and the young lady turned and gave a little curtsey, first to one side of the road and then to the other. The couple cleared the road just as a line of cars eased past heading northeast, and a single RV slowly crawled southwest. Then for the moment, the road was clear once more.

"Maggie, you should let me take a picture of you and Will in the middle of the road," Tess said.

"Oh, I don't know." Maggie said, certain that Will would never in a million years do such a thing.

Before she could say another word, Will took the camera from her, handed it to Tess, and grabbed Maggie's hand. In the next instant, Will was hustling her toward the middle of the road.

When they reached the centerline, he spun her around and pulled her close, then looked to see if Tess was ready. Caught off guard herself, Tess was just getting out into the road when he turned.

Once Tess was set, Will reached down, picked Maggie's hands up, and placed them on his shoulders, then he placed a hand on each of her hips, and looked into her eyes. Trey could hear the clicking of the camera as the shutter opened and closed. Then, without so much as a word, Will leaned forward and gently kissed her lips.

Trey's mouth dropped open and then snapped shut when the crowd began to cheer. It was as if he was watching a scene from a movie, except his grandparents were the stars. When the kiss ended, Will once again took Maggie by the hand, looked both ways, and escorted her back to the edge of the pavement.

As she stepped down from the asphalt lip into the sand, she said, "Goodness gracious, Will, where did that come from? My heart is pounding as bad as it did the first time you kissed me."

"It came from my heart, just like the first time I kissed you," he said and brushed another kiss across her lips.

Tess handed the camera back to Maggie and said, "That was awesome. I got several pictures. I think you're gonna love them."

"I'm sure I will," Maggie reddened a little. "Thank you so much for taking them."

*****

From their first stop at the entrance to Monument Valley to the Arizona state line was a mere twelve miles, but it took them nearly two hours to cover the distance. If it wasn't Maggie pointing out a place to pull off the road, it was Tess. Out of the truck, they would all climb, take a series of pictures, and then load back up. Trey lost count of the times this process was repeated, but there was no doubt his grandparents seemed to be having the time of their lives. He had never seen them act so carefree, laughing and joking and genuinely enjoying the day.

If it hadn't been for his morning phone call hanging over his head like a big black cloud, he would have enjoyed the day, too. But that call continued to eat at him until his stomach felt like someone had tried to kick a hole in it, and the tension in his shoulders turned into a headache. He was half wishing he had not made the call when his grandmother pointed at a little sign to the left of the road welcoming them to Arizona.

"I think we're leaving the valley," she said. "That sure was a lot of fun. Thank you all for the good memories."

Trey muttered a thank you as he looked down at the flip phone in the console. Still no sign of a missed call or a text message.

*****

Shortly after they entered Arizona, Trey saw three horses milling around a large, round, galvanized water tank below a spinning windmill. He had the sudden urge to pull the truck over, jump the fence, catch one of them, and ride it off into the desert.

You don't have a saddle, or a canteen, a pesky little voice in his head reminded him.

I really don't give a shit about a saddle. I'd ride bareback to get away from all my troubles, he told the voice.

Then he was past the horses, and the desert road seem to just roll on and on.

At Kayenta, Arizona, they stopped at Subway for a quick bite to eat and then took Highway 160 west. In the middle of the desert, Highway 160 intersected with Highway 98 near a convenience store.

"Turn right up there before you get to that Shell station," Maggie said pointing over Trey's shoulder.

He did and somewhere, between that turn and the exit to Kiabito, his three passengers all fell asleep. Forty minutes later, the outskirts of Page appeared, and he was forced to wake them because he didn't know where they wanted to stay the night. He sent up a silent prayer that wherever it was, they would have three rooms available.

*****

A very short, thin middle-aged lady with strawberry blonde hair arranged in a very messy bun atop her head informed Will that they had plenty of rooms. When he told her he would need three, she pushed her leopard print reading glasses higher on her narrow nose, turned to her computer screen, and began typing.

Without looking away from the screen she asked, "So what brings you to Arizona?"

"We're here to see Horseshoe Bend," he said.

"Can I give you some advice?" she asked.

"Sure," Will shrugged.

"Wait until just about an hour before sunset," she said, "It's a little cooler and the best time to view it. I've been here nearly fifteen years now, and I make it a point to go out and see it every couple of weeks when I can. And even after all these years, it's still amazing."

"Well, thanks," Will said. "Sure appreciate it."

"My pleasure." She smiled as she handed him the key cards, pointed out the elevator, and said, "All three rooms are on the second floor. I'm here 'til eight, but someone will be here all night, so if you need anything, just ring the front desk."

Will thanked her once again and stepped outside where Trey and Tess were loading the last of the luggage onto a cart, while Maggie gathered odds and ends from the back seat. The final suitcase loaded, Maggie tossed a plastic bag of snacks and her purse on the top of the pile, and Trey rolled it around the back of the truck and pushed it up the slight incline into the hotel. Years of use had worn and loosened the screws holding on the front wheels on the cart and part way up the incline, the front left wheel folded, causing the cart to tip. Trey made a grabbing attempt to stop the shifting luggage from hitting the pavement, but he only managed to secure Granny's purse before an avalanche of suitcases, overnight bags, snacks, and blankets hit the ground.

"My goodness." Maggie stepped over everything to take the purse from her grandson. "You'll have to get another cart and reload it."

Trey stepped back into the motel, and in a few seconds returned with another cart.

Helping his grandfather reload the new cart, he sighed and thought that the whole incident was a pretty good metaphor for his life. After years of trying to please people, after years of constantly rolling along whatever path he was told to follow, his own wheels were becoming a little wobbly, and he feared that, any day now, just like the cart, one would come off, and his entire life would be turned upside down.

"It's okay, it was just a little mishap," Tess spoke beside him, then asked, "What are you thinking about?"

"My life," Trey answered.

*****

Tess's pink suitcase was the last item Trey picked up from the ground. As he placed it on top of the rest of load, Tess thought how much this reminded her of the situation she was in. Two days ago, the plans she had been making for the last year and a half had crashed and burned just like the cart. When Maggie had found her, her life was a scattered mess on the floor of a bathroom stall. And then fate brought her a new cart. Trey gave the second cart a push to get it started, her eyes met his, she smiled, and he smiled back. It was a bit weak, perhaps even a bit forced, but a smile all the same. She felt her heart begin to race and looked away.

When the elevator reached the second floor and the doors began to open, Will handed Tess the keys to her room. She immediately began to dig her wallet out of her purse. Taking a hundred-dollar bill from it, she handed it to Will and ask, "Will this cover my room?"

"Yes, it will," He said, taking the money without argument. He slid it into his shirt pocket. "I'm sure glad they had plenty of

135

rooms tonight. I didn't sleep worth a darn last night with Trey snoring loud enough to wake the dead."

Without even turning to look at his grandfather, Trey said in a calm matter-of-a-fact voice, "I don't snore. You were hearing yourself, not me." He maneuvered the cart off the elevator.

Will winked at Tess and stepped out into the hallway. "How would you know? You were asleep."

Tess tried to hold a giggle in, snorted loudly, and then blushed. Will chuckled at her which caused Maggie to laugh. When Trey stopped at the first of their rooms, the three of them were wiping tears. He did not see a single thing funny about any of it, but then they had all had a nap while he drove. Maybe they weren't as dog tired as he was.

After a quick stop at his grandparent's room and then Tess's, Trey finally reached his own room, opened the door, dropped his bags just inside the door, and started back for the elevator with the now empty cart. He was getting pretty efficient at this little nightly routine. The door to the elevator opened just as he reached it. A man with salt-and-pepper hair who smelled heavily of beer and cigars stepped off, and a woman with jet-black hair, sunbaked skin, and deep green eyes followed him. As Trey eased the cart past them, the woman smiled, showing a perfect set of the whitest teeth he had ever seen. He nodded in acknowledgement but did not smile in return.

The elevator door shut behind him, and he wondered if that was considered rude. He thought perhaps it might be. Rude was not something he had ever intentionally been, and it bothered him to think he might be turning that way. He pulled his phone from his pocket. No messages, no calls. The door opened on the first floor, and as he rolled the cart back towards its place, he flipped the phone open and dialed Lisa's number.

When the voicemail picked up, he hung up without leaving a message. He parked the cart and, on the way back to the elevator, dialed again. Same number of rings. Same result. By the time he reached his room, he'd repeated the process twice more. Inside, he sat down on the edge of the bed and sent a text.

It read: *If we can't talk, we can't move forward. I will be taking my grandparents to see Horseshoe Bend and then out to a restaurant. I should be back in my room by nine at the latest. When you're ready to talk I'm here.*

He lay back on the bed and closed his eyes. An hour later, he awoke to the ringing of a phone.

Chapter 14

"We'll be ready to go in about twenty minutes," Maggie told him when he finally figured out it was the room phone and not his cell that was buzzing. "Why don't you just meet us down in the lobby?"

Trying to rub the sleep from his eyes, he half-mumbled, "Sure, Granny, I'll meet y'all down there."

A quick check of his cell yielded nothing, and he stepped into the bathroom. He put on fresh deodorant and bushed his teeth, then checked his reflection in the mirror. The person looking back at him looked tired. Not it has been a long day tired; more of an I am down, and life is still kicking me in the head kind of tired. A voice in his head that sounded a whole lot like Will Tucker said, *It's your choice. You can either lay there and keep letting 'em kick you or you can pick your ass up off the ground and start kickin' back.*

If it was only that easy, he thought as he gathered what he needed, reached out and switched the bathroom light off, and made his way out of his room and down to the first floor. He was sitting there staring at but not watching the Weather Channel on the lobby television when Will stepped off the elevator followed by Maggie and Tess.

*****

From the hotel to the turn off for Horseshoe Bend was less than three miles. The cost of admission was ten dollars, five if you were on a motorcycle. The walk from the parking lot to the edge of the cliff above the Colorado river was a little over a half a mile, mostly at a decline.

Trey and Tess hiked along behind Will and Maggie. The steady stream of people, both going to and coming from the bend, seemed endless. More than once, their little group found themselves crowding the edge of the footpath as a group eased past them.

"It's a bit warm still," Tess said as she stepped in front of Trey to allow a group of elderly couples to pass.

"I guess so," Trey agreed.

"The sun coming through the clouds is pretty though." She pointed towards the western horizon.

"Yes, it is," Trey said following her gaze.

"Your turn," Tess said, looking over her shoulder at him.

"What?" Trey asked confused, "My turn to what?"

"Say something about something," Tess said. "That is how a conversation is supposed to work. I can't always be the one running the show."

"I think we already had this talk," Trey shook his head. "I'm not really good at discussions. I'm more of a listener."

"And you never will be if you don't try," Tess chided. "You need to practice."

After few silent steps, Trey observed, "The rock formations here are pretty."

"Yes, they are," Tess said and pointed at one ahead and to the right of them. "I especially like that one."

An elderly man headed back to the parking area pointed at Will's Stetson hat and said, "Sure like your lid, mister."

"Thank you," Will smiled then asked. "How was the sight at this time of the evening?"

"Top ten," the guy answered, "And I've seen a bit of the world."

Trey had not seen much of the world but somehow, he doubted that whatever lay at the end of this trail was going to impress him nearly as much as it had that little old man.

But he was dead wrong!

The Colorado River had cut a horseshoe-shaped canyon out of the desert, and people were everywhere along the edge of the cliffs. One young woman in a yellow tank top and pair of black and yellow floral print shorts stood two feet from the very edge, raised her iPhone high above her head, threw up the peace sign, smiled, and snapped a selfie. Unprepared for the sheer depth of the canyon, Trey walked steadily to within five feet of the edge. There he stopped short, slowly backed up several feet, and turned around to check on Tess.

He spotted her some fifty feet back up the trail, staring right at him with nothing short of a deer-in-the-headlights look. He retraced his steps back to where she stood, feeling a little wobbly on his feet as he went. He was not afraid of heights but walking up unexpectedly to the edge of a thousand-foot drop would make even the bravest man on earth a little weak in the knees.

"I don't think you're gonna want to look over the edge," he said. "It was all I could do to keep from getting lightheaded, and I'm not afraid of heights."

"Really?" she feigned shock and then put a hand to her chest and gasped. "You don't think I can handle a thousand-foot drop?"

"How did you know it was a thousand-foot drop?" he asked.

"I did a little research on my phone while we were at the hotel," she answered and then changed the subject. "So, why are you still sporting a flip-phone, anyway?"

"It's a long story," he answered. "Let's just say I had an iPhone when we started on this trip, and it had a little accident."

"What kind of accident?" she asked.

"A *let's-make-a-point Will Tucker kind of accident*," he answered as he lowered himself to the ground a few feet from her.

At the mentions of his grandfather's name, Trey looked quickly in the direction he had seen Maggie and Will go and found them standing side by side near the fence that was supposed to keep people from getting too close to the edge. As he watched them, Will took Maggie's hand in his, and the two of them stood there together, looking out over the landscape.

"I want what they have someday," Tess said with a sigh, and sat down beside him.

"So do I," Trey agreed.

"Someone should really get a couple of pictures of those two," Tess said.

Trey raised an eyebrow. "And I suppose by someone, you mean me?"

"You know I'm not going any closer to that drop of death than right here," she said. "Do you want to use my phone?"

"No, Granny brought her camera," he said as he pushed himself up of the ground. "I'll use it."

"When you're done, would you take a couple of pictures of me with my phone?" she asked as he started to walk away.

He shrugged and said, "Yeah, I guess so."

By the time Trey made it back from taking his grandparents pictures, Tess had moved over next to an outcropping the size of a large trailer, the top of which towered nearly twenty feet above the surrounding area. People working their way up and down a slight incline on one of its sides had worn a narrow walkway into the edge of it. When he reached Tess's side, a group of four teenager guys all shirtless, in athletic shorts, and running shoes were making their way down from it.

"Would you mind climbing up there and seeing what the view is like for me?" Tess's asked.

"Why?" Trey questioned.

"Because if there's a good view of the bend from up there, I thought I might climb up there myself," Tess answered.

"But…" he began.

"But I'm afraid of heights," she interrupted, "but only real high stuff. I've been on the roof of a house before, and while I wasn't crazy about it, I can do it. Please, climb up and see… please," she begged.

"Alright," Trey answered.

What's wrong with you man, a voice inside his head chided, *a pretty girl says please, and you think you have to do her bidding.*

He was halfway up the little ledge before he realized that he had acknowledged, even in his mind, that Tess was pretty. By the time he reached the top, he was in a full-on argument with himself as to whether it was okay for him to think of her as pretty. Did thinking another female was pretty make him unfaithful?

An opinion on the matter does not imply infidelity, he argued with himself. *You're not having impure thoughts about her. You only thought she was pretty.*

"Well?" Tess's voice broke through his thoughts.

When he didn't immediately reply, she repeated it. He looked out over the land, and asked, "You need help getting up?"

"Maybe," she answered, "I might be able to do it myself, but I'd feel better if you were close. If you don't mind, please."

Pretty girls says please and you... he chided himself as he started back down.

He stayed within arm's reach of her as they made their way to the top of the ledge. When they reached it, Tess looked down, and said, "This is a bit higher than it looked from down there."

"And it's smaller than I realized," Trey said trying to give her room to turn around.

Slowly, she turned so the Horseshoe was behind her, took three quick shots and then she handed the phone to Trey.

"You're taller than me," she said, "Stand here beside me and take a selfie with me."

Just as he figured she was fixing to offer up another please, he stepped up beside her, turned around, held the phone up high, tilted it at the proper angle, and started to take the picture.

"That doesn't look right," Tess stopped him, "my head is too far down in the corner." And she stepped up to a higher position on the rock, leaned forward, braced herself with one hand in the middle of his back, placed her head over his shoulder, tilted her head until it was resting against his, then said, "Okay that's better. Take a couple."

With no idea what else he could do, he hit the button three times.

Sweet lord, please, and I mean I'm begging, don't ever let Lisa see these pictures, he thought.

The photos showed a sun that was quickly sinking towards the horizon in the west, causing yellow, orange, and pink streaks across the sky and creating a natural backdrop to the photographs that no painter or photographer could ever do justice. One last long look at her face so close to his, and he handed the phone back to her. He could still feel the pressure from where her hand had rested on his back even after he stepped away and while it felt wonderful and right, it also felt wrong.

*****

"I think we better get down now," Tess said. "My legs are feeling a little shaky."

She had no doubt that it was more than just the height that was causing her knees to knock. The effect of being so close to him was not something she had counted on, not after what had happened to her only a couple of days ago. She figured it would be a much longer time before she would even think about liking someone else. And now, here she was, her heart fluttering in her chest like a middle school girl hoping her crush would ask her to the dance. Only it had been a while since middle school, and she was sure she was not ready for a relationship. Plus, if she was not mistaken, he was taken. At least, he seemed to be very interested in his phone and frustrated that someone was not communicating with him. It was probably for the best. She sure didn't need a rebound relationship right now.

*****

"Don't be too obvious," Will said to Maggie, "but take a gander at that rock outcrop over your left shoulder."

With a slow turn of her head, she found the outcrop, and to her surprise, there were Trey and Tess, heads together, phone held high, taking a selfie. Afraid they would notice her looking their way, she quickly faced forward once again.

Will chuckled, "Yeah, I didn't want to jinx it by staring either."

"Jinx what?" Maggie gave a sharp sniff. "He's engaged. She's heartbroken. They've only known each other two days, and in no more than five days, we'll be dropping her off in Placerville. So, once again, jinx what?"

Unscathed by Maggie's doubt, Will just grinned and said, "Five days is a long time. Who knows what might happen? And honey, remember, I knew I was going to marry you the first time I laid eyes on your beautiful face."

Will pulled Maggie into his arms and gently kissed her there in the warm evening air above the Colorado river as the slightest sliver of sun winked one last time before disappearing below the western horizon, leaving the desert bathed in golden hues. When the embrace ended, he took her by the hand, and they headed back up the path towards the parking lot.

"I don't know what's gotten into you," Maggie grinned, "but I could sure get used to it."

Will put his free hand over the left side of his heart as if she had stabbed him in the heart and with a sly grin said, "You cut me deep. You know I've always been very romantical."

Maggie laughed and nudged him on the shoulder, "Yeah, right, and I'm not even sure you used that word correctly."

"Me neither," Will chuckled, "but you know what I meant."

"What's so funny?" Trey asked when his grandparents joined him and Tess.

"Nothing really," Maggie grinned "Your Pappy here was just trying to convince me he's an old romantic at heart."

"I am," Will declared. "A downright romantical fellow, I am."

He slid a sly wink at Tess and Trey. "And so are my son and my grandson. We're all a romantical bunch of cowboys."

"I still don't think that's the correct way to use that word," Maggie told him.

Will just shrugged in indifference, and the four started up the trail. Halfway to the top, Will stepped over to the small rock pavilion and sat down.

"You, okay?" Trey asked him.

"Need a breather," Will said. "Ain't as young as I use to be, but still a durn sight tougher than most."

"Alright." Trey nodded, knowing very well that he would be hard put to find anyone as tough as his grandfather.

The breather was a short one, and five minutes later, they were climbing the incline once again. Trey had never really considered that as he grew older, his grandparents did too. By the time they reached the end of the footpath and stepped onto the black top surface of the parking area, he had decided, that in the years to come, he definitely needed to spend more time with them. As bad as he hated to admit it, he was starting to think that maybe this trip was a good idea after all.

"I overheard some folks talking about a restaurant called Sunset 89 that's just up the road a little way," Will said when they were all in the truck again. "Let's try to find it."

Before Trey could say anything, Tess spoke from the backseat, "It's on the left just about three miles straight up this road."

Trey shook his head and said, "Unlike me, she has a working iPhone, and she can even tell us how to get to the restaurant."

"I see," Will said accepting the explanation but choosing to ignore the iPhone implication.

When Trey pulled into an open parking space in front of the Sunset 89 restaurant and turned the key in the ignition to the off position, his cellphone vibrated and rang. All eyes turned to him as he dug it out of his pocket and looked at the number.

"I better take this," he told them. "Y'all go ahead. I'll be along in a minute."

Chapter 15

"Hello," Trey said as he watched his grandparents and Tess walk away from the truck. Will's stance and stride told Trey all he needed to know about his grandfather's mood—aggravated.

"I guess you got rid of the slut," Lisa said smugly.

"What?" Trey responded shocked.

"The slut," Lisa repeated. "I guess you got rid of her. Your message said we could move forward, right? And I told you the other night you had to get rid of her or else, so did you or did you not get rid of the slut?"

Trey took a long breath and then let it out slowly. "Lisa, I told you from the beginning I am with Granny and Pappy on this trip. They make the calls. I don't have a lot to say in anything."

"So, what you're tellin' me is that your little tramp is still along for the ride?" Her voice got louder and shriller with each word. "And I guess you still want me to believe you're not doin' her?"

"Good grief, Lisa!" Trey gasped. "What in the world is wrong with you? I am not doin' anyone. I am engaged to you. I have never cheated on you or been unfaithful to you in any way!"

"I don't believe you." Her voice was flat and hollow sounding. "I think you've known this girl for a long time. Your Granny said she was a family friend. I bet you've been layin' it to her every time you got a chance to slip away from me."

"Have you lost your mind?" He lost his temper and screamed into the phone "We've been together six years. In all that time, I haven't been away from you for more than a couple of days… what?… maybe, half a dozen times at the most. And you think some girl would wait around for six years just to see me… Like what?… once a year?"

"Don't you yell at me!" Lisa shouted. "I won't put up with a man who yells at me, and who doesn't know what he has or how good he has it."

"So, I guess, Slade doesn't yell at you, huh?" he asked, "and why did he answer your phone?"

"Really?… That's the best you can do?" Lisa snarled, "We're not talkin' about him. We're talkin' about your little whore."

Trey stared out past the edge of the light of the parking lot and into the darkness not knowing how to respond. When several seconds of silence had past, Lisa, back to her flat, hollow tone, said, "What? Nothing to say? The tramp got your tongue?"

Something deep inside Trey's brain registered the unwarranted insult on Tess for the first time, and suddenly, he realized he didn't like it, not in the least.

"Her name is Tess." He matched Lisa's tone and pitch as well as he could. "She is a person that my grandparents and I have known for two days and two days only. I am not sleeping with her, and as far as I can tell, she is respectable. I have no intentions of sleeping with her. I am engaged to you. I love…"

"No, you don't," Lisa cut him off. "No you don't. Don't say it. I don't want to hear it. If you did, your precious little Tess wouldn't still be with you. So don't even try that, and as far as us being engaged… well…"

Trey felt as hollow as Lisa's voice. "That's not right," his voice cracked, "Lisa, you know that's not right?"

From somewhere in the background, he heard a woman yell, "Lisa you comin'? We ain't gonna wait on you all night."

"I gotta go," Lisa said flatly.

"We need to talk," Trey said around the lump in his throat. "We need to…"

"I'm hangin' up now," She stated coldly.

"Call me later, please." He heard himself saying.

"Don't count on it," She said and at the same time Trey heard a male voice say, "Come on let's go, Lisa."

*****

Will and the ladies had ordered and received their drinks and were waiting on Trey to make it inside before ordering their entrees. Tess watched as Will flipped the menu from front to back several times without actually looking at it. His eyes tracked back and forth between the menu and the front door.

"I'm goin' to the restroom," he said and left the table.

"I'm sorry about all the tension," Maggie apologized to Tess.

Tess smiled and said, "Can I ask you a question?"

"Of course, you can." Maggie reached across the table and patted Tess's hand.

"Who was that on the phone with Trey?" Tess asked.

The smile left Maggie's face. "That would be Lisa, the woman he's engaged to marry."

"Oh." Tess's looked down at the table, and a voice in her head that sounded a lot like her Aunt Alyssa said, *How could you not see that coming?*

She wanted to shout back, *I could see it, I just didn't want it to,* instead, she instantly told herself, *It's all for the best. It would have only been a rebound relationship, and it would have ended badly.*

Maggie patted her hand once again, this time leaving her hand atop Tess's. "Can I tell you something?"

"Of course," Tess said.

"She's not the right girl for him," Maggie whispered.

A whirlwind of thoughts, of what-ifs and maybes, swirled through Tess's mind, and for a fraction of a second, she allowed herself a smidgen of hope. Then in and amongst all the possibilities, memories of past failed relationships began to circle like debris in a tornado, and in a *poof!* all hope disappeared.

"What makes you say that?" Tess asked.

"Woman's intuition," Maggie answered, "maybe a grandmother's instinct, but most likely, just the wisdom the Good Lord has been kind enough to give me."

The two sat quiet for a moment. Maggie removed her hand from Tess's and took a sip of her sweet tea. Tess ran her right index finger along the side of her glass enjoying the feel of its coolness. She was amazed at how comfortable she was with Maggie. From the very moment she had opened the stall door at Clines Corner, Maggie had made her feel like she was someone. Never in her life had anyone made her feel like she was so special.

Maggie set her glass down and said, "Trey is a good man."

Tess simply nodded her head in agreement and looked up to see Will coming back to the table. He eased down in his chair and frowned.

"Trey still not made it in?" He glanced over at the empty chair.

"He'll be here when he can," Maggie assured him. "We're not in any hurry anyway. Why don't we just order an appetizer?"

Will picked up a menu and looked at Tess. "Sorry about this, young lady."

"It's okay," Tess said. "I'm sure he's got things to talk about."

Will scanned the menu and shook his head and thought, *Rome wasn't built in a day, so what makes you think you were gonna be able to dig through six years' worth of bullshit and magically pull your grandson free in just four days?*

"Do you wanna try the fried pork skins?" Maggie asked.

"Yeah, that's fine," he grumbled.

*****

When Trey finally came into the restaurant, his grandfather looked up and said. "Sorry, son, but we ate all the appetizers."

"That's all right," Trey said. Bloodshot eyes and the slump of his shoulders was enough to tell them the phone call had not gone well. When the waitress returned to get Trey's drink order, Will asked if they could move to a table outside on the veranda.

"Sure," the young lady said, "If you will just take your drinks with you, I'll find you when I bring this young man's drink out."

When Trey stood up, Will stepped up behind his grandson and placed a hand on his shoulder. A long-buried memory of his last high school baseball game rose to the surface, and Trey remembered his grandfather's hand on the same shoulder as he ushered him out of the ballfield. Trey remembered the pain of knowing it was the last time he would play as a Mustang. But mostly he remembered the strength Will's hand on his shoulder had given him.

You should have taken the scholarship to Murray State, Trey thought.

Outside, the evening air had already begun to cool, and the sweet fragrance of some desert flower rode a gentle breeze onto the veranda. Maggie led them to an umbrellaed table that sat at the furthest edge of the concrete patio. Had the sun still been up, they would have had a view of the Colorado River far below. In the dark, it was a bit different. A neatly manicured patch of grass extended from the edge of the patio to the edge of the cliff above the river. Strings of lights had been strung along the edge and then crisscrossed over of the lawn. The dimly lit yard faded into blackness that fell away into emptiness at the rim of the canyon. Several small wireless speakers were strategically placed around the area, and soft instrumental music played.

No sooner had they taken their seat than the waitress arrived with Trey's drink. She took their orders and left. After a few moments of awkward silence, Will pushed his chair back, stood, and offered his hand to Maggie.

She looked up at him, a confused look on her face, and took his hand. He pulled her up from her seat and lead her to the center of the grassy area. There in the dim light, he pulled her close, and began to sway slowly to the music. From their seats, Trey and

Tess watched as the two seemed to float in a little circle, dancing along to the rhythm.

"Do you think love like that is still possible?" Tess whispered when Will dipped Maggie. He raised her back up, twirled her out, and then pulled her close so she could rest her head on his shoulder.

"It's possible, I suppose," Trey answered in a low and raspy voice, "Possible, but very rare, especially in today's world. My mom and dad had it. They used to dance around the house when I was young."

Tess let his words sink in and then said, "I want it. I want that kind of love, and if I can't have it then I'll just do without."

Trey looked from his grandparents to Tess. "I hope you find it," he told her. "I really hope you do." And he meant it.

Chapter 16

Eight-thirty Friday morning found Trey driving north on Highway 89 across the Utah state line. He had tossed and turned most of the previous night and had fallen asleep just two hours before the alarm on his phone woke him.

Will stared out the side window at the desert. Trey drove eyes ahead, trying not to think at all. There had been no missed calls or messages when he checked his phone before leaving the motel. A weight, invisible and immense, pressed in on all sides and made it hard for him to breathe.

Maggie touched Will on the shoulder and asked, "Honey, are you okay?"

"I'm fine, darlin'," He answered. "It was just that rough night. My stomach was giving me fits. Must have been those short ribs I had last night."

"Trey, how are you feelin' this morning?" Maggie asked.

Not taking his eyes from the road, he said, "A little tired. I didn't sleep so well last night either."

"Well, maybe you and your grandpa will both do better tonight," she said then turned and asked Tess, "How was your night?"

"I had the strangest dream and woke up just before my alarm went off. In it I was floating along a desert path in a long white wedding dress. It had this beautiful train flowing behind it. When I looked back, I couldn't see the end of it. Then far up ahead on a flat area, I could see people waiting on me. I didn't know them or why they were waiting on me, but I felt anxious because I just knew I was going to be late. I tried to move faster, but no matter how quickly I ran, the people weren't getting any closer. I ran faster and faster until suddenly, the train on the dress tangled around my feet and I tripped. Just before my face hit the ground, I woke up, thrashing in the sheets. It was so strange because I usually don't dream. I wonder if it means something?"

"That is strange," Maggie said. "I don't know anything about interpreting dreams."

"Me either." Tess shrugged and turned to look out the window.

Maggie picked up the Atlas, checked the route, and told Trey, "It looks like we're gonna be in Utah for about an hour, then at Kanab, you'll need to take Highway 89A back down into Arizona. Then we'll make a big half circle back into Utah before heading up into Nevada."

Trey glanced into the rearview with a frown on his face. "Granny, that didn't make much sense. We're going north then circling back south then back north?"

"It's the desert and the roads," Maggie explained. "It's not like back home where there's lots of roads. I guess, if we knew the country, we could take one of these dirt lanes that run off this highway and cut some time off our trip."

Trey was quick to say, "The highway will be fine." He could just imagine getting lost in the middle of the desert if he got off a marked road. *Talk about being completely screwed*, he thought, *You're already mentally and emotionally lost, getting physically lost might just put you over the edge.*

An hour later, Maggie reminded Trey about turning south on Highway 89A as he entered the city limits of Kanab. He found the turn in the middle of the little desert town, and a few minutes outside of town, they left Utah and crossed back into Arizona. He barely had time to set the cruise again before Maggie told him to make a right onto Highway 389 at Fredonia.

"I could use a restroom break," Will said, "I see a Sinclair station up ahead. Let's stop there."

"Okay." Trey nodded and slowed.

As they pulled off the highway, Will turned in his seat, looked over his shoulder at Tess, and said, "I've been thinking about your dream. My mother was part Chickasaw, and sometimes she would interpret dreams."

Trey found a parking space in front of the building and turned to look at his grandfather. Will already had Maggie and Tess's full attention.

"Now, in your dream, the desert, itself, and the fact that you were says that you were feeling helpless." Will pursed his mouth, "Tells me you may be worried that you don't have anyone and are afraid you're never going to have a decent relationship."

"Alright," Tess said.

"The white dress represents a relationship, past, future, or both, I don't know," he continued, "but you running means you are scared, fearful. And the tripping there at the end is you being afraid if you give up control, something bad will happen."

"So, is it telling me to take a chance on a relationship or to avoid them all together?" Tess asked.

"That's for you to figure out," Will smiled. "I'm not Doctor Phil, and to be honest, that's my first try at interpreting a dream. Who knows if I got it right?"

Trey caught a glimpse of his grandmother's face in the mirror and could tell by the look on her faced that she was shocked. He looked back to Will. His grandfather just gave him a shrug, opened the door, and stepped out of the truck.

After a fifteen-minute stop, they were back on the road. Trey found the intersection and turned west. A few minutes later, a small green sign off to the right of the road said they were entering the Kaibab Paiute Indian Reservation. Except for the highway and the utility poles and wires that seemed to parallel it, there didn't seem to be anything but miles and miles of desert with the occasional butte. Trey looked out across the landscape and wondered how something so desolate could be so beautiful.

"So, I guess that first date that you and Will had didn't go all that well, Maggie?" Tess spoke up.

When Maggie did not answer, Trey looked up into the rearview. Maggie's scrunched eyebrows and confused stare told Trey that she had no idea what Tess was talking about.

"You know, the date you and Will went on after you didn't talk to him for two weeks?" Tess said and then twirled her index fingers in a gesture that said the story should continue.

"Oh, that!" Maggie chuckled. "To say he broke nearly every rule of dating would be an understatement. I spent all afternoon getting all gussied up, fixed my hair just right, and put on my best blouse and favorite denim skirt. He showed up right on time in this rusty old truck with a trailer in tow."

"A trailer?" Tess raised a dark brow.

"Yep," Maggie said, "That's exactly what my Momma and sister thought, too. I'll never forget her hollering from the front door, 'Margaret Lynn there is some crazy cowboy out here with a horse trailer. You want me to get rid of him before your date gets here'. I hollered back and said, 'it's probably someone to see Amelia.' That was my older sister."

Trey glanced over at Will who was sporting the biggest grin Trey had ever seen on his grandfather's face. As if someone had cued him, he sang out in a strong baritone voice, "Come take my hand and walk through this world with me."

"Stop that now," Maggie chided. "You're getting ahead of the story."

Trey, who had only ever heard his grandfather sing hymns during church services, could hardly believe that the sound he had just heard had come from the man seated next to him. He would have given up hearing the rest of the story if his Pappy would finish the song.

"When I got to the front door," Maggie continued, "there was Will, standing in the yard at the bottom of the steps with his cowboy hat in his hands. Of course, I was bewildered, to say the least. I said, 'What in the world do you think you're doing, Will Tucker'?"

"And I said," Will broke in from the front seat, "'I'm here to pick you up for our date. Are you ready?'"

"Before I could say yea or nay or boo," Maggie said, "He steps right up on the porch, reaches out and takes my Momma's hand and says, 'and you must be Maggie's sister,' and of course, Momma just fell in love with him right there and then."

"If only I could have won *you* over that quick." Will wiggled his eyebrows.

"If only," Maggie's grinned. "About that time, Amelia came in from the back of the house, took one look at Will through the screen door, and said, 'Momma I don't know that man. To which momma said, 'it's okay, this is Maggie's date'."

Will chuckled from the front seat and Maggie blushed.

"Amelia, my own sister, took one look at him and said, 'Well, damn! Maggie if you don't want him, I'll take him'." Maggie shook her head, "Momma scolded Amelia and told her to go to her room then started apologizing to Will who was just standing there grinning like a shit-eatin'-'possum."

In all his life, Trey had never heard his grandmother say a curse word, and in less than sixty seconds, two had slipped out of her mouth. With his grandfather singing songs and his grandmother cussing, he wondered if sleep deprivation was causing him to hallucinate.

"Where was your dad during all of this?" Tess asked.

"He was dead," Maggie answered. "He was killed in an oilfield accident when I was four."

"Oh, I'm sorry," Tess said.

"Don't be," Maggie told her. "I never knew him, and from what little I heard about him, he wasn't a real nice fellow."

Tess nodded then asked, "What happened next?"

"Well, I was so embarrassed, all I wanted to do was just get out of there," Maggie said, "so I grabbed Will by the arm, told Momma I'd be home before ten and we left."

"That's about right," Will cut in again, "except for the part where we just left. What actually happened there was she came off that porch hard, grabbed me, and was durn near draggin' me across the yard to my truck when I lost my footing and stumbled.

Before I knew it, I was fallin', and because she didn't realize I was goin' down, she didn't let loose quick enough, and next thing I know, I'm layin' in the dirt in her front yard, and she's lying sideways across the middle of my chest."

Tess's eyes went wide. Trey couldn't begin to visualize such a thing.

"Alright, yeah, that happened too," Maggie said, then pointed out the front window, "Look. We're coming into a town."

Ahead on the horizon were buildings, and suddenly as if it had sprouted miraculously from the desert right in front of them, a town appeared. On the right side of the road, a green highway sign let them know they were entering Colorado City and that the town had been established in 1985. Additionally, the sign told them the elevation here was five thousand feet above sea level. What it didn't tell, and what Trey found strange, was the population.

The city itself was east of the highway until they reached the Utah state line. Here the imaginary line that separated the two states, also separated what on a map looked like one large town. To the south in Arizona was Colorado City and to the north of the line in Utah was Hildale. Adding to the separation of states, the number on the road which they were travelling now changed to Highway 59.

Trey thought about the line between him and Lisa. Once he would have said, it was as thin as those between states. Now he was not so sure. It seemed that the space between them was growing. Not just the physical separation of being apart, but also their ability to communicate and resolve conflicts. If he could not find a way to turn it around, all the plans he had made for the future would be for nil.

Will pointed to a convenience store on the left side of the highway just after they crossed over into Utah and said, "I'm ready for something to drink and a chance to stretch."

*****

"So, the date did not start well." Tess said after they had gotten beverages, walked around a bit, and returned to the truck.

Trey could have hugged her for asking. The thought of driving in silence did not appeal to him. He had checked his phone while they were stopped—no messages, no missed calls. Not only was he interested in his grandparent's story, but he also knew he needed to be distracted from the worries that were running through his head.

"No, it did not," Maggie said, then, "All sprawled out in the dirt, we were both a mess. His shirt was covered with dust, and I had torn a rip in the hem of my skirt. None of it seemed to phase Will though. Once we got untangled and into his truck, he drove us right through town, past the diner, past the theater, and then he turned and started out of town."

Maggie brushed the front of her jeans as if she was in Will's truck, straightening out her favorite skirt. Trey thought maybe his grandfather would take up the story, but he didn't.

After a moment, Maggie said, "When he passed the cemetery, I got kind of worried. I thought a date meant dinner or a show, I didn't know where we were goin'."

"I could see she was gettin' nervous," Will finally said, "I was a little afraid she was goin' to open the truck door and jump out."

"I thought about it." Maggie admitted, "especially when he turned off down an old dirt road. I was a bit of a city girl. I hadn't spent much time running the rural roads around Hico, so I was out of my comfort zone, as you kids say these days."

Will said, "I pulled over at an old, gray, weathered barn that hadn't been used in years because the back half of the roof had fallen in. I got out, went around the truck, opened the door for her like a gentleman should, and she refused to get out."

"What did you do?" Trey asked.

"I left her sitting there with the door open and started unloading the horses out of the trailer," Will answered.

"Horses." Maggie said and then repeated, "Horses."

"How was I supposed to know you couldn't ride," Will

threw up his palms defensively. "I mean, I thought everyone in Texas grew up on a horse."

"Well, I hadn't," Maggie declared. "As a matter of fact, I had never even been on a horse."

Will shrugged and went on with the story. "By the time I had gotten both of the horses out of the trailer, curiosity had gotten the better of her, and she had gotten of the truck."

"It wasn't curiosity," Maggie disagreed, "it was fear. You took the keys out of the ignition when you got out of the truck, and I was afraid you were goin' to saddle up, ride off, and leave me stranded. I didn't want to have to walk back to town."

A sign to the left of the road indicated that the next exit was for Apple Valley. Trey looked out across the desert and chuckled at the thought of an apple orchard anywhere near them.

"This is the strangest first date I've ever heard of," Tess stated.

Trey nodded and asked, "Have you ever told my dad about this?"

"Oh, yeah," Will answered.

"I thought so, too," Maggie said continuing her story, "We must have argued for twenty minutes before he finally talked me into letting him help me up on that horse. There I was, straddling a horse in this ripped denim skirt that thankfully was loose enough and long enough that it mostly covered my thighs to the knees. If the town gossips had seen me, I would have lost my reputation for being a good girl for sure."

"She *was* a sight," Will declared, "and if anyone had ever said an unkind word about her, I'd have whipped them from one end of Hico to the other."

"So, off into the wilderness we rode," Maggie smiled, "Me bouncin' all around on that horse, just tryin' to keep from fallin' off. I thought it would never stop."

"In my defense," Will said, "she didn't tell me she'd never ridden before."

"I didn't want you to know," Maggie proclaimed.

"Well, darlin', after the first two minutes, it was kind of obvious." Will grinned.

"I realize that now," Maggie rolled her eyes. "Finally, he stopped and helped me down on a flat place next to this little stream running beside this big old live oak tree."

"You should have seen her eyes when I pulled a big old red and white checkered tablecloth, a pair of white bone China plates, and silverware out of the saddlebags." Will glanced over at Trey.

"That's right," Maggie said, "This crazy man had packed a whole picnic in saddlebags, complete with cloth napkins, long-stemmed glasses, and a bottle of sparkling grape juice."

"Oh my gosh," Tess put both hands over her heart and pretended to swoon. "That is so romantic."

Trey kept shifting his eyes from the road to his grandfather. It was hard for him to imagine this man he had known all his life doing something like what was being described, and had his grandmother not been there, he would have been even more doubtful. Seeing this side of Will gave him a whole other level of respect.

"We had our picnic, and when we finished and had everything packed back on the horses, he took me in his arms." Maggie's smile made her eyes sparkle.

Will started to sing again, and when he finished a few more lines, Maggie went on with the story, "I thought he was going to kiss me, and I was all ready to give him what for, and then he started dancing me slowly around that pasture, all the while lookin' deep into my eyes and singing that song."

"What is the song?" Tess asked.

"An old George Jones tune," Maggie said. "Well, it's old now, but then it was almost brand new. It's called 'Walk Through This World With Me'."

Trey could feel a lump forming in his throat and swallowed hard. Tess wiped at her eyes and then said, "That is the most beautiful story I've ever heard, and after that was it happy ever after?"

"Close, but not quite." Maggie said.

Chapter 17

At Hurricane, Utah, the highway took a sharp, hairpin turn and the ground seemed to just drop away, leaving the impression that they had reached the edge of the world. Tess was staring out her window, probably replaying the story Maggie and Will had told, when Trey made the turn. Caught off guard, Trey heard her breath catch, and watched in the rear view as she moved away from the door.

When they reached the bottom of the grade, they drove down North State Street, crossed the Virgin River, and were in the little town of La Verkin. Trey thought back to Colorado City and Hildale. Twice in less than half an hour, they had passed from one town to another by simply crossing a line. He wondered if life wasn't filled with similar scenarios. Perhaps, he thought, sometimes a person doesn't even realize when they cross the line between one phase of their life and the next. It could be that if one isn't paying attention, they are well down life's highway before they even know the line has been crossed.

Highway 17 turned into Interstate 15 and ran nearly straight north. The flat desert gave away to sandstone, cedar-covered mountain ridges for the next half an hour. At Hamilton Fort, Maggie instructed Trey to turn onto Highway 56. He did and found himself headed west once again.

Tess stuck her pillow against the door, pressed her head into it, and dozed off. A short time later, Will's chin dropped to his chest, and Trey could tell from his breathing that he was out. He looked into the rearview and smiled at his grandmother.

"I think they're both worn out." She smiled back and whispered. "How are you holdin' up?"

"I'm fine," Trey whispered back, knowing that he had just told his grandmother a lie. He was dog-tired and still worried about the situation with Lisa. "You go ahead and get some rest if you want to."

"I'm good," Maggie told him.

An hour later, when they had crossed the line into Nevada and the highway number changed again, he glanced back to find her still awake.

When the city limit sign for Panaca came into sight, population of four thousand seven hundred and thirty-two, established in 1864, Maggie said she was ready for a stop. Trey found a Sinclair station, and as he pulled in Will awoke, Tess did not.

"Should we wake her?" Trey asked his grandparents as he put the truck in park.

"Don't know when we'll stop again," Will said, "probably better."

A soft shake from Maggie and Tess opened her eyes, yawned, stretched, and said, "Where are we?"

"Panaca, Nevada," Trey answered.

As he opened the door and stepped out, he realized he had responded to Tess's question without even thinking. It had not flustered him. *Am I getting too comfortable with her?* he wondered to himself.

*****

Highway 93 was a straight shot north through the desert. Ten minutes north of Panaca, Trey passed an exit for Pioche, and after that, it was nothing but highway and cedar-covered desert. *If life was only as straight forward and simple as this road, I'd have it made*, he thought. But when the traffic dwindled to nearly nothing, boredom set in, and Trey began to count vehicles and measure the distance between curves in the road. Down one stretch that ran straight for twenty-seven miles he counted five vehicles—two cars, two RVs, and an old truck with a camper shell on it. If it hadn't been for the rolling nature of the terrain, the road would have not just been straight, it would have been completely flat, also.

Tired of counting vehicles, Trey asked, "So what happened after the dance?"

Will looked across the truck at his grandson and grinned. Maggie smiled and leaned a bit forward. Tess pepped up and dropped the magazine she had been idly flipping through.

"Your grandmother fessed up to the fact that she didn't really know how to ride," Will said. "I told her that we'd have to fix that 'cause she'd need to know how to ride since she was goin' to be a rancher's wife. That started a whole new argument."

"Yes, it did," Maggie answered and said, "In the end, I agreed to ride back to the truck on his horse with him, so he could show me what I was supposed to be doin'."

"She was a natural," Will said. "Took to riding like a fish takes to water, but she still swore she would never marry a cowboy. From then on, we spent every minute we could get away from our jobs together. I taught her to ride, and we spent a lot of time at that little spot down by the creek."

"Now, they don't need to know everything." Maggie reached up and slapped him on the shoulder. "He took me home from that first date. Walked me up to the porch, and I stepped up on the bottom step thinkin' he would try to kiss me and thinkin' I might just let him."

"I wanted her to know I was a gentleman and serious about marryin' her," Will said, "so, I just took her hand, bowed deep at the waist, and kissed the back of it."

"Oooh," Tess sighed.

"And then he said," Maggie took over, ""I sure had a wonderful evenin'. I hope we can do it again real soon'. And I said, 'I'll think about it, but I'm still not marrying you'."

"And I said," Will grinned, "Okay, you can just be my sweetheart until you change your mind."

"Then he just walked away before I could think of anything smart to say," Maggie said as the road curved slightly to the east and then swung back north. "He has always been annoying that way."

As far as Trey could see, it was nothing but straight flat blacktop all the way to the far horizon. Just as the first car he had seen in many miles came into view ahead of him, his cellphone vibrated in his pocket.

Half expecting it to be spam, he nearly dropped it in the floor when he saw Lisa's name and the message symbol. Needing to know what the message said outweighed any fear he had of aggravating his grandfather, so he slowed the truck and eased over onto the gravel shoulder between the pavement and the beginning of the desert vegetation. When the pickup rolled to a complete stop, he put it in park, set the brake, flipped the phone open, and read the message.

He could feel Maggie and Tess watching him from the backseat. Will had turned to stare out the front window as soon as Trey had pulled to the edge of the road. As he read the message his teeth clenched, then clenched harder, his mouth narrowed, and he felt like his face was on fire. He slowly unbuckled his seatbelt, and eyes still fixed on the phone screen, opened the door, stepped out, rounded the front of the truck, and started walking out into the desert.

*****

It took Tess a minute to realize he was either still reading the text or rereading it.

She looked over at Maggie, saw the worry in her face, and quickly turned back to the see Trey still walking away, out into the sand and shrubs. Phone held out in front of himself, he seemed not to see the vegetation at all.

"Where is he going?" Tess spoke, her voice just above a whisper.

"Looks like he's headed back to Oklahoma," Will said, concern and uncertainty audible in his voice.

Suddenly, Trey stopped. As the three of them watched, he raised his hands above his head, cellphone clutched in both of them, and began shaking it at the blue sky above. He shook the phone so hard his entire body began to quiver. Even without seeing his face, Tess knew he was screaming. With the windows up and the air conditioner running, the sound did not register, but the pain in his posture sure did.

His arms fell to his side, and he leaned forward, hands on his knees. Tess felt tears begin to well up in her own eyes as she watched him. Suddenly, he stood, and once more, hands raised high, began to scream, only this time he kicked furiously at the sand and shrubs. When it seemed like he had run out of air, he dropped his hands to his knees again. Maggie sniffled behind Tess and then tears broke free and streaked down her face.

Tess reached and pulled on the door handle, but before she could push the door open, Will raised a finger above his headrest and in a choked voice said, "Wait. Not yet."

She pulled back on the door and as it clicked back into place, Trey started the process of screaming and kicking once again. Tess was sure her own heart was going to explode in her chest. Slowly, she watched as the anger and frustration spewed out until Trey could no longer hold his arms up, but still he kicked and screamed. A cloud of dust and sand rose from the ground to his knees as he spun in a slow circle, kicking out at anything close. Finally, he dropped the cellphone on the ground, reached down and picked up a rock the size of a small watermelon, lifted it high above his head, and slammed it down on the phone.

The stone crumbled, and the phone shattered into several pieces. He picked up the pieces and hurled them out into the desert. They formed a great arch as they soared through the air and then disappeared into the brush. Before they landed, he collapsed onto his knees beside the broken pieces of the stone and vomited.

That's when Will turned around to Tess and said, "Okay, now you can go out there with him."

Tess was out of the truck and halfway to Trey before doubt and fear hit her. She trudged on, pushing away the worry that he would refuse her comfort. Afraid that her presence would further anger him, she circled the knee-high vegetation, picking a path carefully towards him as quickly as she could.

Trey sat head down, legs crossed, staring blankly at the sand in front of him. Easing herself down beside him, Tess placed one arm crossed his chest, the another against his back, and pulled him close. He let himself be pulled into her body, buried his face into the crook of her neck, and sobbed.

Tess on her knees, held him close, rocked him gently, and cried with him. For a long time, they rocked and swayed and wept. After a while, the tears slowed and eventually stopped except for an occasional sniffle. When Tess was sure Trey was done, she stopped the rocking motion, continued to hold him with one arm while she softly stroked his hair, pushing it away from his face and towards the back of his head.

*****

Maggie and Will watched from the truck. When Tess stopped rocking, Will reached into the glove compartment, pulled out a handful of napkins and handed them over the seat to Maggie. She took them, wiped her face, and blew her nose.

"That hurt," Maggie whispered.

"Yes, it did," Will's voice cracked, "but if it fixes the problem, it was worth it."

Maggie muttered a prayer, "Please, Lord, let this fix the problem," as she watched Tess shift her position until she was sitting beside Trey. One arm still around him, the two sat there until Trey finally picked his head up off her shoulder.

*****

Trey's head felt like it weighed a ton, and for a brief instant, he thought about laying it back down, but then he remembered his grandparents were still in the truck.

"Thank you," He said still staring out into the desert. He wondered why he didn't feel embarrassed or ashamed. Figured it was either because he was too spent or because he knew that in a few days, he would probably never see this girl again.

"You're welcome," Tess whispered. "I'm glad I was here."

"Me, too," he said and realized he wasn't just saying it. He truly was glad she was here.

Pushing himself off the ground, he helped her stand up and then let her take his hand and lead him back through the brush to the truck.

At the truck, Trey opened the door and helped Tess in, then shoulders back and head held high, he rounded the front of the truck, climbed in, and buckled his seatbelt. His grandparents both sat staring ahead.

Without turning his head, Will asked, "Are you okay to drive?"

"I am," Trey answered, not missing the hoarseness in Will's voice—or his own.

As he pulled back onto the highway, he asked, "Where are we staying tonight?"

Tess picked up her phone but had no service. Maggie flipped open her Atlas, and after a quick check said, "Ely is the next big town on the map. If there's somethin' available there we'll stop."

Chapter 18

We're done. Hope you're happy with your choice. Hope the slut is worth it.

The lines of Lisa's text ran through his mind. When he closed his eyes, they rolled like film credits on the back of his eyelids. When he opened them, the words played in his head like the lyrics of an unwanted song he just could not forget.

I know you've been lying to me. I know you've been screwing that bitch.

The pounding in his head made him nauseous, or perhaps it was the sick feeling that was giving him a headache, he couldn't be sure. Life was like walking through a fog—he knew where he was, but nothing seemed real.

Just so you know, I did sleep with Slade. And he's much better in bed than you'll ever be.

He became conscious of the distant hum of traffic. Slowly, it dawned on him that he was no longer hearing the sound of the air conditioning unit and the temperature in the room was still too warm to be comfortable. Caught between, *I don't care*, and *I don't feel like moving, and you're never going to be able to sleep like this,* he forced himself off the bed and made his way across the room to the thermostat.

He pushed the down button until the digital numbers read sixty, stripped to his underwear on his way back to the bed, lay down on top of the comforter, and waited for the room to cool down. The sound of the air conditioner cancelled the noise of the world around him but did nothing to quell the screeching of Lisa's voice in his head.

*****

"What should we do about dinner?" Maggie asked Will as she hurried around the motel room organizing the suitcases and digging out the toiletries needed in the bathroom.

"I'm not really hungry," Will said, "I think I can make it on a pack of those peanut butter crackers you brought up and maybe a Sprite from the vending machine at the end of the hall."

"I'm not all that hungry either," Maggie admitted. "I think I could do the same, but what about the kids?"

"I'd just bet Trey isn't gonna want to be bothered tonight," Will answered. "Why don't you give Tess a call, and if she wants something, I can go get it for her."

Maggie crossed the room and punched in the numbers for Tess's room. Tess answered on the third ring and when Maggie asked her if she need anything she said, "No, I still have food from our last stop, but I'm not sure I'm going to be able to eat tonight anyway. I'm still pretty shook up. Do you know how Trey is doing?"

"We haven't heard from him," Maggie told her. "I think it's probably best to give him a little space."

"Alright," Tess said. "Thanks for checking on me."

"You're welcome," Maggie said, "and thank you for what you did for Trey today."

"I wish I could have done…" her voice broke, "I'm sorry."

"Don't be," Maggie said. "It's what we're all feelin'. If you need anything, give us a holler."

"Okay," Tess said and hung up.

"She says she's okay for the night," Maggie ended the call and turned to Will, "I know it's nowhere near our normal bedtime, but I'm worn paper thin. Do you think maybe we could get our showers and turn in early?"

"It's like you read my mind." Will forced a smile but it didn't reach his eyes.

"Then you must have been thinkin' we really outta sleep in in the morning too." She raised an eyebrow.

He nodded. "You gonna get your shower first or you want me to?"

*****

Wrapped in a large, fluffy, white motel towel, Tess used a second towel to dry her hair. Head tilted to the side, she gently squeezed strands of her dark hair between folds in the towel. Looking in the mirror above the bathroom sink, she noticed the events of the day had left her eyes puffy and a bit red.

She had never been so relieved to reach a destination in her life as she had been when they had finally arrived at the hotel. And she had never felt so sad about leaving someone alone as she did when she watched Trey pushing the cart down the hallway toward his room when she closed the door. Thinking of him and the pain he must being going through brought tears to her eyes again. She wiped them away on the corner of the towel, dropped it on the floor, and shook out her still damp hair. It would air dry before she turned in for the night.

She gathered up her the clothes she had dropped on the floor before showering, stepped out of the bathroom, found the plastic bag she used for her dirty laundry, and stuffed them into it. A hint of desert dust mixed with the musky smell of sweat and Polo cologne brought her up short. It was Trey, or at least the aroma of Trey. In the time she had spent holding him, his scent had soaked into the fabric of her dress. She shoved it into the bag, opened her suitcase and found her nightclothes.

*****

The sound of kids running and screaming down the hallway awoke Trey the next morning. Wrapped in a tangle of bedding, it took him several seconds to free himself, roll to the edge of the bed, and sit up. The alarm clock on the nightstand told him it was thirteen minutes before nine o'clock, and the temperature in the room told him the air conditioner was definitely working.

The last thing he remembered from the night before was lying on the bed, staring up at streaks of light that had filtered through the split at the top of the curtains and onto the ceiling, and thinking it was going to be a long night and praying for sleep to come. At some point, his prayers had been answered.

He rubbed the sleep from his eyes, stood up, crossed the room to the thermostat, and shut the air off. Then he stepped into the bathroom and turned the water on in the shower. Wondering why no one had called to wake him, he crossed to the phone, and while the water warmed up, stood shivering by the desk and called his grandparents' room.

Maggie answered on the first ring, "Good mornin'," she said. "You up and around?"

"Up but not around," Trey told her. "Why didn't someone wake me?"

"We decided last night that we'd all just sleep in this mornin'," Maggie told him. "I don't know what time your Pappy rolled out, but I've only been up about an hour."

"Alright," Trey said. "I'll get around. Should be ready in half an hour."

"We'll meet you downstairs," Maggie said and hung up before Trey could ask her about Tess.

*****

Highway 50 covers over three thousand miles and runs through the heart of the United States from east to west. Starting in Maryland, it ends in California but not before running through the middle of the Nevada desert. Dubbed the "Loneliest Road" by some, most of its length cuts through remote, desolate areas of the country.

After a late start and a stop for breakfast at Denny's, Maggie asked Tess if she had the thing on her phone that could find the best route to Lake Tahoe. Tess said she did, pulled up the app, and showed Maggie the screen.

After a look at it, she studied the Atlas one last time and said, "Looks like it's Highway 50 all the way."

An hour of awkward silence and nearly seventy miles of

desert later, Tess flipped open one of the magazines she had already looked through and began to scan the pictures of its pages again. She was worried about Trey but afraid it would embarrass him if she asked him how he was doing. She thought about asking Maggie how she had ended up in Oklahoma, but she just wasn't sure if the timing was right.

*****

Of them all only Will rode along content. For the first time in months, maybe even years, he felt like the future of his family wasn't threatened and there was, at least hope, for the future of the family's ranch, of his ranch. He had always known Bo would never let it go, but Bo didn't seem inclined to remarry, and even if he did, he was getting a little old to have kids. With Wyatt gone, that only left Trey, and until yesterday, he had been nearly certain Bo would have been the last Tucker to hold the land.

Some folks would say he was a real bastard for making Trey take this trip with them, but he did it out of love for his grandson and the ranch. Even with Lisa seemingly out of the picture, there was always a chance that Trey would never want the ranch, but it had been in the family for three generations, each generation building onto what the previous generation had left. In times when everyone else was selling and downsizing, the Tucker's had bought. What would happen to it once he was gone really shouldn't matter, but it did to Will. In his heart, he regretted his part in the pain his grandson was feeling, but if given the chance to do it over again, he would do it the same. He knew Trey was strong and that he would get through the pain. Whatever path his grandson chose, the young man would have a better life because of what had happened. As they passed through mile after mile of desert, Will studied the landscape and prayed Trey would forgive him.

From the sounds coming from behind him, Will could tell that Tess had tired of the magazine and had begun to play with her phone. He would never understand why kids these days were so glued to those things, but then most folks would call him an old dinosaur. When Trey slowed at the edge of Eureka, Will noticed a softball field. The outfield that was dark green with grass seemed an odd sight against the desert, almost as if someone had accidently spilt green paint in the wrong place. A block later they passed another field, this one for baseball. Will wondered if they would even be making this trip if Trey had taken that scholarship to play at Murray State and how different his grandson's life would be now if he had.

Will pointed at a gas station and said, "Let's go ahead and fill'er up."

"We've got between a half and three-quarters of a tank," Trey said.

"In the desert, you never know when you'll get a chance again," Will told him.

"Alright," Trey said.

The store behind the three gas pumps was not much bigger than some walk-in closets Will had seen, and the selections of food and beverages were minimal. The restrooms were in a separate building around behind the station. While Trey topped off the tank, Will and the ladies made their way around to them. Well before they made it back, Trey was finished and waiting.

"You might want to use the facilities," Will told him. "The man that was on his way out when I was going in said it was quite a ways to the next stop."

Even though it did not seem to be a pressing matter, Trey took his grandfather's advice.

Outside of Eureka, they passed a stretch of land where someone was using circle-irrigation to grow crops. To the north of the highway and as far as Will could see, there was one round patch of green after another. Then the desert swallowed them once more, and the view was much the same as they had been seeing all morning.

An hour passed before they reached Austin. With its population of one hundred and sixty-seven, it slipped by on the right almost before Will could blink. Far ahead on the horizon, a mountain peak covered in white appeared and then disappeared as the road dipped into a low spot. Another ten minutes passed before they topped over the rise, and Will saw it once more.

Below the snow-capped mountain and much closer to them was what looked like a gigantic patch of snow that appeared to shimmer. The word *mirage* came to Will's mind, but the spot did not seem to vanish or change in shape or size as they drove towards it.

Finally, Will pointed it out and asked, "Do you see that white spot ahead?"

"I do," all three of the others said at the same time.

"Is it snow?" Trey asked. "I'm pretty sure that's what it is, but does snow fall in the desert?"

"Guess we'll just have to wait 'til we get closer to tell," Will answered.

Thirty miles later and after much speculation, they reached the edge of a large salt flat. Along the edge of the road, travelers had arranged large gray rocks into various letters and words. Tess began to read aloud the ones from her side of the road, and pretty soon, Maggie joined in from her side.

"Cory," Maggie said.

"M.J.," Tess said. "I wonder what that stands for?"

"Tanner." Maggie pointed to another one.

"I heart New York!" Tess squealed. "I'd love to see New York some day."

"Really?" Maggie turned. "They wrote all of that out?"

Tess giggled, "No it was an I, then a heart-shape, and the letters N and Y."

"I see," Maggie said and then touched Trey on the shoulder. "Find a place to pull over."

Trey tapped the brake, and as the truck began to decelerate, Will turned and asked, "Why?"

"Someone left a pile of rocks back there on the highway and I want to put my initials in the salt," Maggie answered.

Will turned back forward knowing from her tone that there

was no sense arguing with her, and Trey began to watch for a place to turn around. A quarter of a mile further along, the highway widened on both sides giving him enough room to make a three-point turn.

Just past the rock pile, Trey checked for traffic, pulled off on the side of the road, stepped out of the truck, and opened the door for his grandmother. From the other side of the truck, he heard Tess say, "Oh my goodness. That's not good."

"What is it dear?" Maggie asked across the bed of the truck.

"This stuff is like white mud," Tess answered. "I think I've ruined my sandals."

*****

Trey turned around to see that his grandfather's boots looked just fine. "Why aren't your boots a mess?" he asked.

"I saw what happened when she stepped out in that stuff," Will said, "so I stayed up on the pavement."

By that time, Tess was coming around the back of the truck, both feet caked with the dirty white mixture of salt and sand. With her hands on her hips and pure disgust written on her face, she looked down at her feet. "What do I do? I can't track this into your truck."

"We better see how hard it is to get that off." Maggie opened the truck door, reached in, and gathered up three bottles of water.

While Tess sat on the tailgate, Maggie and Trey used the water to clean Tess's feet and shoes. When they had removed the last of the mud, Tess stepped down and then immediately hopped right back up to where she had been seated with a look of surprise on her face.

"What?" Trey asked.

"It's hot!" Tess slid her still-wet sandals back on her feet.

"What about the sand?" Will asked.

"It was a little warm," Tess answered, "but nothing like that hot pavement."

"I'll shed my shoes then," Maggie said, "It'll be like when we were kids and waded out in the pond. Can't be much different than the muddy bottom."

"I don't know about ponds," Tess said. "I've never waded in one, but I'm game to 'shed my shoes' as you call it. At least now we know the salt and sand won't be too hard to get off our feet."

Maggie laughed, "Who else is brave enough?" she asked, challenging Will and Trey.

Trey watched in disbelief as his grandfather leaned against the edge of the tailgate and began the process of removing his boots. He had expected an argument, had been sure his Pappy would simply refuse, and then he could follow suit. With no idea of how to get out of it now, he began to tug off his own boots.

"I think me and Will should use that space right past Cory there," Maggie said, "I think there's plenty of room."

"Okay." Tess said looking for an open space for herself.

Maggie pointed at a spot further down the road and said, "See that big open space just before the I heart New York, I bet there's enough space in there for both you and Trey to put your whole names."

"Really?" Tess raised an eyebrow.

"I think so," Maggie said. "Both of your names are pretty short."

Trey pulled his socks off and stuffed them in his boots. Will stepped into the salt and mud, as the mixture oozed between his toes and encased his feet, he picked up a rock in each hand, and began forming the letters of his initials in the space Maggie had chosen. Trey stared down the empty road and thought how strange this little scene was going to look if anyone happened by. Then following his grandfather's example, he stepped into the muck, gathered as many of the stones as he could manage, and started down the road to where Tess was already laying rocks for the first letter of her name.

It took less than half an hour for the four of them to finish their tasks. Will's initials, a capital W beside a capital T sat above Maggie's initials, a capital M and a capital T. That much was Maggie's plan, but Will had other ideas and spaced rocks around their initials in the shape of a big heart.

"Will Tucker, you are too much." Trey heard his grandmother say as his grandfather laid one final stone in place.

"You don't like it?" Will asked.

"I love it!" Maggie said, "It's perfect!"

"Yes, it is," he agreed, "Perfectly Romantical." And they both laughed.

When Trey set the last stone down, he and Tess's names were spelled out beside each other with a space between them. A larger space separated Tess's name from the I heart NY.

Their names finished, they all returned to the truck. Trey hotfooted it around and grabbed what was left of the case of water so they could all sit on the tailgate and wash their feet.

While they did so, Maggie wandered back down the road to take a picture of the place where Tess and Trey's names were. By the time she made it back to them, Will and Trey had already pulled their boots back on and rolled their pants' legs back down. A barefooted Tess sat on the tailgate, feet swinging in the hot sun, waiting for it to dry her sandals.

"Let me help you get your feet cleaned, Darlin'," Will said as he picked Maggie up and set her on the tailgate.

"If you insist." she said, wiggling her encrusted toes at him.

"I insist," he said as he poured the first bottle of water onto her left foot.

When he had finished cleaning both feet, he helped her into the truck and then slid into his own seat. Tess slipped on her damp shoes long enough to get around the truck, hop into her seat, and quickly kicked them off onto the floor. Trey closed the tailgate, carried the five remaining bottles of unopened water around and gave them to his grandmother, climbed into the driver's seat, and started the truck.

*****

His shirt had not even had time to dry before he was fighting to keep the sound of Lisa's voice out of his head, repeating the lines of yesterday's text over and over. Their little project with the rocks had kept him busy and his thoughts on what he was doing, but now, back behind the wheel, the nightmare returned. The frustration built fast, and just about the time he thought his head would explode, Tess's voice broke through from the backseat.

"Did you see that?" she asked.

"See what?" Maggie asked.

Tess pointed back over her shoulder. "There was something hanging in that tree back there, but we were going too fast for me to make it out."

Trey looked to his grandfather, and all thoughts of Lisa disappeared. Will gave a nod, and Trey started looking for a place to turn around. He found it in the form of a dirt road that led across a rusty cattle guard and off into the desert.

The tree where Tess had seen something hanging was not hard to find since it was the only deciduous tree for miles. An area large enough to park several vehicles sported tire tracks, making it obvious that others had been there recently.

Hanging from the branches of an old cottonwood tree were thousands of pairs of shoes of every kind. Trey could not begin to count the number of running shoes tied together by their laces and dangling from the tree's limbs. Ladies' high heels, men's working boots, hiking boots, kid's snickers, and in a crook of the trunk a lonesome pink flipflop was wedged. Trey could identify a pair of Nikes by the swish and a pair of Adidas by the three bold stripes. Someone had even used bailing wire on a pair of cowboy boots and tossed them onto one of the tree's highest limbs.

"I gotta get a picture of that." Maggie opened her door and stepped down from the truck.

"Me, too." Tess followed her lead.

Trey looked at Will who grinned at his grandson, shrugged and unbuckled his seatbelt. By the time the two men made it out of the truck, the ladies had found an opening in the fence that led to the edge of a gully above the big tree. Tess and Maggie were both snapping pictures when Trey reached them and looked down into the gully. The area below the tree was covered with a pile of shoes. Trey realized that most of them had, at some point, hung in the tree, but over time, the laces had rotted away until they had fallen into the gully. A kid's red rubber rain boot caught his eye. Someone had used white paint and written the date on it: April 27, 2018, and the words: DODGE and Hilmar, CA.

"How cool is this?" Tess turned to face him.

"It's definitely different," he said.

"Let's take a selfie." She grabbed his arm and turned him to face away from the tree.

His first thought was that a selfie wasn't a good idea, and then he remembered there was no longer any reason he shouldn't. As Tess twisted and worked to get the right angle, Trey studied the lines of her face. She found the angle she wanted, evidently noticed that he was staring at her and blushed. Her finger pressed the button while her face was still red.

"You'll have to send that to me when I get another phone," Trey said.

"I'd be happy to," she said, wrapping a hand around his elbow.

When he realized she wasn't going to let go, he crooked his arm, placed his other hand on hers, and escorted her back to the truck. Maggie was still snapping pictures of the tree, but when she looked up and saw them, she quickly raised the camera and captured the moment.

*****

Trey was still trying to wrap his mind around the sparks that seemed to run through him anytime Tess touched him when a sign came into view ahead. As they got closer to the sign, he saw that it read Welcome to Fallon—The Oasis of Nevada—Historic Main Street Just Ahead. After nearly four hours in the desert, the place truly seemed like an oasis. A quick look over his shoulder at an exhausted Tess, and he began to wonder if she was his oasis, that little place of hope and cheer in an otherwise bleak, barren, unforgiving land.

"Looks like we need gas," Will said and pointed to the gauge.

Trey did not hear him over the thoughts in his own head. *Kind of feeling sorry for yourself, huh,* a voice said. *Got bucked off and now you can't decide whether or not to lay in the dirt and cry or cowboy up.*

"Earth to Trey," Will said finally breaking through, "we need gas."

At Will's request Trey pulled into a convenience store and topped off the gas tank while everyone else went inside. When he finished, he pulled the pickup into a space in front of the building and went in himself.

Inside, he scanned the room for his group. Will was visiting with one of the store clerks, a big burly man with a heavy grey beard that reached to the middle of his chest. As he passed them on his way to the restroom, he caught enough of the conversation to realize his grandfather was picking the man's brain about the area around Lake Tahoe.

"Carson City is your best bet for a motel this time of year," the man was saying. "Lake Tahoe is usually full, and even if you can find something, it's going to be at least twice as expensive."

When Trey came back from the men's room, his grand-mother caught him by the sleeve and told him to grab whatever he wanted and meet her at the counter. After a quick trip along the coolers in the back for a drink, up the candy aisle for a couple of Snickers, he joined everyone at the front of the store.

"I can get mine," Tess said, placing her drink, a small bag of chips, and a Butterfinger on the counter.

As the cashier began to ring up the items, Maggie unloaded

what she was carrying into the space left and said, "Let me get it this time."

The man scanning the purchases hesitated when Tess argued, "But we agreed that I would pay my own way."

Trey set his candy bar and drink in front of the cashier, stepped back to wait beside his grandfather, who was looking on with a grin, and said, "This could get interesting."

"Ya think?" Will chuckled.

"No, you and Will agreed to that, not me," Maggie said, motioning for the cashier to continue.

Exasperated, Tess turned to Will and Trey. They both gave her a shrug and a smile.

In the end, Maggie paid for everything.

On the way out, Will said, "I was talkin' to the fella in there, and he said it would be better to stay in Carson City tonight and drive over to Lake Tahoe in the morning."

"Why's that?" Maggie asked.

"He said the motels around the lake fill up pretty fast, and they are more expensive," Will answered.

"In that case, I reckon me and Tess better see if we can find some rooms in Carson City." Maggie said.

Once back on the road, the girls got busy. Well before they reached the town, their combined efforts had found them three rooms at the Holiday Inn Express and Suites.

Trey found himself wondering if his and Tess's rooms would be connecting.

Chapter 19

Their rooms were connecting. After an early dinner Trey lounged on the motel bed and flipped through the channels on the television. Nothing really looked all that interesting, but he refused to turn it off for fear thoughts of Lisa would once again find their way into his mind and haunt him for the rest of the evening.

C-Span, CNN, Fox News, he clicked through quickly. ESPN, ESPN2, ESPN Classic would normally have had something he would watch, but nothing grabbed his attention. He passed up a rerun of *Law & Order* on NBS, skipped through commercials on several channels, and then a young Sandra Bullock in a cowboy hat appeared on the screen. A cowboy was asking her to dance, and she was telling him she couldn't dance anymore.

The cowboy said, "Dancin's just a conversation between two people. Talk ta me."

As Trey watched the cowboy two-step Sandra's character around the floor, he wondered if Tess knew how to two-step. He closed his eyes and imagined what she would look like in boots and how she would feel in his arms.

*****

Several doors down from Trey, Will reclined in the middle of the bed, leaning back on a stack of pillows, watching the same scene, one arm around Maggie who sat next to him, her head resting on his shoulder. As the dance ended, Will gave her a little squeeze and asked, "You think we could still dance like that?"

Maggie shifted so she could look up into his eyes, laid a hand on his chest just above his heart, and patted him. "I think we're probably a bit rusty, but I don't see why not."

"It *has* been a while," Will said.

"You think?" Maggie asked.

"We should go," He suggested.

"Go where?" Maggie frowned.

"Go dancin'," Will smiled and brushed a stray strand of hair away from her face. "You know, like on a date. Whatta ya say, sweatheart?"

"I say, I think you've lost your mind, Will Tucker." she giggled, tapping his chest with each word.

"We'll see." He tapped her gently on the nose with an index finger and kissed her on the forehead.

*****

At the commercial break, Trey clicked the info button on the remote and found that the movie he was watching was *Hope Floats*. He watched it to the end and then wished he had started it from the beginning. Making a mental note to do that the first chance he got, he began to surf through the channels again. Twenty minutes later, unable to settle any particular show and bored with the process, he decided a soak in the motels hot tub might relax his sore muscles and help him fall to sleep.

He dug a pair of black Nike swimming trunks out of the bottom of his bag, stripped off his clothes, and pulled them on. A faded East Central University t-shirt with a tiger on the front, a pair of worn tan Hey Dudes, and he was ready. Grabbing a room key, he stepped out in the hall, made sure the door shut behind him, and started for the elevator.

A curly-headed teenager in the traditional blue-shirted uniform of a Domino's pizza delivery person stepped out of the elevator and started down the hall as Trey approached it. Picking up the pace, Trey managed to stick a hand in the doors before they closed.

At the first floor, the doors opened to an empty lobby. A right down the hall past the exercise room, which was also empty, Trey found the pool and hot tub area. A woman somewhere in the center of middle age was stretched out on one of the four white chaise lounges arranged haphazardly around one end of the pool. She scrolled though her phone, ignoring the two young boys who were throwing a small red and black nerf football to each other. As Trey eased around her and along the far side of the pool, one of the boys threw a pass too high and it landed with a thud in front of him.

"Ball help," the closest youngster shouted from the water.

Trey picked the ball up, faked a flip at the closest kid, then with a quick turn threw a perfect spiral to the young man at the other end of the pool. The boy caught it in a spray of water, held it over his head, and then slammed it down like he was spiking the ball. Trey laughed and shook his head.

"What do you say?" the lady asked the boys without looking up from her phone.

"Thank you, sir," the boys shouted in unison.

Trey nodded, strolled to the hot tub in the back corner of the room, removed his shoes and shirt, stepped over the edge, and down into the warm water.

A few minutes after Trey got settled into the hot tub, the woman hustled the two boys out of the pool. Left alone, with only the bubbling of the water jets and the soft splash of the pool water, Trey sank down until he could rest his head of the tub's edge and closed his eyes.

The smell of chlorine and the warmth of the water on his skin was threatening to lull him to sleep when the sound of the door across the room opening caused him to open his eyes. A young woman in a red bikini under a transparent, white chiffon kimono coverup had stopped at the towel rack. She removed a towel, laid it on the top of the cabinet, pulled a hair scrunchy from her wrist, and using the window for a mirror, pulled her hair into a bun atop her head.

Trey let his eyes wonder the length of her body, from her elegant alluring neck, down the soothing arch of her back, over the well-defined curves of her hips and along the length of her perfectly formed legs. When she finished with her hair, she retrieved the towel, and turned. Trey's eyes focused on her legs began to trace a path upward across a flat stomach and ample breasts. He couldn't help but wonder if she was going to join him in the hot tub.

Reaching the end of the pool, she turned, and his eyes widened as they met hers and he realized he had been looking at Tess. She paused midstride, brought the towel up to cover her breasts, and he thought for half a second that she was going to turn and leave.

Then blushing slightly, she crossed the few feet to the hot tub and said almost apologetically, "I didn't realize anyone was in here."

"No problem," he said, trying hard to keep his eyes on her face, and hoping the hot water was hiding the redness creeping up from his neck. "The water's nice. Come on in."

She stood there holding the towel and then gradually bent down, laid the towel down, eased herself into a sitting position on the edge of the tub with her feet down in the water. "It does feel wonderful.".

"Yes, it does," Trey agreed.

Casually, in a graceful fluid, motion, she slipped from the edge into the water, removing her coverup as the water flowed up and around her. One instant, she was perched on the edge, the next, Trey was staring across the bubbles on the surface of the water into her beautiful brown eyes, and the coverup was laying on top of the towel.

"How long have you been here?" she asked as she settled into a comfortable position directly across from him.

"Maybe fifteen or twenty minutes. Long enough that I'm completely relaxed," he answered.

She pulled the towel into a position where she could use it as a headrest, leaned her head back onto it, and closed her eyes. For several minutes Trey watched her peacefully soaking up the warmth of the water.

"Thank you for yesterday," he said finally breaking the silence.

"You already thanked me," Tess said, not opening her eyes, "but you are welcome."

"I don't usually act like that," he said. "Maybe I could have handled it better."

"Well, maybe that would depend on what *it* was exactly." Tess opened one eye and looked across the water at him. "Do you want to talk about *it*?"

"I don't know… maybe," He stammered.

"I know what you mean," she opened her other eye. "My *it* was when your grandmother found me in the bathroom."

Trey sat up and asked, "Do *you* want to talk about *it*?"

Tess smiled and said, "You first."

Trey watched the foam dance across the top of the water while he gathered his thoughts, then began by saying, "My fiancé… well I guess technically she's my ex-fiancé now… sent me a text… but you kind of knew that already… Anyway, it was a text to tell me she was sleepin' with someone else, and we were through."

"That's awful!" Tess said, "just awful! No wonder you lost it!"

Trey was amazed at how good getting that much out made him feel. "I think the biggest problem was I had never been through anything like that before, so I didn't know how to react. I didn't know how to handle it, and I completely lost it."

"So, you've never been through a breakup before?" Tess asked when it was obvious, he was finished.

"No, not really," Trey answered. "Lisa was the first real girlfriend I ever had. I mean, I had the grade school and middle school crushes kind a couple of times, but no real relationships until her. We started dating when we were sophomores in high school. She was the first and only girl I've ever been with and…" he stopped, suddenly realizing what he had just said and thinking that perhaps he had shared too much.

"That's beautiful and sad all at the same time," Tess straightened up, "and at the risk of sounding bad, I wish I had met someone when I was young and only been with them my whole life. I'm a bit jealous of you. It sounds like this fiancé of yours had no idea what she actually had, but on the other hand, maybe you're better off without her."

"Maybe," Trey agreed then asked, "So, how about you?"

"I spent most of my high school years working at the same job. It was at a little restaurant and bar, kind of a classy joint in Placerville, called the Main Street Tap Room. My Aunt Alyssa got me a job there washing dishes as soon as I was old enough. Anyway, a little over a year ago, the man I was travelling with just before you grandmother found me in the bathroom came in and… well let just say, he became a regular, and after a while we started to date. He told me he was from Nashville but had been working for a casino in Kentucky. He had gotten a divorce, and right after that, his bosses sent him out to Nevada and California to visit the casinos out here. Long story short, at the end of a year, he told me he was going back to Kentucky, and he wanted me to come with him. Said he was sure he could get me a job at the casino, and I could work my way up to head cook in no time. I said okay, packed up, and thought I was finally going to get out of California and start a life."

She stopped there and chewed on the corner of her mouth for a moment before tears began to slide down her cheeks and into the warm water.

When she didn't continue, he asked, "What happened?"

After a long moment, she looked up at him, wiped at her eyes and said, "He told me he was divorced when we first met, but when we got to that gas station where you guys found me, he told me that he hadn't been completely honest. He admitted that he was only *separated* from his wife, and they had been talking about giving it another try. Then, you know what he had the nerve to say to me?"

Slightly unnerved by the steel in her voice, Trey asked, "No, what did he say?"

"He said," the disgust practically dripped from her voice, "I could still go with him to Kentucky, and even if things did work out with his wife, we could still see each other, and if they didn't well then…" she stopped.

"I'm sorry," Trey said. "That is terrible."

The look on her face softened, and she moved across the hot tub to his side. Tossing her legs across his, she laid her head on his shoulder, reached up and pulled his arm around her back and said, "I think it's *your* turn to hold *me*."

He pulled her close and whispered, "Fair trade."

Later, outside the door to her room, Trey found his hands laced in hers, and he had no idea when that had happened. They had left the hot tub, dried off, and then walked to the elevator and down the hall. It had all seemed so natural, so easy, but now he felt the awkwardness creeping in.

Fearing rejection, he leaned in, and she met him halfway. The simple kiss on the lips he had planned evolved quickly into a much longer much deeper embrace that left them wrapped in each other's arms and breathless.

"Oh," Tess panted, "that was nice."

"Yes, it was." Trey agreed after he'd drawn a long breath.

"I better go," Tess untangled her arms from around his neck. "Thanks for holding me. And thanks for this," she touched a finger to his lips, "but I better go." And she opened the door to her room, stepped inside, and quickly closed it behind her, leaving Trey standing alone in the hall.

Relaxed from the hot tub and tired from the day's escapades, Trey lay on his motel bed and waited for sleep to come, the kiss still on his mind.

Chapter 20

During the short drive to Lake Tahoe, not much was said. The long hours of travel had finally caught up with the four of them, and they had all slept the night through for the first time since New Mexico. Worried that the kiss from the night before would make things awkward, Trey had said little during breakfast. Tess had been quiet throughout the meal as well. Will and Maggie acted as if they didn't notice and chatted away about whether they should shop or sightsee once they reached The Lake.

The area around the lake was crowded. Traffic moved slowly, and there were people everywhere. Trey found a public parking area near the water. A slow circle of the lot turned up no empty spaces, and he was about to pull back onto the road when Will saw the reverse lights come on a big Silver Dodge Ram four slots away.

Trey managed to navigate into the empty space. A short walk along a well-traveled path brought them to the edge of the clearest water Trey had ever seen, and the view in every direction was spectacular. The lake water disappeared at the foot of snowcapped mountains. Tall pine trees and granite rocks decorated every landscape. Everywhere he looked reminded him of a scene from a postcard.

"This is beautiful," Trey said. "It may just be the most beautiful view I've ever seen."

"It is quite a sight, but I don't see cattle anywhere." Will smiled.

"Cows in the picture is all it takes to make you happy?" Maggie asked.

"Nope," Will answered. "I need you there, too. Cows and you… a view of the lake would be nice, but it's not as important as you and the cows."

"So, you prefer Oklahoma to Lake Tahoe?" Tess asked.

"Give me a horse in the middle of Nowhere, Oklahoma, and I'm as happy as a meadowlark on a crisp summer morning," Will said. "This is beautiful, but it ain't home."

"Well I'm glad we came," Trey spoke up. "I know I wasn't keen on the idea at first, but I'm sure glad I got to see this view."

"I've seen this one before," Tess said, "and it is special, but I think The Arches were my favorite. I've sure enjoyed the trip, and I am going to miss you all when you drop me off. I'll never forget the arches or the horseshoe down in Arizona. I don't know that I'll ever see Oklahoma, but Mr. Will, you sure make it sound nice."

"It's not for everybody," Will said, "but to me, it's my own little piece of heaven on earth."

"I want to thank you for all you've done for me," Tess looked around at each of them, "I am so glad that Miz Maggie found me when she did."

"The Lord works in mysterious ways." Maggie smiled.

From that stop, Trey drove north around the lake. By noon he had lost count of the number of times one of his grandparents had instructed him to pull into this or that parking spot, but suddenly it didn't matter how many times they wanted him to stop. He was enjoying the trip.

Maggie snapped pictures of everything. Wherever she went, Will was right beside her. Trey and Tess spent most of the day trailing along behind them. Trey had the urge to take Tess's hand in his several times but decided against it. Neither of them should get involved so soon after such painful breakups, he thought.

When they reached the northern end of the lake, Trey drove west for a short distance, crossed over into California, and then started south. Maggie liked the looks of the pier attached to the Gar Woods Grill.

"Can we eat there," she pointed, "and maybe walk out on the pier after lunch."

"I don't see why not," Will said and Trey pulled into the parking area.

Once inside, they were told there was no wait and led to a table overlooking the lake. Tess and Trey nearly bolted for the door when they received their menus and saw the prices.

"This one is on me," Will said, "and I don't want you looking at the prices."

"Too late," Tess told him.

"Are you sure about this, Pappy?" Trey asked.

"Yes," Will smiled.

"I may get indigestion if I put something this expensive in my stomach," Tess whispered.

"We'll get you some Pepto," Will grinned, "so figure out what you want."

The food was exceptional, and Will insisted they all try the deep-fried Oreos for dessert. Before they left, they all walked the length of the pier. Tess took pictures of Will and Maggie leaning against the rails at the end of the dock. When Tess handed the camera back to her, Maggie asked, "Would you let me take a picture of you?"

"Yes, I would," she said and took Trey by the hand and led him to the exact place Will and Maggie had posed.

As they turned around for their picture, Tess slipped her arm around Trey's waist leaving him no choice but to wrap his arm around her and rest his hand on her shoulder. The surprised look on his grandparent's faces was priceless. After Maggie snapped a couple of photos, he took Tess by the hand, and together, they followed Will and Maggie back along the pier. Her hand felt good in his, not just good, but right--and comfortable.

He wondered why it had never felt this way with Lisa, then scolded himself for the comparison and reminded himself it was over. Thinking of her, of the past, would hold him back, he realized. It was time for him to close the door on that era of his life and move forward, whatever that might mean.

It was nearly dark by the time they made it to the southernmost shore of the lake. Will insisted that they try to find a motel in the South Lake Tahoe area. The first three they stopped at had no vacancies, but on their fourth try, they found rooms at the PlayPark Lodge. Once again, Tess insisted she be allowed to pay for her own room, and just like before, Will took the hundred-dollar bill and slid it into his pocket.

"Tess, how big of a hurry are you in to get home?" Maggie asked as they unloaded their bags from the back of the truck.

"Not in any kind of hurry," Tess answered. "Actually, we're only about an hour and a half from Placerville. If I need to, I could probably get my aunt to drive over here and get me."

"Oh, no," Will stepped in. "Me and Maggie wanted to spend some time doing a little shopping tomorrow and then maybe have a night out before we start for the wedding. We wanted to know if you would mind spending another day here with us."

Trey's chest tightened, and he held his breath waiting for her response. When she looked his way, his eyes locked with hers.

Finally, she asked without blinking, "So, would we stay here again tomorrow then?"

"Yes, we would," Will answered.

"And what about rooms tomorrow night?" she asked.

"I booked rooms here for two nights," he grinned. "I was hopin' you'd say yes."

She pulled another hundred from her pocketbook. Will held a hand up to indicate it wouldn't be necessary. With a look of determination Tess said, "This is the only way the answer is yes. You all have already done too much for me."

Will took the bill, and as he slipped it into his pocket beside the other one, he said, "Lady, you drive a hard bargain."

Maggie slipped an arm around Tess and hugged her tight.

Trey took a deep breath, felt a sharp desire to dance a little jig, and knew he was in trouble.

Over dinner that evening at Bert's Café, Tess asked Maggie and Will how they had gotten from Texas to his parent's ranch in

Oklahoma. Maggie looked to Will, but he shook his head and said, "This one's all you, darlin'."

"Well, okay," she smiled at him and turned to Tess, "it was the end of the summer, nearly fall, when he finally proposed proper, not that he hadn't been hinting and asking for months. He had already gotten permission from my Momma and had called his parents and told them to be ready."

"So, you had an all-out wedding?" Tess asked, her half-eaten Bueno Burger completely forgotten.

"Yes, we did." Maggie was all smiles. "I didn't want anything fancy. I actually tried to get him to just go to the courthouse, but he wasn't having any of that, so he arranged it all. The only thing I had to do was find a dress and make sure I had a bridesmaid."

Tess looked from Maggie to Will.

Will just shrugged. "This is her part to tell."

"So, on the day of the wedding, Will's dad picked me and my sister up in his truck and Will's little brother drove my mother. I had no idea where we were headed or how big the whole shindig was going to be." She shot a grin toward Will.

"They drove us out to 'our tree'." Maggie paused and took a sip from her glass of sweet tea, "the tree where me and Will had our first date. We'd spent so much time there that we had begun to call it 'our tree'. Everyone from the ranch where Will worked was there and everyone from the restaurant was, too. I couldn't believe it, but Will had talked them into shutting down for the evening."

"So, did you have to ride horses from the road to the tree?" Tess asked.

"Oh, Lordy, no!" Maggie giggled. "What a sight that would have been. Me on a horse in my wedding dress. I'm sure glad Will didn't think of that 'cause, if'n he had, I'm sure he'd have suggested it."

"So how did you get there?" Tess asked.

"We just drove out there in the trucks. The pastures in that part of the world are pretty flat and not too rough if you drive slow," Maggie explained. "When we arrived, everyone was all around and under that old oak tree. The justice of the peace was standing in the very spot where Will had laid the tablecloth on our first date. We got married right there. It was a short and quick ceremony, just the traditional couple of verses and our vows."

"Who was your bridesmaid?" Tess asked.

"My sister, Amelia," Maggie answered, "and Will's brother was best man."

"Did you have a reception?" Tess asked.

"You bet we did," Maggie chuckled herself. "It was out at the ranch Will was working on. There was a live band, and we danced and danced."

Trey had long since finished his B.L.T. and was enjoying watching the glow on his grandmother's face almost as much as he was enjoying watching the excitement on Tess's face as the story unfolded. He fought the urge to reach out and take her hand in his.

"We honeymooned at a hotel near the stockyards in Fort Worth." Maggie smiled across the table at Will and with a slight blush, said, "I wonder if it's still there?"

Will shrugged again. "I'm not sure. To the best of my recollection, it was still standing the last time I was through there." Trey wondered if that would be the end of the story, but then Maggie said, "From there, we moved to the ranch."

"And then it was happily ever after?" Tess asked.

"Not quite," Maggie's smile faded. "We moved into an old hunting cabin while Will cleared a place for our home, but the very day he got it cleared, his brother got drafted into the Army." She paused, then, "Will told me he couldn't let him go over there alone. He told me he was going to enlist so he could go with him and make sure he got back home. Not long after their boot camp, they were both sent to Vietnam."

"Oh, my!" Tess gasped.

"I was heartbroken and scared out of my wits, but I

respected his decision. I spent the next three years helping on the ranch and building the house. When he got back, we started our family, and if you must insist on a happily ever after ending," Maggie said with a grin, "I guess that's about where it started."

"I do." Tess returned the smile and looked to Will. "What about your brother? Did he make it back?"

For a minute, Trey didn't think he was going to answer, then finally his grandfather softly spoke, "Yes, physically he made it back but not really mentally. We saw a lot of wickedness over there, and his mind didn't deal with it well. I, too, had a lot of trouble keeping it together in those first few years after we got back, but he didn't have a good wife and, soon after, a son that needed him like I did. I was the lucky one."

Trey realized that this was the only time he had ever heard his grandfather talk about his brother and the war. He couldn't help but wonder how this girl they had just met and hardly knew somehow had the keys that seemed to open up every door of their family history.

*****

At eight-thirty, unable to stop thinking about Tess, Trey finally found the courage to knock on her door. He counted a silent five and was just about to leave when she eased the door open and peeked out. With a smile that melted his heart, she pushed the door closed, and he could hear her removing the security chain. When she swung it open again, she stood just inside the door, still dressed in the white lace sundress she had worn all day.

"I had about given up on you," she said. "I was fixing to get ready for bed."

Trey hadn't even thought about seeing if she wanted to talk until half an hour ago, so how in the world did she know he was going to show up?

"Well," he said, "I'm glad I didn't wait any longer. You

wanna go for a ride. Maybe see what the lake looks like under the stars."

"I'd love to," She answered pulled the door shut, and followed him the short distance to the truck.

He helped her into the vehicle, and as they pulled from the motel onto Emerald Bay Road, Tess reached over and took his hand. Neither of them had spoken during the drive, but when they stopped at the Pope Beach parking area, they were still holding hands. With a little squeeze, Tess released his hand and started to open her door.

"Hold on just a second," Trey said.

Before she could respond, he stepped down out of the driver's side of the truck, walked around the front of the pickup, opened the door, and offered her his hand. "Aren't we the gentleman?" She smiled and took his hand.

"Pappy taught me well." He flashed a brilliant smile. When she was on the ground, he opened the back door, and retrieved two throws from the back seat. Hand-in-hand, they walked to the beach. A breeze off the lake had already caused a drop in the temperature, and by the time they reached the sand, Tess had started to shiver.

Trey quickly spread one of the blankets on the beach, and when Tess sat down on it, he wrapped the second one around her shoulders. When he eased down beside her, she slid and arm around his waist and pulled him into the covers with her. He draped an arm around her shoulders, and for a long time, they sat there, staring out at the stars reflected off the lake's surface.

Finally, Tess leaned her head on his shoulder and said, "Trey, I'm scared."

"Of what?" he asked.

"The feelings I am developing for you," she answered.

So, there it was. Trey tried to think of a way to express his own feelings for her, but he was worried that she would think less of him if he admitted how he felt so soon after his breakup with Lisa.

"I've been struggling with my feelings for you, too," he admitted.

"Should we talk about it?" she asked.

"I think so, but I don't know how to begin?" he answered and then grew quiet.

"I think I could really fall for you, but we've only got tonight and tomorrow and then the next day you're going to drop me off, and I don't know when or if I'll ever see you again," Tess said in a rush, then took a deep breath and went on, "and I've never been good at long distance relationships."

"That pretty much lines up with what I've been thinkin' myself," Trey admitted.

"So, what do we do?" Tess asked.

"I'm not sure," Trey answered. "I haven't been able to stop thinkin' about the kiss we shared the other night, and the more time we spend together, the more I want to kiss you again but…"

He stopped and searched for a way to finish. Finally, Tess finished for him, "But another kiss might lead to something more."

"Yes," he said, "and, well…" he stammered. "First, we haven't known each other that long… and second, I respect you… and third… well, I don't know… I guess… well…"

"It's too soon after breaking up with Lisa," she finished for him.

Trey just nodded, and Tess said, "I know what you mean. I'm having trouble with the fear that it would only be a rebound relationship for me … or you… or maybe both of us. And, well… I'm not that kind of girl."

"So, what do we do?" Trey asked.

"I don't know," Tess raised her head from his shoulder, "but I think we probably shouldn't sleep together."

"Agreed," Trey said.

"Good," Tess said. "So, now that we've got that out of the way, I would really like it if you would kiss me."

Chapter 21

By noon the next day, Trey was beginning to wonder if Tess and his grandmother were actually going to visit every store in South Lake Tahoe. He had never really enjoyed shopping, but as the four of them moved from one business to another, he had to admit that it wasn't all that bad. That the day was not really about him and his grandfather became apparent well before they broke for lunch.

"She's always wanted a daughter to spoil," Will whispered.

"Looks like Tess has been as good for her as…" Trey stopped.

"As she has for you?" Will raised an eyebrow.

"I was going to say as this trip has been for her, but I got tangled up," Trey said.

"Yeah, right," Will grinned.

At noon, they back tracked for a quick bite at Izzy's Burger Spa, and then started shopping their way once again along Highway 50. They were nearly to the Nevada state line when Maggie found a little western wear store called the High Chaparral.

"I think this is exactly what I've been looking for," Maggie said as she opened the door and stepped out of the truck. "I'd bet you a plug-nickel we're in the right place now."

By the time Will and Trey rounded the back end of the truck, both women were halfway across the lot, hurrying towards the store entrance.

"I've gotta a feelin' we might be in this one for a bit," Will told his grandson as they made their way to the open door.

"I'm in no hurry," Trey said. "I've got nowhere pressin' to be."

"Glad to hear it." Will smiled.

Once inside, his grandmother led Will and him to a couple of old wooden chairs near the fitting rooms and disappeared with Tess. It wasn't long until the women were back with several outfits for Tess to try on. Maggie hustled her into a fitting room, then sat down in a third chair to wait with the guys. After several minutes, Tess stepped out wearing a floor-length tan dress that buttoned down the front and split on the side to just above her knees. A turquoise necklace hung perfectly framed in the low-cut blouse and matched the aqua-blue in the stitching of her light-brown western boots.

"What do you think?" she asked and twirled around.

"It's beautiful," Trey said, "and you're beautiful."

Tess held the dress out to her sides, crossed her right foot behind her left, and curtsied. Trey couldn't keep his eyes off of her, and right then, he didn't want to even try.

"Stunning." Will smiled as Maggie began to fuss with Tess's hair.

After several more trips into and out of the dressing room, Tess had tried on everything Maggie had gathered up. Some of the items of clothing had to be modeled multiple times since they coordinated well with more than just one other piece. Trey didn't mind at all. For the first time in his life, he found himself thinking that shopping could be fun.

"Which one did you like best?" Tess asked Trey when she stepped from the dressing room in the last outfit.

Maggie looked at Will. Will gave her a half-grin and winked, and they both turned to see what Trey would say.

"I like them all," he answered, "but my favorite was the very first dress you had on."

"Then that's the one I'll get." Tess stepped back into the dressing room.

"Go ahead and pass out what you want to keep, and I'll hold it for you," Maggie said.

When Tess handed them to her, Maggie passed each item over to Will, and she and Will took off for the front of the store.

"Where's Will and Maggie?" Tess asked when she stepped out of the dressing room.

"They are somewhere in the store. I waited on you. You sure looked gorgeous in all those outfits," Trey said.

"You quit that," Tess told him, "You're going to make me blush."

"Well, I guess you better get used to being red," Trey grinned, "because I'm not fixin' to quit any time soon."

With a quick look to see that no one was watching, Tess crossed the space between them, tip-toed, gave Trey a quick peck on the cheek. She had barely made the first step away when he spun her back around, wrapped her in his arms, and kissed her soundly.

Breathless, she looked around once again when the kiss was over and said, "Goodness."

Trey smiled, "Guess we better find Granny and Pappy."

"I guess so," Tess agreed taking his hand and leading him towards the front of the store.

After a friendly debate, Maggie convinced Tess to let her buy the outfit as a gift for keeping her company on the trip. Tess was still thanking her when they made it back to the truck and started for the hotel.

*****

When Will informed Trey they would be going out for the evening, he had no idea it would be to a bar or that he would be required to dance. He wasn't sure which surprised him more, the fact that his grandparents were actually going to a bar, or that they planned to dance the night away at their ages.

Following along behind Will and Maggie, Trey and Tess walked hand-in-hand across the parking lot towards the front entrance of the Slick Whiskey Saloon. Tess wore her new outfit. Trey wore his best white Wrangler pearl snap shirt, creased

Wrangler jeans, and a pair of black ostrich boots. Will's outfit matched Trey's. Maggie had picked out a long-sleeved, white Wrangler shirt with crystal snaps and an ankle-length denim skirt which had a row of buttons down the right side.

Once inside, Will led them to a table along the front wall not far from the door. Trey found it strange that his grandfather seemed to be completely comfortable, not only entering the bar, but locating what appeared to be the seats he wanted.

"Would either of you ladies like something to drink?" Will asked as he pulled a chair out for Maggie.

"Just a water, please," Maggie answered.

"Same for me, please," Tess said when Trey pulled a chair out for her.

Will nodded to Trey to let him know he should follow, turned, and headed for the bar. Trey noticed that there were very few customers in the saloon and no one on the dance floor at all. He wondered if it was just too early, or if it was because it was a Monday night.

"What would you like?" Will asked when they reached the bar.

"I don't know," Trey asked, "What are you havin'?"

"I'm gonna stick to water tonight, but if you want something stronger, I can drive us back to the lodge," Will answered.

"I'll just have a Dr. Pepper," Trey said, "if they have it?"

"Let's see," Will said and turned to the young lady who had stepped to their end of the bar, "I need three waters and a Dr. Pepper if you have it."

"Glasses or bottles?" she asked in a drawl that said she had grown up somewhere in the deep south.

"Bottles." Will said, then asked, "When does the band start playin'?"

"That'll be nine dollars. and they've already started. They're just between sets. Should be back at it in another five minutes or so," she answered.

Will passed her a ten, told her to keep the change, handed one of the bottles of water and the Dr. Pepper to Trey and started back to the table. They set the drinks on the table about the same time the sound of a guitar being strummed caught Trey's attention, and he noticed that the band members were making their way back to the stage.

The band started the set with George Strait's "Marina del Rey", and Will led Maggie out onto the dance floor.

Trey offered his hand to Tess, and said, "Would you dance with me?"

"I would love to," she answered and put her hand in his.

As they two-stepped around the dance floor, he held her close and listened to the lyrics of the song. It might be South Lake Tahoe instead of Marina del Rey, and they may have just cuddled on the beach, but the song seemed to be telling their story. It only took one trip around the dance floor for Trey to know that Tess not only knew how to two-step but was a perfect match for him.

When the song ended the band went straight into "You Look So Good In Love," Trey adjusted his step and continued to dance Tess around the edge of the dance floor. For the next three songs, they danced together, and then "Boot Scootin' Boogie" ended, and he cut across the floor and led her back to their table. Will and Maggie had danced through a couple of songs and were back at the table.

"Y'all havin' fun?" Maggie asked them as they fell into their chairs.

"We sure are," Tess answered. "How about you?"

"Yes," Maggie said. "We're just not as young as we used to be. Had to take a break."

The tables around them had begun to fill up, and the whole place was beginning to get a little crowded. By the time Tess stood up, took Trey's hand, and tugged him towards the dance floor, there was not an empty table in the place, and the dance floor was pretty well crowded. Even with the additional people, Trey guided her smoothly around the dance floor.

Twice in the next four songs, they passed Will and Maggie. At the end of the fourth song the band leader stepped to the mike and announced they would be taking a short break. Tess took Trey by the hand and started back to their table.

On the way, they passed by a table full of rough looking young men. One of them, a bearded fellow in a sweat-stained, Motley Crue t-shirt with the sleeves cut out, winked at Tess. Trey moved closer to Tess, blocking the man's view.

"Everything alright?" Will asked as Trey pulled Tess's chair out for her.

"Just an idiot being an idiot, Trey answered.

"Okay," Will said, "It's about time for us to call it a night anyway. Me and your Granny ain't as young as we use to be. As soon as we rest a minute, I'm gonna spin her around the floor one more time, and then you kids better take us old folks on to our room."

The band came back from their break, and Trey and Tess made it around the floor twice without being noticed by Mr. Motley Crue, but as they passed his table on their third trip, he gave a wolf-whistled and shouted at Tess, "Save me a dance, sexy."

When Trey stiffened, Tess pulled him closer and whispered in his ear, "Ignore him. It's not worth it, and besides, this is the last dance. Let's just enjoy it."

They made a couple of more rounds before the song ended. Each time, Trey guided them well out of eye shot of Mr. Motley Crue and his buddies. The guitars had done the lead-in for another song when Will motioned towards the door. Trey nodded and turned that way, only to find the way blocked by Motley Crue and two of his companions.

"Time for that dance," the man said, and reached out a hand to Tess.

Trey stepped between him and Tess.

"Sorry, but we were just leaving," Tess said.

"Not before I get my dance," Motley Crue said. Friend Number One stepped up on his left side and Friend Number Two did the same to his right.

"Take Tess to the truck," Will leaned close and whispered

in Maggie's ear then stepped around Tess to Trey's side. Maggie took Tess by the hand, stepped back, and the two of them disappeared into the crowd.

"We don't want any trouble." Will's eyes locked with Motley Crue's, his voice calm and even.

Motley Crue looked from Will to Trey and then back to Will. "Old timer, if you don't get out of my way, I'm going to fu…"

The sentence went unfinished.

Will's right uppercut started at the hip. When it collided with Motley's chin, Trey heard the crack, saw the lights fade from the man's eyes, and watched as his legs turned to rubber and he began a slow crumble to the floor. Just before he crashed onto the hardwood, Friend Number One threw a left hook that landed just above Trey's right eye. Dazed and bleeding from a deep cut, Trey's instincts took over. Both of his hands shot up, and he turned in time to take the incoming jab on his forearms.

Friend Two watched Motley hit the floor, drew his right hand back, and set up for a jab at Will. When he stepped forward to throw it, Will gave him a short, quick kick to the front of his knee. He grabbed his leg, screamed in pain, and dropped to the dance floor with a thud loud enough to stop the band.

Friend Number One had just thrown a flurry of punches. In a defensive stance, Trey had his face covered and took the strikes all on his shoulders. Number One ended the combination with a left uppercut that left his chin exposed. His friend's scream was the last thing he heard as Trey rolled everything he could muster into a right hook that broke Number One's jaw. The force of the blow toppled him over the motionless body of Motley and onto the moaning, withering torso of Friend Number Two.

"Let's go," Will said to Trey as a circle began to form around the three prone figures on the floor.

Trey did not need to be told twice. When the crowd parted to let Will through, he followed. Halfway to the door, a big fellow that Trey guessed was probably a bouncer passed them moving towards the commotion. The cut above Trey's eye caught his attention and he started to say something, but someone across the room hollered for his help and he kept going.

*****

Maggie and Tess had just reached the truck and realized they didn't have the keys when they saw Will and Trey coming across the parking lot. Neither of them was running, but the hurried gait of both men told Maggie plenty. When Trey was halfway there, she saw him dig the keys out of his pocket and hit the button to unlock the doors.

Trey started for the driver's door, and Will stopped him with a hand on his shoulder and took the keys from him, "Maybe I better drive this time."

Trey rounded the front of the truck, opened the door, and slid into the passenger's seat. Will handed him a handkerchief, and Trey pressed it against the cut above his eye.

When the light from inside the truck washed across Trey's face, Maggie shrieked, "You're bleeding. Will Tucker what have you done?"

"We'll talk about it later," Will said as he started the truck. "Keep pressure on it. Maggie, have you got anything back there bigger than this hanky?"

She handed up one of the Navajo blankets. Trey wadded up one corner, switch it out with the blood-soaked kerchief, and pressed it tight against the wound.

Will backed out of the parking space, drove off the lot, and back onto Emerald Bay Road. Two blocks from the saloon, Trey started to chuckle. Slowly, the chuckle turned to a laugh then the laugh turned into a cackle, and by the time they took a left onto Lake Tahoe Boulevard, he was howling.

"What in the world has gotten into you?" Maggie asked.

"Pappy… he…" Trey managed two words between bouts of laughter and dabbing at his eyes with the opposite end of the blanket.

"What is he goin' on about, Will Tucker?" Maggie asked.

Before Will could answer, Trey started again, "He… hit the ground…" then laughed so hard he choked, "so… so hard."

"Oh, good Lord," Maggie's face paled, "are you hurt Will. What happened in there?"

"I'm just fine," Will answered her gently, and then his tone sharpened as he spoke to his grandson, "You're scarin' your Granny. Get ahold of yourself, Trey."

Even with the roughness of his grandfather's command, it took Trey a few minutes to curb the flow of adrenaline and quiet down. When Will pulled to a stop in front of his and Maggie's motel room, Trey looked over at his grandfather and said, "Thanks, Pappy. This would be a lot worse if you hadn't been there."

"You're welcome," Will said then added, "but you better get out before you get blood on the seat."

Maggie insisted that Trey come to her and Will's room so she could check his cut, but as they rounded the front of the truck, Will doubled over, grabbed his stomach, braced himself against the vehicle, and vomited violently. Caught off guard, the other three stood speechless. When he finished and could stand again, he wiped the sleeve of his shirt across his mouth.

"Guess maybe I am gettin' too old for bar fights." He grinned, but the humor didn't quite ring true.

"Bar fights?" Maggie's eyes narrowed. "Just exactly what happened back there?"

"Pappy knocked…" Trey started, but Will shut him down with a wave of his hand.

"Another time," Will said, "I don't feel so good. I think I need a shower."

Tess who had quietly made her way to Trey's side, said, "Maggie, I'll check Trey's cut. Why don't you get Mr. Will on inside?"

"Maybe that would be best," Maggie agreed, looking a little pale herself. "There's a first aid kit under the seat in the back if you need it." She took Will's hand and lead him to the door.

*****

"This probably needs stitches." Tess pinched the cut over Trey's eye shut.

Trey took the first aid kit from her and rummaged through it. He located an unopened box of butterfly strips and a half tube of Dermabond. Moving to the bathroom, he stood in front of the mirror and talked her through how to close the wound.

"How did you know how to do that?" she asked when the last strip was in place.

"Sometimes, we fix minor cuts on livestock that way," Trey told her. "I've helped Pappy and dad do it hundreds of times."

"We really haven't talked about family much. Do your parents live on your grandparent's ranch?" Tess asked as she began to gather up the bits of trash left from the strips.

"Dad does," Trey told her, "but my mother passed away when I was in high school. Before she passed life was about as perfect as it could be. Her and dad had the same kind of relationship that Pappy and Granny do. Two people that just seem to complete each other. I remember some folks talking once when they didn't know I was listening. They wondered if the 'illness' as they called it would change them. It never did."

"I'm so sorry," Tess said, "I didn't mean to bring up…"

"It's okay," Trey threw up an open palm. "I've made peace with it. She had cancer, but she's not hurting now."

"Still," Tess said, "I'm sorry."

"So, how about your folks? Mom and dad waitin' on you over in Placerville?" Trey asked.

"No," Tess answered, and she stared at the floor for a few seconds before saying, "Just my aunt."

"Oh," Trey said, "I'm sorry, I didn't mean to pry."

"It's okay," Tess said, "You didn't know."

"Maybe we should talk about something else," Trey suggested.

Tess gave it some thought then raised her head and said, "No, I want you to know. I never knew my dad. He came up from Mexico to work and met my mother. They had a summer fling, and she didn't know she was pregnant until after he went back. When she finally managed to get in contact with an uncle of his, she found out that he had been shot and killed. It kind of messed her up, and when I was born, she left me with my aunt Alyssa, her older sister, and just disappeared."

"I am so sorry." Trey reached out to pull her close.

"It's okay," Tess said. "I won't say I've made peace with it, but for the most part I guess I've learned to live with it."

"So, you've never seen your mom?" he asked, and then immediately wanted to take it back.

"She came back when I was six and again when I was fifteen," Tess told him, "but she only stayed for a couple of hours each time, and then she was gone again."

Not knowing how to respond, Trey simply closed his eyes, pulled her closer.

After a few minutes, she pushed away from him and said, "I think we both need a shower."

His eyes popped open and he winced in pain.

"That's what you get for thinking those kinds of thoughts," Tess told him. "What I was saying is you should get a shower. I'm going to my room to get one, but I would really like to drive back down to the beach again tonight. That is if you feel up to it."

"I do." Trey pulled her close, gave her a kiss, said, "I'm going to get undressed now so unless you…"

"I'm going." She said as she wiggled out of his arms and made for the door.

*****

The throbbing cut over Trey's eye could not even begin to match that of his breaking heart. Sitting cuddled up with Tess on the same beach for the second night, he wished time would just stop. Or that he and Tess had met at a different place in a different time, a time when there was a chance that a relationship between them could work. Tomorrow, they would drop her in Placerville. Should he get her phone number, maybe try to stay in touch with her, or would that just be delaying the inevitable breaking of their hearts?

"What are you thinking about?" Tess asked him.

"Tomorrow," He answered honestly. "What about you?"

"Same," She sounded sad, "and I was wishing we had more time."

"Me, too," Trey said.

She leaned in and placed her head on his chest and said, "I've been trying to figure out if there is a way for us to… well, I don't even know what the word for it would be… maybe… I just don't know." And then she pulled his head around for a kiss.

When the embrace was over, Trey looked down into her eyes and said, "I don't know, too."

Tess smiled, "Maybe we should just enjoy the night and give thanks for the time we've had together. Like Miz Maggie said about God working in mysterious ways—maybe our paths crossed for this little while so we could help each other through our rough patches."

"Lots of kissing might help," Trey suggested.

"Yes," Tess giggled, "but you know a part of me wants more."

"Hmm, really?" Trey asked.

"Yes, really," Tess said, "but…"

"But neither of us are really the one-night-stand type," Trey finished for her.

"Exactly," Tess sighed.

"Lots of kisses?" Trey offered.

"Fair trade?" Tess said with another giggle. Trey wasn't sure if it was a question or a statement. And as her lips met his once again, he realized it really didn't matter.

Chapter 22

Like the thoughts and feelings running through Trey's mind the next day, the road from Lake Tahoe to Placerville was filled with twists and turns. Little had been said as they loaded their luggage into the back of the Silverado. Will was pale and Maggie worried over him throughout the morning. Tess stared out the window, not really seeming to see the passing countryside.

For the first time since they had left Nowhere, Oklahoma, Trey found himself in no real hurry to return home. Now that there was no longer a fiancée in Oklahoma for him to go back to, the thought of living in Tulsa really didn't appeal to him. He played with the idea of taking his grandparents' home after the wedding, and then making a trip out to Placerville. After half an hour of chasing the notion around in his head, he decided it wouldn't work.

In his heart, he knew Oklahoma was where he was supposed to be, maybe not in Tulsa, but definitely somewhere in the state. He thought about Fort Cobb where he had graduated. His father, Bo, had mentioned a math position that hadn't been filled at the high school, but that seemed almost a waste of his degree. Still, it was worth checking into when he got back.

As if Will had read his mind, he said, "Son, you sure you want to live in Tulsa? Your dad hates doing the bookwork on the ranch. We could sure use an accountant to take over that part of the business, and with your daddy away with school and coachin' so much, I could use another hand around the ranch. I'd pay you well."

"I do like the sound of that, but I'd like to think on it a bit before makin' any decisions," Trey answered, "if that's okay."

"It's always smart to worry something that big around in your head for a bit," Will answered. "You take as much time as you need."

Time is one thing I seem to be running out of at the moment, Trey thought and glanced back at Tess. *Maybe she could come to Oklahoma.* The thought surfaced and surprised him. Why hadn't he thought of it before? *Because*, he reasoned, *if she had any desire to go to Oklahoma with him, she would have brought it up, or at least suggested it during one of our talks*. She might not have been in a hurry to return to Placerville, but she had not once mentioned going to Oklahoma.

*****

The Tap Room restaurant where Tess asked them to drop her was still an hour and a half away from opening when Trey pulled into a space beside a silver Toyota Camry with an I Love Cats sticker on the back glass. Tess got out of the truck, crossed the parking lot, and knocked on the front door. After a short wait, the door opened and a middle-aged woman with platinum-blonde hair and a runner's body stepped out. Tess turned and pointed towards the truck, and the two women started their way.

Trey heard Maggie's door open as they approached and decided, that maybe he should get out himself. Will came around the back of the truck and stepped up beside Maggie just as Tess reached the three of them.

"This is Alyssa, my aunt," Tess introduced them to the woman, "Aunt Alyssa, this is Miz Maggie."

Alyssa extended a hand and Maggie took it.

As they shook, Maggie said, "It's so nice to meet you. You have such a wonderful niece."

Tess blushed, turned to Will, and said, "And this is Mr. Will," then to Trey, "and this is Trey."

When the handshaking stopped, Alyssa turned back to Will and Maggie and said, "Thank you so much for making sure she got back home safely."

"It was our pleasure," Maggie assured her. "We're going to miss her on the trip back home."

Trey thought he saw sadness in Tess's eyes when she locked gazes with him, but he wasn't sure. Maybe he was just projecting his own feelings.

"I'll miss you all, too. It's been a wonderful trip." Tess said.

"I better get back inside," Alyssa said and handed a set of keys to Tess. "It was nice to meet you all."

"You, too," they all three responded.

Maggie took Tess into her arms for a farewell hug. When she released her, tears welled up in both their eyes. Will stepped up next, and after a quick embrace, he handed her a sealed envelope with instructions not to open it until later. Tess started to argue, but Will gave her a weak smile and started around the front of the truck. Maggie was already stepping up into the vehicle when Trey realized he only had moments left with Tess, and he couldn't find any words.

"I guess we should get your suitcase out of the back," he finally spoke, took her hand in his and led her to the back of the truck.

"Yes, I guess so," Tess agreed.

Trey lowered the tailgate, reached in, pulled the suitcase out, and placed it on the pavement. A flood of emotions whirled through him as he pushed the gate back into position and turned to look at Tess. When he couldn't find words, he simply reached out and pulled her close.

"I'm going to miss you," she whispered.

"I'm going to miss you, too," Trey told her. "I don't want to go."

"You had better before you make me cry even harder," she said.

With a quick kiss, they parted.

She headed across the lot. He slid into the driver's seat.

"What was in that envelope, Pappy?" Trey asked.

"All the money she gave me for hotel rooms, and your phone number," Will answered.

*****

Forty-five minutes from Placerville, Trey hit the first of the Sacramento traffic. It was well past morning rush hour, but the eight lanes of traffic were still busier than Trey would have liked.

"This is what driving in Tulsa would have been like," Will said.

"I don't think I'll be going there after all," Trey said as he settled into the second lane from the left and made a mental decision to stay there if at all possible. It seemed to be his safest bet. The vehicles in the lane to his left seemed to be auditioning for the Grand Prix, and incoming traffic from on ramps kept the two lanes to his right playing a game of automotive musical chairs.

"I'm glad you're driving," Will said as a little red Porsche 911 zipped by in the fast lane.

"Don't worry, Pappy," Trey assured him, "I'll get us there."

Trey slowed as a black Ram 1500 truck cut across the lane in front of him from his right all the way into the lane behind the Porsche. The median widened, hiding the east bound lanes behind tall bushes filled with white and purple flowers. Removing four of the eight lanes from his immediate view did little to help Trey's anxiety level, but the flowered shrubs were much nicer to look at than the vehicles flashing by.

"I guess you have some decisions to make then," Will said as Highway 50 merged onto Interstate 80.

"I reckon I do," Trey agreed, glad to see the traffic seemed to be thinning as he left Sacramento. As the city faded behind them, the landscape changed. High rolling hills rose along either side of the road, hills that back in Oklahoma would have been left for grazing had furrows where farmers were preparing the ground for crops. Others were vineyards with vine-covered arbors running down them in neat tidy rows. Will pointed out a small herd of cattle grazing high up near the top of one of the taller hills. From the road, they looked more like large dogs than full grown cows.

"Did you get Tess's number?" Will asked.

"No," Trey said.

"Why not?" Will asked him and, in the same breath, turned to Maggie, "Did you?"

"No. I kept hoping maybe she would just go home with us," Maggie answered.

"You gave her my number. I guess the ball is in her court now," Trey shrugged.

"Well, I'll be damned," Will's frustration was clear, "That girl looked at you like your momma used to look at your daddy." He shook his head, then confessed, "I only gave her the number to the house phone at the ranch. I didn't know your new cell number; you should have, at least, gotten her number."

"Maybe I should have, Pappy," Trey responded, the frustration in his voice, more at himself than his grandfather, "but I don't think things work these days like they did back when you met Granny."

"Hmmph," Will returned, "It ain't that things don't work like they did back then because things ain't what do the work. It's men who do the work, and if men don't do the work, it don't get done. If I hadn't put the effort into courting your Granny, we wouldn't be where we are today. And you wouldn't be here today, either."

Maggie sat silent. Trey reddened. Will shook his head and turned to stare down the road ahead of them.

"I don't belong in California," Trey finally said, "and I don't think Tess wanted to move to Oklahoma."

"Did you ask her?" Will asked.

"No, Pappy," Trey answered. "No, I did not."

"Then how do you know what she might want to do?" Will said.

*****

Will stared out the window at a small herd of Belted Galloways cows, or Belties as some folks called them. They had

214

always reminded him of Hampshire hogs with their black bodies belted by a wide white stripe, but one of the cows in this herd was brown and white, and he had never seen one like it before. He was trying to figure out the genetics of the brown one when Trey broke the silence.

"Maybe I should have asked her," he said. "Maybe she would have said yes, maybe no. I liked her, and she liked me, but I don't know that either one of us was really in love."

When Will acted like he hadn't even heard, Trey asked, "Did you hear me?"

"Yes, I heard," Will spoke, his voice sharp as he turned his head to look at Trey. "Love is something that happens as you get to know someone. Do you think your Granny loved me when I told her I was going to marry her?"

Trey didn't know if he was supposed to answer or not, so he remained silent.

"No, she did not," Will went on. "As a matter of fact, I'm pretty sure she didn't even like me much right about then, but once she got to know me, she decided I wasn't so bad. And to tell you the truth, I wasn't in love with your Granny when I told her I was going to marry her. I saw something in her that seemed to pull me in. She was spunky and tough and spoke her mind, and I liked her for that as much as I liked her because she was beautiful, but I didn't know her well enough to be in love with her." Will paused to let that sink in, then after a few seconds and in a softer voice, he continued, "Trey, love is something that begins with like and then grows. And if you work at it long enough and hard enough, it will grow strong enough to get you through those times when you really don't even like each other much. And believe me there will be some of those times. Me and your Granny are where we are today because we gave each other a chance, and that chance grew into a love that has seen us through the years, a love that we worked hard to build. Now, I don't know what your future holds, but I know that we are only given so many chances at lasting relationships. You should really think on that."

*****

Trey was still thinking about what his grandfather had said when he pulled into the driveway of a sprawling, grey-bricked, two-story house. The smell of flower blooms filled the air as he stepped out of the truck and opened the back door for Maggie. The manicured shrubs and the white rail fence that ran along the edge of the lawn gave the whole property a very regal appearance. Trey was still surveying the yard when the front door flew open, and a lady who bore a striking resemblance to Maggie hurried down the front steps.

His grandmother met her halfway across the yard, and the two hugged and danced around like teenage schoolgirls. They broke free of each other just as Will and Trey reached them.

"Trey, this is your Great-aunt Amelia," Maggie introduced her sister to her grandson.

"My goodness, you do favor your grandfather." Amelia looked Trey over then turning to Will, "I see you're still as handsome as ever. If I'd known you were going to age this well, I might have tried harder to steal you away from Maggie here," she said will a chuckle.

"Good grief, Amelia," Maggie said. "This is why we don't get together more often." They both giggled as Amelia lead them up the stairs and into her house.

*****

It was late afternoon before Trey and his grandparents made their way from Aunt Amelia's home to the hotel rooms they would call home during their stay. Amelia had begged them to allow her to re-do the sleeping arrangements so they could stay in the house with her, but Maggie had refused, saying they didn't want to be a burden. Trey had been introduced to more kinfolks and friends of kinfolks in the short time they had been there than he would ever be able to remember.

He was fairly certain that two of the bridesmaids had been whispering about him across the room at one point. When the bride-to-be pointed directly at him, they had both blushed and turned away giggling, and he was sure enough glad his grandmother had decided to stay at a hotel.

After Trey helped Maggie and Will into their room and dropped his bag in his, he made his way back to the hotel's office. The young woman behind the front desk gave him direction to the nearest AT&T store. He made the two-mile trip there, purchased a new iPhone, and returned. It would have taken him less than half an hour, but the store was short staffed, and a rather short, obnoxious blonde-haired man had both the clerks tied up, trying to fix some problem with his phone.

Back in his room, he started the slow process of setting the phone up to his liking. There was no doubt in his mind that he was messing with the phone to keep his thoughts away from Tess. He was also mentally kicking himself for not, at least, getting her number. When he had the phone the way he wanted it, he called his dad.

"Trey?" Bo asked hesitantly.

"Yes, Dad, it's me," Trey said. "I bought a new iPhone to replace the one that was broken."

"So, this is your new number?" Bo chuckled.

"Yep," Trey smiled, "new phone, new number, new life."

"Your Granny told me a little about what happened with Lisa," Bo said, then asked, "Are you okay?"

"I guess so," Trey answered. "It's been a very confusing trip."

"Well, I almost hate to mention it, but Lisa's been callin' here the last couple of days. She's back from the Bahamas. She asked me to tell you she needs to talk to you when I heard from you." Bo said.

"That's just great." Trey sighed, "I thought after Lisa's last text things with her were sure enough over. And now Pappy seems to think I'm makin' a big mistake for not givin' Tess a chance."

"Tess?" Bo said, "The girl y'all picked up in New Mexico."

"Yes," Trey answered, "and Pappy thinks she's the one."

"What do you think?" Bo asked.

"I don't know," Trey said. "I like her but it's complicated."

"It's always complicated, Trey," Bo said, "but it's not up to me or your Pappy, it's up to you. *You* decide what you want because if you don't, you'll aways wonder if you did it for yourself or for someone else, and that's not fair to the other person."

"I'll keep that in mind," Trey said.

"How are your Pappy and Granny?" Bo asked.

"Granny seems to be doin' fine. She's as spry as ever. I think she's really enjoyin' the trip." Trey paused, thinking maybe he should not worry his father, then decided to be honest, "Dad, I'm a little worried about Pappy. He hasn't been eatin' like he usually does, and the other night he got sick and puked. Plus, he seems pale to me."

"Your Granny was tellin' me the same thing last time I talked to her," Bo said. "She said, she wants him to see a doctor as soon as he gets back home. She wants me to help her talk him into it. I hope it's not appendicitis. It would be just like that stubborn old man to wait until it burst to go to the hospital."

"I'll keep an eye on him," Trey promised, "and on Granny."

"Call if you need anything," Bo said, "Love ya, son."

"I will. Love you, too," Trey said and hung up.

*****

It took twenty minutes of arguing with himself before Trey was convinced that a call to Lisa was necessary. In his mind it was over, and a conversation was not needed. That she had called and wanted to talk would indicate the end of the relationship was not as clear in her mind, so he sat down on the edge of the motel bed and keyed in her number.

"Hello, who is this?" Lisa asked after picking up on the first ring.

"It's Trey," he answered, "Dad said you wanted me to give you a call."

"Yes," she said quickly, "I'm back in Oklahoma and I was wondering when you would be back home."

"Why?" Trey kept his voice steady.

"What do you mean?" Lisa seemed genuinely confused.

"I mean," Trey answered, "Why is it any concern of yours when I get back? You broke up with me? You slept with another man? So again, I ask why?"

"But I only did it because you slept with her." Trey could hear the chill in her voice, "You slept with her. I slept with him."

"That's not the way it works. That's not the way I work." Trey said managing to keep his voice low and even, "And just so you know, I didn't sleep with Tess."

"I don't believe you." Lisa's voice cracked.

"And I don't care." Trey felt cold and empty as he added, "It's over."

"But what am I supposed to do now?" Lisa's whined.

"Call Slade." Trey suggested.

"He's gone back to Texas," the chill in her voice returned, "and he's engaged."

After a moment of silence, Trey said, "I'm guessing he didn't tell you that until after you slept with him."

"Why does that matter?" Lisa's voice was pure venom once again.

"It doesn't," Trey answered, then added, "Goodbye, Lisa."

As he took the necessary steps to block her from calling his phone, a calmness and peace slowly replaced the uncertainty and anger that had plagued him since he had received her awful text. It was over. It was done. The future was in front of him, and he had decisions to make.

Long after the sun had dropped over the western horizon Trey lay staring at the ceiling. Before he drifted off to sleep a question surfaced. Should he ask his Pappy if they could go home through Placerville?

Chapter 23

Will groaning in his sleep woke Maggie early Wednesday morning. She sat up in bed and gently shook him awake. Groggy, he turned from his side to his back and looked up at her.

"You were groaning. Are you okay?" she asked.

Rubbing the sleep from his eyes, he told her, "It's just a little pain in my stomach, I'll be fine."

"We really never talked about the trouble in that dance hall," she said, "Did you get hit?"

"No Ma'am. I may be old, but I'm not dumb enough to let some young buck hit me," he said and smiled up at her.

"No, just dumb enough not to know when you're too old to be fightin' in the first place," she chided, "Maybe we should run you by an E.R. and have you checked."

"You worry too much," he said and sat up in the bed. "I'll tell you what, let's get through this wedding and back home and I promise I'll go see a doctor then."

That he had even suggested he might be willing to go see a doctor worried Maggie. It had taken all she could muster to get him to agree to annual checkups after they both reached sixty. Will's first appointment had been on an April first. He had made the trip to Anadarko by himself, and when he returned home and Maggie asked him how it went, he told her not so good. When she asked why, he told her that the doctor said he was pregnant, then roared with laughter and said, "April Fools."

It had become a yearly joke that he was going to Anadarko to get his pregnancy test, and she could not remember the last time he had been to a doctor, other than for his annual checkup.

*****

The ringing of the room phone woke Trey out of a sound sleep. It took him a minute to figure out that he was hearing the phone, and not an alarm clock.

"Hello," he said, his voice still hoarse from sleep.

"You awake?" Maggie asked.

"Am now," he answered. "What time is it?"

"A little after eight," she answered. "You want to get around and go find some breakfast?"

"I can be ready in half an hour," he answered and then asked. "Is that okay?"

"No hurry," she told him. "Your Pappy isn't feeling well so it's just you and me and I'm not starving yet."

*****

Will was up and sitting on the room's loveseat with his socked feet propped on the coffee table watching the Weather Channel when Trey and Maggie returned from eating in the hotel dining room. On their way back Maggie had insisted on stopping by the hotel pantry for Saltine crackers and Sprite.

"You are going to at least eat this," she told her husband.

Will didn't protest, but merely obeyed her.

"You goin' to be okay, Pappy?" Trey asked.

"I reckon I'll make it through the day," Will teased, "that is if the Good Lord's willin'."

Maggie shook a finger at him. "Will Tucker, that's not funny."

"Not even just a little bit?" He held up a hand, his thumb and forefinger slightly apart.

"No even a little bit," she answered and closed her index finger and thumb firmly together to illustrate just how not funny it wasn't.

"You're a little pale," Trey told his grandfather.

"Probably just caught a bug," Will said. "I reckon I'll be fine by the rehearsal dinner."

"I didn't think we'd be goin' to the rehearsal dinner," Trey said with a questioning look at his grandmother.

"Traditionally, we wouldn't," she told him, "but Amelia never has been much on tradition, and she insisted that we be there since we've traveled the farthest to attend the wedding."

"Okay, just so I've got this straight," Trey said, "the bride is your great-niece, so that would be your sister Amelia's granddaughter?"

"Yes, that's right," Maggie confirmed.

"Seems like she's having a lot of say in this wedding," Trey said.

Will chuckled. "That's Amelia for you. I'm glad I got the right sister of the family."

"My sister has always been a bit of a controller. From what I gather, when she married her late husband and moved out here, she was the one with the head for business. Her savvy and no-quit attitude are the main reasons the family has done so well financially."

"And what business would that be?" Trey asked.

"Well, they started with a vineyard, then bought a winery," Maggie told him, "after that Amelia branched out into anything that looked like it would make money."

"So, she's like the matriarch of the family, huh?" Trey asked.

"Pretty much," Maggie said, "and I'd even go as far as to wager she's probably springin' for most, if not all, of this wedding. So, if she says she wants us to be at the rehearsal dinner, I reckon it will be okay."

*****

Since they weren't actually a part of the wedding procedures, they didn't have to be at the venue until seven o'clock. Trey dropped his grandparents at the front entrance and circled back to the parking lot to find a space. Will was still pale but said he thought he could make it through the dinner. He and Maggie were both seated by the time Trey made it into the dining room.

Trey's wedding experience was limited to the nuptials of a few college friends and one of Lisa's cousins. He had never been a part of any of those weddings. Lisa had been a bridesmaid in her cousin's wedding, so he had been forced to attend the rehearsal. The dinner that followed had been in the backroom of the local steakhouse and was nothing at all like what was laid out before him as he stepped through the door and looked around the room for his grandparents.

The venue itself had been partitioned off with temporary, six-foot tall, black-framed fabric-surfaced room dividers. Large round tables that sat eight were arranged so that a spacious center aisle made the two long rectangular tables at the back of the room easily accessible. White linen table clothes covered the tables, and there were centerpieces of white roses and blue hydrangeas flowing from wine bottles.

Most of the tables where already occupied, and it took Trey several seconds before he spotted his grandmother waving him towards a table near the front of the room. Feeling a bit subconscious and way too underdressed in his pressed Wranglers and white pearl snapped shirt, he made his way down the center aisle and eased into the seat beside her.

Amelia, dressed in a long flowing, white V-neck jumpsuit and gold, single-strapped, four-inch heeled sandals was in the seat on Trey's other side. Will sat beside Maggie, leaving the four seats across from them empty. Theirs was the only table for four, and it faced the bride and groom's table. With no one in front of them, their view wasn't blocked.

"How do you like California, Trey?" Amelia asked as the servers began to arrive with drinks.

"It's beautiful," Trey said, "but it's just not home."

"Honest and straightforward," Amelia chuckled, "Must get that from ole Will over there, but I know what you mean. It took me nearly twenty years before I really thought of this as home. In my mind, I was just a poor girl from Texas."

"Really?" Maggie chuckled. "I don't believe you ever thought of yourself as a poor girl from Texas, even when you were just a poor girl from Texas."

"Touché." Amelia held up her glass of wine. "Dearest Maggie, I believe you may be right."

"I did see my first ever real palm tree yesterday." Trey told Amelia as a waiter took the navy-blue cloth napkin from his plate and spread it in his lap.

Unready, unsure, and unaccustomed to such a practice, Trey nearly turned his chair over trying to get out of the man's way before he realized what was going on. Amelia placed a hand on his shoulder, and said, "Good Lord, Maggie, you've got to get this young man out of Oklahoma more often."

Trey could feel the flush of blood in his cheeks and along the collar of his shirt as the man turned to helped Maggie with her napkin. Before the waiter had a chance to move over to Will, his grandfather had placed his napkin himself. "I'm surprised you didn't stuff it in your shirt like a bib," Amelia told Will.

"Don't tempt me," he reached for his napkin.

"Don't you dare," Maggie warned and then to Amelia, "and don't you encourage him."

*****

Maggie noticed that Will picked at his Italian-seasoned French baguette but barely touched his creamy lobster linguine. He wasn't as pale tonight, but his color was still a bit off. She found herself worrying that she or Trey would catch whatever bug was plaguing him before they made it back home.

"You've barely touched your pasta," she leaned in and whispered. "Are you okay?"

"Stomach is still a little off," Will smiled, "but the bread tastes good."

"You want mine?" she asked.

"No," he answered, "Mine is enough." He nodded toward the table next to theirs. "A couple of those young ladies there sure have taken an interest in Trey."

On hearing his name, Trey followed his grandparents gaze and made eye contact with one of the two bridesmaids who were staring at him. She said something he couldn't hear, and both of them looked away giggling. When he looked back at his grandparents, they were both watching him and grinning. It was going to be a long night.

*****

As the evening wore on, Trey's thoughts drifted to Tess. He wondered what she was doing at that very moment and wished she was sitting here with him. He looked around the room with all its eloquence and felt very out of place.

"Excuse me. I need to use the restroom," he said as he rose from his seat.

"It's just outside the door and to the left." Amelia pointed over her shoulder and down the aisle.

"Thank you." Trey felt like all eyes were on him as he made his way from the room.

When he came out of the men's room, a woman was standing in the corridor right outside the door. Trey recognized her as one of the bridesmaids who had been watching him earlier.

"Hey, cowboy." She smiled, "I'm Natalie. And you are?"

"I'm…" Trey stammered, "I'm Trey… Trey Tucker."

"Well, Trey Tucker," Natalie said, "this is your lucky night. "I'm in the middle of my hot girl summer, and I think it's about time to add a cowboy to my list."

Slowly, what she was suggesting began to sink in. Trey searched her face to see if she was joking. With a flourish, she raised one arm over her head, did a slow turn, then curtsied and with her best smile said, "I'm all yours."

"My apologies," Trey smiled back at her, "but I'm afraid I'm goin' to have to pass."

Shocked she sputtered, "Are you gay?"

"No, ma'am," he answered, "I'm not gay."

"Then what's the matter," she asked running her hands down her length. "Don't like what you see?"

"It's not that at all," Trey told her. "You are very pretty… even sexy…"

"Then what?" She seemed bewildered, "Is there someone else."

"You could say that," Trey nodded.

"Really, so does this someone have a name?" Natalie looked deflated.

"It's Tess," Trey told her, excused himself, and returned to the dining room.

Chapter 24

At nine twenty-three on Thursday morning, Trey rolled over, opened his eyes, and stared at the red digital numbers on the hotel alarm clock until the three changed to a four. He couldn't believe he had slept so long. Even more astonishing was the fact that his grandmother hadn't called to wake him. Worried that something was wrong, he sat up quickly in bed and rang his grandparents' room.

"Hey, Granny, it's Trey," he told her when she answered on the second ring. "Is everything okay?"

"Your Pappy's still a bit under the weather," she told him, "so we decided to sleep in. He's in the shower now."

"Okay," Trey said. "Just scared me a bit when I woke up this late and you hadn't called."

"We're okay," Maggie said but she sounded tired. "I just wish your Pappy could shake this bug. It's really tirin' him out."

"Maybe we should take him by an Urgent Care," Trey suggested. "They do have those out here, don't they?"

"Yes," Maggie said. "We passed one the other day comin' into town, but he's already said he'll be fine. He promised to see the doctor when we get home, if he's not better by then."

"Granny, that's like what… two maybe three days, depending on how long we drive each day." Trey decided not to mention going back through Placerville until he knew his grandfather was feeling better. He had used his phone before going to bed last night and found that the quickest routes back home did not go anywhere near Placerville. Since stopping to see

Tess would definitely be out of the way, if his grandfather did not get well, he just did not see it happening.

*****

The day seemed to drag by for Trey. Amelia had made arrangements to have lunch with them since she would be busy most of the afternoon, helping make sure everything was set up correctly for the wedding. When the time came, Will said he didn't feel much like eating, and Maggie did not want him staying by himself, so Trey offered to stay while the two sisters left for lunch.

As soon as they were gone, Will waved Trey out of the room. "I'm gonna lay down for a nap. You don't have to stay, I'll be alright."

"I promised Granny I'd keep an eye on you." Trey dropped into the armchair and pulled out his phone.

"I won't be able to sleep with you starin' at me all the time," Will snapped, "Go on back to your room. I'll be fine."

"Tell you what," Trey said, "give me your room key so I can check in on you, and I'll go."

"I don't need you to check in on me," Will snarled.

"I promised Granny." Trey stood his ground. "It's either give me the room key or I'm sittin' right here."

"Fine!" Will said, digging for his wallet. "You know who this reminds me of?"

"No, Pappy, I don't," Trey answered, "but I bet you're gonna tell me.

"Yes, I am, smartass," Will said and handed him the hotel key card. "Tess. You're actin' just like Tess. Now, get on out of here and let an old man take a nap."

Trey took the key from his grandfather and smiled, "Have a good nap, Pappy," he said and made his way out of the room.

The next two hours crept slowly past. Every half hour, Trey eased the door to his grandfather's room open and stepped far enough into the room to make sure Will was still resting. Between times, he scanned through channels on the television in his own room. He couldn't find anything that interested him, but it gave him something to do while he thought about every possible outcome of a trip back to Placerville.

In the first scenario, he asked Tess to return to Oklahoma with him, and she said yes. As the morning turned to afternoon, the idea played out in his mind a dozen different times with as many different outcomes. He tried to find the perfect dialogue but couldn't.

Number two, which deep in his heart seemed like a much more realistic possibility was where she was happy to see him but not willing to just up and run off to Oklahoma with him. He didn't like this one much but could understand, with the experience she had been through with the last fellow who promised to sweep her out of the state, why she would be leery to try it again.

The third, and last possibility was the one that had him completely tied in knots. What if he drove all the way to Placerville only to find out that Tess had no interest in Oklahoma or him or even a long-distance relationship. He was pretty certain that this would not be the case, but then, what did he know about the thoughts of women. It was less than two weeks ago when he had no doubt that he would be spending the rest of his life with Lisa.

*****

At exactly seven o'clock, the pianist began to play 'Canon in D' as the wedding processional began. Trey watched as the minister, Bible in hand, walked up the aisle in the dignified manner that bespoke his station. Next, Amelia was escorted down the aisle by one of her grandsons whose name Trey couldn't recall. The groom's grandmother and grandfather followed. Next came the teary-eyed bride's mother on the arm of her oldest son. The groom had both a father and stepmother, and a mother and stepfather. Trey wondered if that had made the occasion awkward. If it had, the groom who followed along behind his mother and her husband, showed no signs of it.

As soon as the groom was in his place, the pianist stuck a chord and then played 'Falling In Love'. On cue, seven bridesmaids, each escorted by a groomsman, marched down the aisle, separated at the altar, and took their places. The ringbearer, a towheaded, freckle-faced youngster with pure orneriness in his eyes, and very shy little flower girl came next. When the two of them where in place, the pianist once again hit a musical transition chord and then began playing, "Here Comes the Bride", and everyone stood and watched the bride, escorted by her father, begin her stroll down the aisle.

As the bride passed by him, Trey's wondered if Tess would want a big fancy wedding like this one. That thought lead him down a mental trail that he had still not found an end to when the minister pronounced the newlyweds man and wife. As the groom kissed his new bride, Trey knew he would regret it forever if he did not return to Placerville. If Tess said no, so be it. At least, he was going to give it a chance.

*****

The photographer and his assistant organized the family members for wedding pictures, and the guests began to slowly drift down the corridor that led to the room where the reception would be held. Trey followed along behind the other wedding guests, lost in thoughts of Tess.

Will tapped him on the shoulder and said, "I'm not feelin' well. Maybe you could run me back to our room."

Maggie said, "I'm going with you. If Trey wants to come back to the reception, he can."

"You don't have to do that," Will argued.

"But I want to," Maggie said, "Let me tell Amelia. I don't want her to worry if she can't find us."

"I'll stay with y'all," Trey said. "I've had enough of this wedding stuff. I'll have the truck around front in just a minute."

By the time his grandparents made it out of the venue, Trey had pulled up to the entrance. He noticed that his grandfather seemed to be having trouble getting up into the truck and offered to help him, but Will waved him off.

"You look like you need to see a doctor, Pappy," Trey said.

"Just get me back to the hotel so I can lay down," Will told him. "I just need to rest. I'll be fine."

"Will Tucker," Maggie's voice was soft and stern at the same time, "you need more than rest. We are taking you to the emergency room."

"No," Will said, "the hotel."

A left across the Napa River and a right into the hotel parking lot, and Trey pulled the truck to a stop at the front entrance. Will swung his door open and used it for support to step down. He managed one step, staggered badly, and started to fall. From the driver's seat, Trey watched as Will's body landed with a sickening thud, and the right side of his face smacked hard against the concrete.

"Oh, Will!!" Maggie gasped and then yelled at Trey. "Call an ambulance!"

Trey pulled the phone out of his pocket and dialed nine-one-one as his grandmother hurried around the front of the truck. He did not remember leaving the vehicle himself, but when the dispatcher answered on the second ring, he was standing over his grandparents. Maggie was seated with Will's head cradled in her lap repeating, "Oh, Will. Oh, Will." Over and over again.

"They're on the way, Pappy," Trey said past a lump in his throat. "Hold on."

Chapter 25

Will had regained consciousness by the time the ambulance arrived, but he was still too weak to set up. Trey had moved the truck out of the driveway, so the emergency personnel had room to park and work.

"I thought I could make it home," Trey heard his grandfather tell his grandmother in a low voice as they loaded him into the ambulance.

"Can I ride with him?" Maggie asked the nearest EMT.

"Yes," he told her then with a glance at Trey, "but there's only room for you."

"I'll follow in the truck, Granny," Trey said and started for the Silverado.

The ambulance was already backing out by the time he got the truck started. He managed to get turned around and catch up to it in less than a block. The trip to the hospital took less than five minutes, and by the time Trey found a parking space and made his way into the emergency room lobby, his grandparents had already been taken back. Not sure what the procedures were, Trey stopped at the front desk and asked where they had taken his grandfather. After answering several questions, he was escorted down a long corridor to a sliding glass door with a blue-green curtain pulled across it.

The attendant leading Trey, opened the door, held the curtain back and motioned him into the cubicle. A young Hispanic man who didn't look much older than Trey was asking Will a series of questions as he examined his abdomen. Maggie sat to the side, her face almost as pale as Will's.

"How long have you been feeling this way?" the doctor asked.

"A few days," Will answered, "but there's something you need to know."

"And what would that be?" the young man asked stepping back.

"First, I need a moment in private with my wife and grandson," Will said.

Trey felt like the bottom was about to fall out of his world. A numbness began in the center of his chest and spread outward until he felt like it was going to strangle him. To see his grandfather, the man who had always been his rock, lying there looking so pale and helpless shook him to his core.

The doctor glanced over at the nurse who had just finished hanging an IV bag on the aluminum pole at the head of Will's bed. With a shrug and a nod, the doctor stepped to the door, slid it open, and allowed the nurse to step out first. Then he turned and said, "I'll be back in a few minutes."

Will motioned Maggie to his side, reached out, took her hand in his, and held it for a long moment. Trey made his way to the foot of the bed. He wasn't certain, but it looked to him like whatever was the IV bag was already helping his grandfather since he seemed to have a little more color in his cheeks.

"Maggie, I'm sorry," Will finally said.

This had to be serious because a tear escaped from the corner of his eye and slid slowly down his cheek. Trey's breath caught in his chest. He had never seen his grandfather cry except at his mother's funeral.

"You've nothing to be sorry for," Maggie wiped the tear away. "We all get sick from time to time."

"I'm not just sick." Will squeezed her hand, "And I'm sorry I didn't tell you sooner, but I knew you would have never come on this trip if you knew."

"Will, you're scarin' me." Maggie said.

"I know," Will said, "and I'm sorry."

"Please, quit sayin' that and just tell me what's wrong." Maggie voice trembled as she spoke.

"Sweetheart, I have stage four pancreatic cancer," he said.

Trey's knees went weak. Through the fog that filled his mind, he forced himself to step to his grandmother's side. She leaned against him for support, took Will's hand in hers, and began to sob. *This can't be happening. There's been a mistake.* Kept running through Trey mind over and over again.

*****

"Why are you in California?" was the first question the doctor asked when Will told him about the cancer.

"That's a good question," Maggie said.

She still held Will's hand. He gave it a gentle squeeze, and said, "I had my reasons, sweetheart. We'll talk about them later, but right now, I need to visit with the doctor here."

Trey, who had stepped to the end of the bed, fought back tears. He had to be strong for his Granny, but right now, he needed someone to be strong for him, too. He should call his father as soon as possible and ask him if he knew about this.

He tried to remember what he knew about pancreatic cancer but he couldn't remember specifics. He seemed to remember that it was incurable, and the life expectancy of a person with stage-four cancer wasn't very long.

Will looked up at doctor. "I did not expect this to progress as quickly as it has. I thought I would be back in Oklahoma before I got bad enough that I had to tell anybody."

"I see," the doctor said.

"So, Doc," Will continued, "I need to know what has to be done so I can get back there as quickly as possible."

"It would be best if you did not travel," the doctor said, "but if you must, then I suggest that as soon as you are stabilized and well enough, you book a flight. It would not be a good idea for you to try to drive back."

"Okay," Will managed a half smile, "I don't know what we have to do to get me stabilized, but let's get to it."

The doctor laid out a plan for bloodwork and several tests and ordered a round of intravenous antibiotics. He told Will to get some rest, and that he would see him in the morning. The next couple of hours were filled with the process of admitting him and making sure that he got all the tests the doctor had ordered for him. It was after midnight before everything was finally done and they got him settled into a private room with a window seat that doubled as a twin-size bed. Maggie refused to leave, so a nurse brought the linens needed for her to stay the night. They sent Trey back to the hotel with instructions to return as early as possible in the morning.

Two blocks from the hotel a mixture of sorrow, guilt, and frustration overcame him and he had to pull to the side of the road. No longer able to hold back the tears, he let them go and with them, the gut-wrenching sobs that come with real pain. His grandfather was dying, and he could do nothing about it. He had not wanted to come on this trip and now the guilt he felt was threatening to eat him alive. Spending time with his grandson was part of the reason Will had planned this vacation, and now all Trey could think about was how much time he and his Pappy were going to have left. Trey wept so hard he could not get enough air and began to choke. When he was once again able to breathe, he put the truck in drive and continued to the hotel.

All thoughts of Tess and Placerville were pushed away as he lay in the hotel bed, waiting for sleep to overcome him. The knowledge that his grandfather was going to die lay heavy on his chest, threatening to suffocate him. He wanted to scream, wanted to hit something, but there was no one and nothing to scream at and nothing to hit. Tears begin to flow once again and continued until sleep finally came.

*****

235

Friday morning, the sun came up in the east and began its slow trek across the sky just like it had every day of Will's life. People got in their cars, drove to their jobs or wherever their daily routine took them, and life went on. Will was not surprised. He was not upset. It was the natural order of things.

"Why, Will?" Maggie asked him.

He had watched her slowly fold the linens and place them on the pillow at one end of the window seat. Then she had pulled the room's only chair up to the side of his bed and taken his hand in hers.

"Memories." He raised her hand to his lips and kissed her knuckles. "First and foremost, memories."

"And here I thought it was all about Trey," Maggie said, "What do you mean memories?"

"Maggie, sweetheart, I know you're angry," he told her, looking into her eyes, "I knew when Doc. Spiller told me I had cancer, that you were going to be angry with me, at the cancer, at the world."

"I'm not angry," she protested and looked away.

"Maggie, look at me," he said.

After a second, she looked back into his eyes. "You *are* angry," he said. "We've been married over fifty years. I know when you're angry, and I know when you're happy, and I know when you're sad, and right now you're angry."

"Okay, you're right," she admitted, "I'm angry you have cancer. I'm angry you didn't tell me as soon as you knew. Why didn't you tell me as soon as you knew?"

"Because you would not have agreed to this trip," he confessed, "and because I needed time to wrap my own mind around it first."

"But I thought we made this trip for Trey," she groaned. "We could have figured out some other way to get his attention."

"Trey was only a small part of the reason we needed to come on this trip." Will squeezed her hand.

"Okay, so explain to me the other part, please." Her voice quivered.

"Memories," he said again.

"What memories," the frustration was clear in her tone, "and why?"

"The good memories, the one's we made on this trip," he explained. "Right now, you're angry. In a few months I'll be gone, and…"

"No, Will." Fresh tears flowed down her cheeks. "Please, don't say that."

"Maggie dear, I love you, you know I do, but there's no sense beatin' 'round the bush about this," he said. "It's gonna happen, and when it does, there are gonna be times when you get plumb mad, madder even than you are right now. And when that time comes, I want you to remember the memories we've made on this trip."

"Will, I've got fifty-plus years of memories stored up," Maggie sniffled. "What makes you think I needed this trip?"

"Because all those memories are going to be too far removed from what's comin', darlin'," he explained, "but these memories, the ones we've made in the last few days, they're fresh, they're new, and they're the ones I want you to think on when the time comes. Okay?"

"Okay," Maggie managed through the tears, "but I can't promise you I won't still be angry with you."

"I know… I know." Will said, holding back tears of his own.

*****

When Trey got to Will's room, he found his grandfather arguing with the doctor. Will said that he was feeling better, and therefore, should be discharged. The doctor and Maggie disagreed and felt like another day on the IV would help immensely. Dehydration and an imbalance in his electrolytes seemed to be a recurring theme as the disagreement circled round and round.

"What's the plan on getting back home?" Trey finally asked.

"You heard the doctor last night," Will said in a gruff voice. "He thinks I should fly back."

"Yes, Pappy," Trey said calmly, "but when and from where do y'all plan to fly is what I'm askin'. And also, I'm just guessin', but I figured you would want me to drive your truck home."

"I want to go home, so me and your Granny will fly out as soon as this here doctor says it's okay. What do you think, Maggie? Think you can make us some arrangements to leave this afternoon?" he asked.

"I think you need to listen to the doctor," she answered.

The doctor picked up Will's chart and looked it over one more time. "Mr. Tucker, if you would agree to stay through until tomorrow morning, I promise to have you out of here by noon. You should be able to catch a flight out of Sacramento and be back in Oklahoma by bedtime tomorrow."

"I guess I can do that," Will said. "It's not like y'all are givin' me much choice anyway."

"Okay, now that we have that settled," the doctor said, "I'll let the nurses know, and you can figure out your travel plans."

As the doctor turn to leave the room, Will stopped him and asked, "How much time do I have?"

"That's hard to say with this type of cancer. Typically, three to five months but with treatment sometimes… well… miracles do happen sometimes." He shrugged.

"Thank you, sir." Will said and turned to Trey, "Do you think you could get us plane tickets for tomorrow afternoon?"

Trey was still trying to work through the three to five months and did not answer right away. The idea that his grandfather had less than a year to live refused to register.

"Mmm… yeah… yes, sir… I guess I can." He stammered when he was finally able to speak.

"Thank you," Maggie said visible shaken, "You will have to drive us to the airport and then drive the truck home. I'll call Bo and let him know he'll have to pick us up at… Oh, Lord…"

"What is it Granny?" Trey asked.

"Bo," she said and then, "He doesn't know. I haven't talked to him since we left Ely. We've just been so busy and I just…"

"Don't worry, Granny," Trey said. "I'll call him."

*****

Maggie stood near the hospital room door, talked on the phone, and watched her husband resting. Trey sat in one of the two chairs provided for visitors.

"Amelia will be here in a little bit," she told her grandson when she hung up. She pulled a chair up close to Will's bed and sat down. Will opened his eyes reached out and took her hand in his. Like water over rapids, her emotions slammed her one way and then another. Lack of sleep and exhaustion were taking their toll. She just wanted to go home. She just wanted to *be* home. And once there, she never wanted to leave again.

"Trey that truck is yours," Will said, "bought and paid for. The title is in your name and when the paper tag runs out, I'll get your tags for you. Consider it a late graduation gift."

I would much rather have you healthy, Trey thought but said, "Thank you, Pappy, and don't you worry about the ranch. I'll stay on and help Dad run it."

Then as if Will had read his mind, he said, "Trey, I'm sorry about all of this… sorry I've been a bit rough on you lately… sorry I didn't tell you… well, hell… I guess what I'm tryin' to say is that I'm sorry."

Trey crossed the room, kissed his grandmother on the forehead, put his hand on his grandfather's shoulder, and said, "I love you, Pappy. And it's okay."

Chapter 26

Trey pulled up to the American Airline terminal at one o'clock. The quickest flight he could book for his grandparents left at two forty-five, had a forty-minute stopover in Salt Lake City, Utah, then arrived in Oklahoma City at seven thirty-five. Trey figured it would take him two days of hard driving to make it home.

As he carried their luggage to the baggage check in, everything seemed surreal, almost like a dream, a bad dream. And just like a bad dream, he wanted to wake from it. But it wasn't a dream, it was real, and he was awake.

And life sucked.

"You got everything you need?" Will seemed like a new man except for a slight yellow tint to his complexion.

"Yes, sir," Trey answered, "I should be home in a couple of days at the most."

Will smiled and asked, "Why don't you take an extra day?"

"Why?" Trey asked.

"Well, because Placerville is a little bit out of the way if you're headed for Nowhere." Will grinned.

"Pappy, you've got cancer," Trey said. "I need to get home as soon as I can."

"Really? I hadn't noticed," Will winked at him. "Trey, you and me, we've still got time, but I have a feelin' you'll never make it back out here to sunny California once you get home. Settle things with Tess, one way or another, so you won't get to the place I'm in and have regrets."

Trey glanced over at his grandmother.

"He's right, Trey, you don't go now, and you'll probably never go."

"But I don't even know if she's… well…" he stumbled over the words.

"And you'll never know," Maggie said as she held her arms out for a goodbye hug, "if you don't go ask her."

Trey wrapped his arms around his grandmother. When she released him, he turned to his grandfather and stuck out his hand. Will ignored the hand and stepped in for a hug of his own. Hugging had not been a part of their relationship since Trey was a little fellow—a handshake, a pat on the back, but not hugging.

When Will stepped away, he looked Trey in the eye, gave him a firm nod, and said, "Go."

*****

The GPS on Trey's phone gave him two choices for routes back to Placerville. The first took him back through midtown. The second caught Dwight D. Eisenhower Highway around the town proper before meeting back up with Highway 50, but it would take seven minutes longer. Trey took the second option.

Even with the extra seven minutes and catching every red light possible along the route the trip, only took an hour and twelve minutes. The first half of it, Trey still hadn't completely convinced himself that he was making the right decision. Somewhere along the way, he crossed that invisible line between you can turn back whenever you want to, and you've come too far to turn back now.

Once he was over that line, he had two problems. First, he had to find her. Of course, the Taproom would be his starting place, but there was a chance that neither she nor her aunt would be working. Surely, someone there could, at least, point him in the right direction. The was really not much he could do until he got there and found out, so onto the next problem.

What to say to her when he did find her? He spent the rest of the trip trying to script out the right combination of words, so he did not fall flat on his face. By the time he pulled into the parking area at the restaurant, the only thing he had managed to do was to completely frustrate himself. He had no idea what to say or how to say it. Fifteen minutes of watching the time click slowly by on the truck's clock got him no closer. Every idea, every speech that he started in his head ended up sounding either ridiculously sappy or just plain stupid.

Finally, he decided to tackle problem number one first. He shut the truck engine off and took a deep breath. *Now or never,* he thought as he opened the door and stepped out. The sweet aroma of food filled the air, and he remembered he hadn't eaten since breakfast. He decided that, even if she wasn't here, he would at least have dinner.

On his way into the restaurant, Trey looked for a silver Toyota Camry with an I Love Cats sticker but didn't spot one and wondered that even if Tess's aunt was at work, would she remember him. He crossed to the front entrance, opened the door, and stepped inside. His eyes grew accustomed to the dimmer lighting as he scanned the place and finally noticed that there was only one customer in the restaurant—a man sitting at the bar.

Tess's aunt faced the back of the bar and was taking a bottle of vodka down to fix the man a drink, but shouted across the room, "Come on in. I'll be with you in a minute. You can sit at the bar or take your pick of the tables."

Trey chose the closest booth, slid in, and put his Stetson down on the seat. After Tess's aunt had fixed the drink and placed it on the bar in front of the customer, she started his way. She stopped at the podium near the front door long enough to pick up a menu on the way to his table.

"Well, if it ain't Mr. Heartache-in-a-Hat?" she said with a big smile.

All Trey could manage was a nod and a weak smile.

"I figured you would be halfway back to Texas by now," she said, "Did you just stop by to eat, or did something else bring you back to Placerville?"

Trey found his voice and said, "Well, Miz Alyssa, it's not

something, it's someone, and that would be your niece, Tess. But I'd like something to eat, too, if that's okay."

Alyssa slid into the booth across from him and laid the menu on the table. Before he could pick it up, she laid her hand on top of it, and the smile disappeared. Trey looked up, and the two locked eyes. He felt like he was being tested, or maybe like she was searching his soul.

"Tess isn't here," she finally said, taking her hand from the menu and pushing it towards him, "but I can give her a call if you want."

"I would sure appreciate it if you would." Trey figured he had passed, at least, one test and wondered how many more there would be.

"Why don't you go ahead and take a look at the menu, and I'll be back in a minute." She said as she slid out of the booth.

*****

"Tess, I need you to bring me another pair of shoes, please," Alyssa said when Tess answered the phone.

"Why?" Tess asked.

"The ones I'm wearing are hurting my feet," Alyssa lied. "If you aren't too busy moping around the house, I could really use my favorite Nikes. The black ones with a white swoosh."

"Are they in your closet or in the living room?" Tess asked.

"In the closet. You can't miss them. They're the only black ones," Alyssa told her. "Please, hurry so I can change them before the dinner rush."

"I'll be right there," Tess said, then before she hung up the phone added, "and I'm not moping."

"Oh, yes, you are," Alyssa said, and the line went dead.

*****

Alyssa had come and gone to his table twice, but Trey had still not ordered when Tess walked through the front door carrying a pair of shoes. He closed the menu and laid it on the table. Heart beating fast, he wanted nothing more than to gather her into his arms and hold her close. Alyssa came from the bar and took the shoes from her and then pointed toward the booth where Trey was sitting.

"Someone would like to talk to you," Alyssa told her loud enough for Trey to hear.

"Who?" she followed her aunt's finger and locked eyes with Trey.

Trey didn't know if he should go to her or wait for her to come to him. He was still trying to decide and hoping she would not turn and leave when she started across the room towards him. Every word he had thought about saying disappeared from his mind. The only thing that he could think about in the seconds before she reached him was the story of how his grandparents first met.

Just before she stopped, he smiled and said, "Well, hello, Sweetheart."

Her chin began to quiver, the next second, the tears were flowing. He stood and she stepped into his arms. With her face pressed into his chest, the whole world seemed to disappear, and for the first time since he found out about his grandfather's cancer, hope filled his heart. He had the strength to face the future, and he never again wanted to be away from this beautiful woman who brought so much peace to his soul.

Tess finally leaned back, looked him in the eye and whispered, "You came back."

"I did," he said and kissed her on the end of her nose. "I needed to see you. Needed to talk to you."

"Okay." She pulled his face down and pressed her lips to his.

When she gave him a chance to talk again, he said, "Tess, I know you said you didn't want a rebound relationship, and I don't want that either. And I know we've both been down some bad roads, and what we thought was love turned out to be something awful. I won't lie to you, I have no idea what love is even supposed to look like at this point, but I do know this, I like you and I think you like me. And if you would give us a chance, we could start with the way we feel right now and build it into a love like my grandparents have."

His heart thumped like a bass drum as he waited for her to say something. Alyssa watched from across the room, forgotten by both Trey and Tess.

"I would like that, too," Tess finally said. "What do you have planned."

"Dinner," Trey answered.

"And then what?" she asked.

"I guess we'll figure it out over dinner," Trey said honestly, "I wasn't sure how you would feel about seeing me again, so I didn't really plan past this point."

"Okay," Tess glanced around the dining area. "Where are Miz Maggie and Mr. Will?"

"They had to fly back," Trey told her. "I don't know an easier way to tell you this, so, I'll just say it. Pappy has pancreatic cancer. He's only got a few months."

"Oh, my," Tess gasped, "Oh, poor Maggie… oh, Trey, I'm so sorry."

As hard as it was for him to tell her about the past two days, it was even harder for her to hear. When he told her what Will had said about him needing to come to Placerville and give their relationship a chance, she teared up again.

"Is everything okay?" Alyssa asked as she approached them.

Tess wiped away her tears and said, "Yes and no."

"What do you mean?" Alyssa asked as Trey stepped back.

"Yes, because Trey came back," Tess answered, "and no, because Mr. Will has cancer, and it's not the curable kind."

"I am so sorry," Alyssa said.

"As soon as we're done eating," Tess told Alyssa, "I'm going to have Trey take me by the house so I can get my things, and we're going to Oklahoma."

"Are you sure about this?" Alyssa asked.

Tess looked from her aunt to Trey then back again and said, "Yes, Aunt Alyssa, I'm sure."

*****

They made it as far as Fallon, the Oasis of Nevada, before Trey stopped for the night. On the three-hour trip from Placerville, they had played the what's-your-favorite game. Trey knew her favorite color was teal green, her favorite food was Italian, her favorite holiday was Christmas, but when they stopped at the Holiday Inn Express and he left her in the truck while he checked to see if there were any rooms available, he realized he still didn't know how many rooms to request.

"Give me just a second," he told the lady behind the desk when she said she had rooms available.

Back in the truck, he took Tess's hand in his, "Everything has happened so fast, and we've discussed a lot but there are still things I just don't know and…" he stammered.

"About what?" Tess asked.

"Rooms," Trey answered, "I don't want to rush you. For that matter, I'm not even sure I'm ready, but we do need to decide how many rooms to rent tonight."

Tess smiled. "I have been thinking about that off and on since we left Placerville, and I can honestly say, as bad as I'd love to curl up next to you right now, just like you, I'm not sure I'm ready."

"Then I'll get us each a room for the night," he told her.

"Okay," she said, then asked, "but can we maybe soak in the hot tub and share lots of kisses before we go to them?"

"You betcha." Trey grinned as he opened the door and stepped out of the truck.

Chapter 27

Monday found them heading back east through the desert. They made a stop at the Shoe Tree and tossed the pair of shoes Tess had been carrying when she came into the Taproom up into it. When Trey asked her about them, she told him how her aunt had used them to get her to the restaurant, and then when she tried to give her the shoes had said they were an old pair she just hadn't got around to throwing away.

"So why did you bring them?" Trey asked.

"I figured this was the route we would take, and I wanted to throw them up in the tree for luck," she answered.

"So, you think you're gonna need luck to put up with me?" He placed his hand over his heart as if he had been shot.

"No, but I'm pretty sure you are going to need all the luck you can get to put up with me," she answered, "so I brought them along for you to throw."

Trey took the shoes from her and tossed them high into the tree. They caught on a limb near the top, swung briefly, and then settled into place. "Not that I think we're gonna need it, but here's to luck for both of us,"

They sealed the luck with a kiss and then started down the road once again, only to stop not long after that in the salt flats where they had written their names in stones. Trey slowed when they spotted the first set of initials, and since there was no traffic, they were just inching along when they spotted the heart with Will and Maggie's initials in it. He stopped on the side of the road and both he and Tess snapped pictures with their cellphones.

Then they walked down to where they had placed their names, and discovered a heart made from seven stones between the two names. Read from left to right it said Tess—Heart—Trey. Tess gave Trey a questioning look.

With a shrug he said, "Wasn't me."

"Then who?" she asked.

Trey noticed the heart missing from between the I and the NY. The indention where the heart had been was still there but the rocks were gone.

Trey smiled and said, "Granny."

Tess said, "Miz Maggie. She knew all along."

*****

Highway 50 took them across Nevada and well into Utah. Just south of Salina, they caught Interstate 70 and followed it until the iPhone GPS instructed them to turn south on the 190 towards Moab. As he drove the route from Moab to Monticello and on down to Cortex, Colorado, Trey thought how odd it seemed that it had been less than two weeks since he had last traveled this way—and yet it felt like a lifetime ago.

They rolled into Cortex at dusk to find the Holiday Inn Express was booked up, but the Hampton just down the road had vacancies. At the desk, Trey asked the clerk if they had rooms available.

"Yes, sir," the young man said, "How many do you need?"

Before Trey could answer, Tess wrapped her arms around his arm, smiled, and said, "Just one, please."

Trey looked down into her smiling face and asked, "Are you sure?"

"Very sure," she said.

*****

Later, they lay on the hotel bed in tangled sheets. Both of them completely exhausted. Tess raised her head off Trey's chest, propped herself on an elbow, and with her finger, began to trace an invisible heart on his stomach. As her finger moved across his abdomen, his moved along in the same motion across the middle of her back. When she realized what he was doing, she smiled and wrinkled her nose at him.

"What time do we have to leave in the morning?" she asked.

"Early, I think," Trey told her, "I would like to make it all the way home tomorrow."

"How early?" She shifted her eyes from his face to the clock sitting on the nightstand.

He followed her gaze, and the red digits told him it was almost eleven.

"I'd like to leave by six o'clock, if that's okay with you," he said. "How much time do you need to get ready in the mornin'?"

"Not long, maybe, half an hour," she answered.

Trey tilted his head sideways and gave her a *yeah-right* look. The finger she had been running up and down along his ribs stopped, and she said, "Look here, mister, I don't know what you are used to, but I don't spend a lot of time in front of the mirror in the morning. So, it doesn't take me long to get ready. And if I say a half an hour, then it will be a half an hour."

Trey raised a hand in mock defense and said, "Yes ma'am, don't get your panties in a bunch."

Tess tapped him on the nose, giggled, and said, "I'm not wearing any, sweetheart."

"Mmm, so you aren't." He raised one eyebrow and smiled, then asked, "So, if I set my alarm for five o'clock, will that give you enough time in the bathroom?"

"Yes, but I'd rather you set it for four-thirty," she answered with an impish grin on her face.

"Why is that?" he asked.

"Because I'm going to want to… well…," she looked him in the eye and ran her finger down the length of his abdomen stopped just beyond his navel, raised one eyebrow, and tapped her finger against him twice.

*****

The top of the sun crested the horizon as they made their way east out of Cortez. The iPhone GPS had given them three choices of routes. Trey chose the one that took them back to Pagosa Springs and down through Sante Fe to Interstate 40 because he did not want to go through Albuquerque. It would put an extra half an hour on their trip, but he had had enough of city traffic.

A quarter before noon, Trey pulled up beside the same gas pump at Clines Corner that he had used on the trip west. He and Tess had spent the morning discussing their plans and hopes for the future. Everything about their relationship seemed to flow so naturally that Trey began to wonder when or if they would ever find something to disagree on. As he pulled the nozzle from the gas pump, it dawned on Trey that the last time Tess had been here, she had been abandoned. When he finished gassing up the truck and got back into it, he looked at Tess who was fiddling with her phone and said, "I wasn't thinkin' when I stopped here. Sorry."

She looked at him confused and asked, "Sorry for what?"

"Well, this place and the last time you were here can't exactly bring the most wonderful memories," he said.

She reached out and took his hand. "Trey, this is where I met you. That is the memory that I chose to hold on to. Aunt Alyssa once told me that we have a choice of which memories we get to hold on to and which ones we get to let go of, and years from now, when we're old and gray and I tell our story to our grandkids, I will tell them this is the place where you found me."

"Grandkids, huh?" Trey questioned.

"Yes, sir, Mr. Tucker," she said, "I want kids, plural, and lots of grandkids."

*****

From Clines Corner, Trey caught Interstate 40 and stayed on it through New Mexico, the Texas Panhandle, and into Oklahoma. When he got to State Highway 283 just south of Sayre, he was sick of the traffic and decided Tess should really see some of rural Oklahoma. He took the smaller, less traveled road down to where he could catch Highway 9, the road that would take them home.

It felt good to be back in familiar country and he wondered how his Pappy was doing. When they got to the city limits of Gotebo, he slowed.

"Gotebo?" Tess said, "and I thought we had weird town names in California."

"I reckon every state has a few," Trey said. "This one is named for a Kiowa War Chief. You'll find lots of towns in this state are named after Native Americans."

As they drove through Carnegie, Trey asked, "How many?"

"How many what?" Tess frowned. "Names of towns?"

"Kids, how many kids?"

"At least four," she said without hesitation, "but if you want more, I'd be okay with that too."

"Goodness, sweetheart," he chuckled.

"What?" she looked worried. "You do want kids don't you? Please, tell me you want kids."

"Yes, Tess, I want kids. I've always known I wanted kids. I just never, until right now, thought about how many. I guess you've thought about it some, huh?" he asked.

"Yes, I have," she admitted. "I grew up an only child. I didn't have cousins close by, so I didn't have anyone, and I decided when I had a family, I wanted it to be big enough so no child of mine would ever feel alone."

"Makes sense," Trey agreed. "I guess we're of a same mind then. So, when do you want to start on this big family?"

"Well to be honest," Tess said, "I think I'm going to be a little selfish with you for a while. I kind of want you all to myself for a bit, but let's not wait too long."

"Okay," Trey agreed and thought that if hearts could smile, his would definitely be sporting a mighty big grin.

*****

Just north of Fort Cobb, Trey turned north towards Lake Fort Cobb. When they passed by the Nowhere Store, Tess noticed the water tank. Painted white it had large red faded letters on it that read NOWHERE, OKLA.

"Oh goodness," she exclaimed, "Miz Maggie was serious when she said you all lived in Oklahoma in the middle of nowhere. I thought it was like when we say someone is from B.F.E. but you really do live in Nowhere."

"Yes, Ma'am," Trey said as he made the right turn that would take them to the ranch, "I guess I should have been a bit clearer as to where I was planning on takin' you. You still think you wanna spend the rest of your life here with me?"

"There's nowhere I would rather be," Tess said.

Chapter 28

On the second Wednesday in August, Will Tucker rolled out of bed, dressed slowly, slipped his feet into his favorite pair of boots, and found his way to the coffee pot. When Maggie came looking for him, she found him rocking gently on the back-porch swing, staring out across the land. He smiled, slowed the swing to a stop, and Maggie slid on beside him.

He took her hand in his and whispered, "Maggie, I wish I'd told you more often how much I love you."

"Will, you always made me feel loved," she squeezed his hand, "and that's more important than words."

"Thanks for letting me do this my way," his voice quivered.

"Like I had a choice." She patted him on the knee. "Think I'll have a cup of coffee now. You want a refill while I'm up?"

"I'm good," he said. "Maggie, I love you."

"I love you, too." She patted his knee once more.

The wooden screen door slapped shut. Her favorite coffee cup retrieved from the dishrack, she poured it nearly full. Careful not to spill it, she retraced her steps to the door. The swing was still. Will's chin rested on his chest, and his hands lay in his lap. Maggie eased the door closed, set her coffee down on the porch rail, and returned to his side. For a long time, she sat silent, staring out past the barn at the land. Then with eyes still fixed on the distance, she took Will's hand in her own. As the first tear of many escaped, she whispered once again, "I love you, too."

*****

On Saturday, Will Tucker was buried in the family cemetery that was located on the northwest corner of the ranch. It was bordered by a three-rung, split-rail fence and overlooked Fort Cobb Lake. It was one of the most beautiful views on the ranch.

"Trey," Will had said a few days before he passed away, "I learned a long time ago that horses have a lot more feelin's than most folks give'm credit for, so when I'm gone, I want you to make sure Red is there, so he knows I won't be around anymore, and he has some closure. And after that he's yours. He's a good horse. You take care of him for me, okay?"

Fighting the lump in his throat, Trey had agreed.

While the preacher read Will's favorite verses from his Bible, Trey held Tess's hand in one hand and Red's reins in his other. After the preacher finished and everyone had said their last goodbyes, Bo and Tess helped Maggie back to the truck they had all ridden in from the ranch house to the family cemetery.

Tess walked slowly back to where Trey stood beside Will's grave. "I'll meet you back at the house," she said and gave him a kiss on the cheek.

"Alright," he said. "Thank you."

"For what?" she asked.

"For helpin' Granny," he said, "and for helping me."

"I love you." She reached out and squeezed his hand.

As she turned to go, he said, "I love you, too."

Trey watched as a multitude of vehicles disappeared over the rise, heading back to the house. He took his Stetson off, and except for the horse, stood alone beside the grave. Through tears, he said, "Pappy, I never thanked you proper for all you did for me. I know you'd have just waved it off and said it was nothin' 'cause that's just how you were, but we both know if you hadn't made me drive you all the way out to California… well, my life would be very different now… and not in a good way. I guess, what I'm tryin' to say is thank you for saving me from myself. If you think about it, it's kind of crazy that we had to go all the way to California just so I could figure out where I belong. Who knew the road to nowhere could be so long? Anyway, thanks again, Pappy."

Placing his hat back on his head, he turned and pulled himself into the saddle. As he rode slowly along the ruts that lead back to the ranch, he watched for tracks in the dirt until Red started to pull at the reins.

Back in the corral, he pulled the saddle and blanket from the horse's back, put them away, and began the task of rubbing Red down. A footprint in the dirt caught his attention, and he realized it must have been left there by Will the last time he came to visit his old friend. Trey knew the prints would fade in time, but the memory of his grandfather would stay with him for the rest of his life.

Kneeling down, he traced the outline of the boot print, "Pappy, you left some mighty big boots to fill, but I'll do the best I can."

Dear Reader,

This story, in many ways, makes me think of Kenny Chesney's song "Don't Blink." As the dad of seven and the pappy of nineteen, I can tell you that they all grow up to fast. Protecting one's children and grandchildren from themselves is perhaps the most gut-wrenching battle many of us will ever face. To ensure their happiness and safety most of us would fight the fires of hell with a burlap sack and a shovel. Sometimes we succeed, sometimes we fail, but as long as we draw breath we have not lost.

Taking this story from an idea to the reality of a book, took two years and a number of special people. With that in mind, I would like to thank my mother, whose 'you can do this' attitude drove me on whenever I wanted to throw in the towel, my father for all the commas, editing, and encouragement he provided along the journey. A big hearty *Thank You*, to my developmental editors, Joani Hartin and Denise Sanders. And a special thanks to my agent, Erin Niumata, and her beta readers.

And a special thanks to you. Without you, the reader, this book is simply pages of words glued together. It took you reading it to make it what it was meant to be—a story I wanted to share.

Until next time,
Charles Lemar Brown

About the Author

Charles Lemar Brown is a retired high school science teacher, who now spends much of his time writing and traveling. He is also an avid photographer whose photographs have been sold around the world. He lives in rural Love County, Oklahoma, where he enjoys spending time with his seven children and nineteen grandchildren. Left alone too long, he is likely to be found making TikTok's, working out in his home gym, or kicked back with his cat, Tilee, watching whatever football game he can find on the television. His favorite quote is—what doesn't kill you makes you stronger and I ain't dead yet.